Praise for *The* ⌐

"*The Dead Don't Sleep* is a skillfully plotted, fast-moving thriller brimming with a believable cast of characters, especially the indelible Frank Thompson, an old-school hero who I hope to see more of."

—David Swinson, author of
Trigger and *The Second Girl*

"Russo's *The Dead Don't Sleep* is a pulse racing, chest thumper of a novel."

—Reed Farrel Coleman, *New York Times*
bestselling author of *What You Break*

"Imagine if Rambo had lived a quiet, undisturbed life in Maine until, many decades later, the ghosts of the Vietnam War came after him. That's roughly the premise of *The Dead Don't Sleep*, a gripping, highly readable contemporary thriller with a strong emotional undercurrent. Steven Max Russo has done a magnificent job rendering the unique hold Vietnam continues to claim on thousands of its veterans."

—Brad Parks, international bestselling author

THE DEAD DON'T SLEEP

ALSO BY STEVEN MAX RUSSO

Thieves

STEVEN MAX RUSSO

THE DEAD DON'T SLEEP

Down & Out Books
3959 Van Dyke Road, Suite 265
Lutz, FL 33558
DownAndOutBooks.com

The characters and events in this book are fictitious. Any similarity to real persons, living or dead, is coincidental and not intended by the author.

Cover design by Zach McCain

ISBN: 1-64396-051-2
ISBN-13: 978-1-64396-051-7

This one's for you, Pop.

PROLOGUE

Nui Ba Den, Vietnam, 1969

This is not war, he thought; it's murder.

The first killer crouched silently along one side of the well-worn trail. His face was painted dark green with intersecting black lines to blend into the jungle. He had a razor sharp SOG Bowie knife, which he held at his side in his right hand, just slightly out in front.

The warm air was heavy with humidity. There were intermittent clouds letting through only occasional starlight and moonlight. A gray mist was discernible swirling lazily in the darkness about a foot or two off the ground. The whole area was shadows, dense with jungle foliage.

There was a small village up ahead about a half kilometer from his location. He could smell the wood smoke from the morning cook fires mixed in with stale odors of cattle dung and swine wallowing in their pens. He had been in-country for two tours now, much of that time spent out in the bush, and to him the smell was not unpleasant—was in fact comforting.

He concentrated on the sounds around him, the buzzing of insects and the calls of birds, the occasional howl of monkeys waking off in the distant trees.

It was early morning, probably somewhere between 3:30 and 4:00 a.m. He could feel the temperature beginning to climb even though the sun was still at least a full hour from starting its rise. His fatigues clung to his body, heavy with sweat and dew from the plants he had brushed against as he moved slowly and quietly through the jungle.

He heard a soft, sharp hiss from just up ahead on the other side of the trail. It was a signal from the other killer, who also waited, crouching silently in the dark.

Someone was coming.

He slowed his breathing and looked down at the ground, not wanting any light from a break in the dark clouded sky to reflect off his eyes.

He closed his eyes, squeezed them shut tight for a second and tried to concentrate on the three essential elements that could mean the difference between life and death.

Speed. Precision. Surprise.

Faint footsteps approached in the distance. The target was supposedly a VC courier that the spooks had identified. This was his preferred route, the time and day supplied by informants.

A *supposed* VC courier.

Shit. He tried to clear his mind.

The steps were rhythmic and measured. Not hurried at all, but not exactly cautious either. Not yet at least. Probably thinking he was still safe this close to the village.

The killer's fingers tightened on the hilt of his knife.

This is not war; it's murder.

That thought again, the words like a whisper echoed softly in his head.

The footsteps became more discernible as the man approached. The killer could sense more than hear the soft padding of sandals on the jungle floor, the occasional rustle of vegetation being gently pushed aside.

He had done this before. He had killed from ambush, up close and personal, with his hands, his knife, silent and deadly. He was good at it. He had done it willingly, with no remorse or regrets, understanding that it was necessary. Had even trained other men to do it.

But things had changed.

The target was getting closer.

He stood slowly, careful not to make any sound, and nestled up close to the trunk of a large Hopea tree that sat right in front of him just off the trail. He could now clearly hear the footsteps, and he put his face close to the tree, his nose almost touching, eyes open. He could smell the damp, living wood, see small ants and other insects crawling along its bark in the darkness.

The footsteps stopped. The target was standing perhaps ten or so meters away. Why had he stopped? Did he see or hear something? Could he intuit the danger he was in?

The killer waited, not breathing. He had a sidearm, his M1911 if needed, but that would alert the whole village making their evac from the area dicey. He was not alone; the killer had a small team of men to think about. He would rather eliminate the target by hand.

There was no sound for perhaps ten seconds; ten long seconds. The footsteps began again, one tentative step, then another, and then one after the other more rhythmically, though certainly more slowly than before.

He waited, still not breathing, for the man to pass. Then, in one quick motion, he stepped out from behind the tree, reached around the man's head and cupped his left hand tightly over the smaller man's mouth, pulled back hard and drew the blade of his knife across the man's exposed throat.

The man kicked and tried to scream, but the killer held tight to his head, pulling it hard to his chest, squeezing his face to muffle the noise. He could feel warm blood squirting onto his hand; hear it as it splattered like gentle raindrops on the leaves and trees and bushes all around him. He had a sudden recollection of the very first person he had killed like this, another small man in black pajamas along another trail. It had been daylight that time and he was amazed at how much blood there was, how it had squirted like a small fountain as he watched it splattering the trees several feet from where the man had fought and died there in his arms.

The struggle didn't last long. He slowly brought the man down to the ground, blood gurgling and streaming down his chest still, but no longer squirting as it did before. He kept his hand over the man's mouth but began to relax his grip.

He heard another soft, sharp hiss from up the trail. He sheathed his knife and quietly drew his sidearm from the holster at his side, never fully letting up the pressure on the target's mouth.

He was in the trail, right in the middle of it, and someone was coming. The footsteps approached quickly, like someone running, no regard to avoiding the branches and leaves along the trail, not trying at all to move silently through the jungle.

He kept one hand on the dying man's mouth and raised the gun with the other, sighting it down the trail from where the noise was coming.

Clouds were moving overhead, and a small break allowed moonlight to shine through. The trail was suddenly illuminated in a soft glow.

Shit.

Too late to move and nowhere to go. He waited.

A small child suddenly appeared, a little Vietnamese girl. She ran along the trail directly toward him, head up. She saw the killer, gun straight out and pointed at her small head. She stopped dead in her tracks.

He heard a gasp, a sharp intake of breath. The child's eyes were shining; he saw them sparkle in the moonlight. She opened her mouth, perhaps to scream, and a hand shot out of the jungle grabbing her hair, pulling her small head back. Another hand, quick, a flash of shiny metal, and then she stood there, wobbling slightly, making a gurgling sound as blood began to sputter out her throat, around her chin, running down her small chest saturating and staining her blouse dark black in the moon's pale light.

A man stepped out of the jungle. He carried an M16 rifle in

one hand, a knife in the other. It was his partner in the killer squad. He stepped carefully past the bleeding child. He turned and faced the first killer. The man with the M16 smiled and nodded, knelt down and slid the bloody knife back into the sheath on his right leg and then turned and faced back down the trail, his M16 at the ready to guard their evac out of the area.

The killer held the gun steady, still pointing down the trail.

The child swayed once, then fell face first onto the trail.

This is not war, he thought; it's murder.

Without thinking, he took careful aim at the man with the M16 guarding their flank. Then he pulled the trigger.

RECOLLECTION

New Jersey, Present Day

Bill watched his Uncle Frank, standing there a few feet away wearing jeans and a black, short-sleeved T-shirt. It was a beautiful Saturday afternoon in early April, the sun was out, and the temperature hovered right around sixty degrees.

Jacket weather thought Bill absently, not T-shirt weather

"Why don't you put that gun down, Uncle Frank? There's a rack right over there. Come and sit down for a few minutes. We've got to wait for these guys to finish up."

Uncle Frank stepped a little closer to where Bill sat, the old Fox double-barrel shotgun hanging business end down in his left hand.

"I'm all right holding it, Billy. You know I don't like to put my weapon down."

"Why, you think someone is going to take that old shotgun home with him?" He said it with a smile.

Uncle Frank shook his head slightly, and then looked out at the other shooters taking their turns on the line.

"Aren't you cold? I've got an extra sweatshirt in the truck."

Uncle Frank took a small step closer to Bill. "Where I live, this is like summer. You never came up to visit us too close to either side of winter. When I left home three days ago, it was sixteen degrees in the sun, and that's no lie. Had what we call a warm spell. This, heck, this is downright balmy. I'm going to head home all tan and tell people I just came back from a tropical vacation." He smiled his easy smile, and it made Bill feel good to see it.

Bill didn't see his uncle often. Less and less it seemed, as they both got older. Frank was nearing seventy, though he could pass for ten years younger. He was tall, about six-one, with broad shoulders, salt and pepper hair that was still relatively thick, and arms that looked fit and strong. He had the beginnings of an old-man paunch around the belly that Bill was sure was a testament to his aunt's hearty cooking. Well, his late aunt. Bill, now in his early forties with a wife and two growing boys, just didn't have the time to travel up to Maine, where his reclusive uncle seemed to have always lived with his wife.

Frank's wife of more than forty-five years had passed away several weeks earlier. No one knew she had died until Uncle Frank called Bill two days after she was put in the ground. Said he didn't want a big thing made of it, people driving or flying up to that little town where he lived up in the wilds of Maine. He had asked Bill to let the rest of the family know that Aunt Sadie had passed, explain how things were, ask folks not to call him for a while, let him settle in. Bill had offered to drive up with his wife and the boys, stay with him for a few days, but Uncle Frank had declined. Said he needed a little space and some time alone to get used to things. Said not to worry, he was fine.

But Bill had worried.

The loud reports of the shotguns stopped abruptly. The five shooters began picking up their spent plastic shell casings and dumping them into buckets scattered along the shooting stations and then made their way back off the trap field to where Bill and his uncle waited along with three other shooters they did not know, who would round out their set.

"Looks like we're up, Uncle Frank."

Bill slipped a box of twenty-five neatly stacked target loads into a small ammo basket that he had purchased at a Dick's

Sporting Goods store last year. The little basket was made to hold one box of shotgun shells and had a belt loop for securing it tight to your waist making it easy to reach and to reload. He watched with amusement as his uncle ripped open his box and began stuffing shells into the pockets of his jeans. When his box was empty, Uncle Frank's pockets bulged to about bursting.

"You gonna be able to walk with all those shells stuffed in there like that?"

"You mind your own business, Billy Boy. It's not the fancy gun or the pretty ammo basket knocks down those birds. It's the man behind the trigger." He gave a smile and a wink, and they headed to their positions on the shooting line.

They shot three rounds. Bill hit seventeen of twenty-five on the first round, then fifteen, and then nineteen. Frank hit thirteen the first round, then began feeling more comfortable with the old Fox as he got reacquainted with it and hit twenty-two and then twenty-three in the final round.

After picking up the spent shells and dumping them into the buckets, they went back to the bench. Bill laid his Beretta semi-auto in the rack and began loading his protective shooting glasses, ammo basket and noise suppression headphones into his bag. Uncle Frank stood a little ways off and pulled out the foam plugs he had stuffed into his ears with his right hand while holding onto his old Fox with his left. He threw the plugs into the large garbage can and stood watching the men who were shooting or milling about behind the firing lines waiting their turns.

When they had finished gathering their things, they walked over to the field house. Bill went inside to pay for the six rounds of trap they had shot. There were chairs and tables on the porch of the field house, and Frank waited in one of them watching their gear. When Bill returned from inside, he found a hot cup of coffee waiting for him. His uncle was sipping from a can of Coke. Bill sat down and sipped his coffee. It felt good going down, taking away some of the chill of the day even though Bill was wearing a thick sweatshirt. Frank seemed totally unbothered by the temperature as he sat with his big hand wrapped around his frosty can of soda.

"You really started knocking them down after that first round. What were you doing, using both barrels?" Bill looked over at Frank. Frank answered without turning to look back at him, instead staring straight ahead at the men shooting.

"I should have used both barrels. My eyes, they're not what they used to be. That gun, the old Fox, it's nice. I bought that before you were born. It's gotta be over fifty years old now. Used to use it when I went hunting with your father, when we were young. Haven't shot it in years. The old guns, they made them out of higher quality metal back then. That's why they last."

"It's a beautiful gun. My dad used to tell me about that gun, about when you and he went hunting and sometimes you'd load up both barrels with double ought to take down a rabbit. Said there'd be nothing left but scraps of bloody fur."

"Yeah, that's true. Thought it was funny then, not so much anymore."

"You still hunt?"

"No, I lost my taste for killing things a while back. Was pretty good at it for a long time though. Always enjoyed the stalking part, the tracking, the waiting. Never really liked pulling the trigger. But when I did kill, I tried always to harvest what I could. What we didn't eat, we gave to neighbors or donated to those less fortunate."

"Except those rabbits, I guess." Bill said it with a smile.

"Yeah, except maybe those rabbits." Frank didn't smile back.

"I thought you still went on those trips with Aunt Sadie's side of the family. Didn't you tell me that you went to hunting camp with them last year? Geez, I remember going with you and Dad when I was just a kid."

"Well, that camp has changed some since you were there. We built a cabin about ten or so years ago. Put up one of those prefab log jobs. Real nice, ran electric and everything, keep a small gas generator in back so they can actually heat the place, plug in lights and a radio and such. And yeah, I still go. But I don't hunt. I keep camp; you know, do the cooking and make sure those boys don't drink. Hell, it's dangerous enough traipsing around in the woods with all of those tourists during the hunting season. I know you've read about them getting all excited and shooting someone's cow thinking they're bagging a moose or something. Those stories are true. I know some people paint the word *cow* on the side of their livestock in big white letters, just to let them know. Still lose animals every year."

"Wow, that's funny."

"Pathetic more like it."

Bill noticed that even though his uncle was talking to him, his eyes were on something or someone out in one of the trap fields.

"What are you looking at? You see someone you know?"

Uncle Frank stood up, grabbed his shotgun off the rack with his left hand, and then reached over and grabbed Bill's shotgun with his right.

"Let's head back, Billy. I just got a chill."

Without another word, he turned and began walking briskly toward the steps that led to the lot where Bill's 2011 Jeep Cherokee was parked.

Bill had the rear hatch open and was loading his shotgun into its soft padded carrying case when he heard a voice that he didn't recognize say "Hey, don't I know you?"

Bill turned around to see an older man smiling, or perhaps sneering at him, it was hard to tell which. He wore dark, mirrored aviator sunglasses and had on a dark ball cap with no insignia on it. He was on the short side, around five-six or five-seven, had on a blue, long sleeved T-shirt with some sort of union emblem under a camouflage shooting vest. His blue jeans were old and worn, as were his scuffed black motorcycle boots.

Bill pulled his head out of the back of the Jeep and turned to face the man.

"I don't know, sir. You don't look familiar. My name's Bill." He smiled and extended his hand to the stranger, but the man ignored it.

"Not talking to you son, I'm talking to him." The man nodded his head and Bill turned around to see his uncle standing a few steps behind him. His uncle stood erect, his right arm holding the old double barrel shotgun pointed slightly downward. His left arm hung loosely at his side, like an old-time gunslinger. The look on his face was something that Bill had never seen before; it was totally blank. Even his eyes seemed dark and lifeless, like those of a shark.

"I've seen you before," said the man, stepping around Bill so that he was looking up directly into Frank's face. "Just can't seem to grab hold of it yet. Blast from the past, you know what I mean? Still a little fuzzy around the edges. But it will come to me. I'm good with faces. Not good with names, but I'm damn good with faces. It will come."

The men looked at each other, not more than two feet apart, neither saying anything for a few long seconds. Bill noticed the shotgun start moving ever so slightly upward.

Finally, Frank broke the silence. "You're mistaken friend, you don't know me. I'm not from around here."

He stepped past the man and laid the old Fox next to Bill's Beretta in the back of the Jeep, then slammed the gate closed. The man continued to watch Frank, stepping close and invading his personal space, like a dog sniffing at someone, that strange smile never leaving his face.

Frank turned and looked down at the man. Then he stepped closer still; leaning down and in until they were just inches from each other, face-to-face. The other man conceded no space; they were like two bulls snorting at each other. Bill thought that one or the other might take a swing and without really thinking about it, readied himself in case he might need to step between them.

"We'll be leaving now." Frank spoke so softly that Bill almost didn't hear him. Then he said much louder, his eyes never leaving those of the other man, "Let's get going Billy, and leave this gentleman to his recollections."

Frank turned away from the man and walked to the passenger side door, opened it, and got in. Bill looked at the stranger for a second more, but the man just stared at where Frank had disappeared into the Jeep, that same strange smile on his face. Then Bill checked the tailgate to make sure that it was shut properly and walked around to the driver's side door, opened it, and got in.

"What the hell is with that guy?" he asked his uncle as he turned the key and started the engine. "I thought you two were gonna start brawling right there in the parking lot."

Frank patted his nephew on the thigh gently, looking straight ahead. "Why don't you get us out of here?"

As Bill put the transmission into reverse, the man with the mirrored sunglasses and the weird, scary smile stepped around to the passenger side window. He peered in, his face inches from the glass. Uncle Frank did nothing for a second, then pushed the button on the door's armrest, and the window lowered. He turned his head slowly and looked at the stranger but didn't say anything.

"It's starting to come to me, out of the haze of the past. I know your face. You were in the shit, man, I know you were. You were in the shit. Am I right? Am I right?"

Uncle Frank sighed, and then said, "It's all shit, partner, isn't it?" He pressed the button again, and the window rose slowly. He looked at his nephew and said, "Drive, Billy Boy, drive."

Bill backed out of the spot carefully, turned the wheel and headed out of the parking lot toward the road. He looked in the rearview mirror and saw the man staring after them. As he watched, the man reached into his vest pocket and pulled out what looked to be a small pad and a pen and began writing something down. Bill continued watching, keeping one eye on the road in front and one eye on the mirror as the Jeep reached the end of the lot, and then the road. He stopped and looked both ways preparing to exit the parking lot onto the roadway, but before he did, he stole one last look in the mirror. The strange man was gone. He turned the wheel to the left, hit the gas, and they began the drive back to his house in Hackensack.

After a few minutes of driving in silence, Bill said, "You gonna tell me what that was all about back there?"

Uncle Frank looked out the window as they drove east along Route 46. The road was lined on both sides with an endless succession of strip malls.

"I'm not really sure. Didn't have a real good feeling about that one, you know? He was watching me, it seems, right from when we first got there. Guess he thinks he knows me from somewhere. But he's mistaken."

"What'd he mean when he said that you were in the shit?"

"I believe he meant the war. I can't stand it when those old guys go all Hollywood. Lots of them never even fired a shot in the war. Not every Vietnam veteran was out there in the jungle with a rifle. Leastwise, I bet most of them Hollywood types weren't."

"So, he thinks he knows you from the war?"

"Yeah, I guess." Uncle Frank turned away from the side window and looked straight ahead.

"Does he?"

"Does he what?" Now Frank turned and looked at his nephew.

"Does he know you from the war?"

Frank shook his head and looked down at his lap. "Hell, I don't know. I served two tours. Ran across a lot of people. I sure as hell don't remember him. I didn't like him much, though. Something about him made me real uneasy. It was something he gave off, an aura, like bad body odor. That was why I wanted to get out of there. He was trouble for sure."

"Was he really a Vietnam veteran? I mean, could you tell? Maybe he was just some guy acting out. He seemed pretty strange to me. Actually, I thought he seemed crazy. I mean like insane crazy. He had that weird smile, not happy at all, more menacing than anything, like a psycho smile, you know? And he kept getting in your face. I thought you were going to hit him, I really did."

"Well, I come pretty close to taking a swing, that's no lie. Seems a bit irrational now that I think about it from a distance. Still, you get some crazies. It's best to leave them be and get on your way. Guy like that hanging out at a gun range, and you ask me why I never put down my weapon. But to answer your question, I'd say probably yes. Was about the right age anyway."

"Were you in the, uh, field, Uncle Frank? In Vietnam I mean."

"You mean was I in the shit?" Both men smiled.

"Well, I was for a while. I guess you know I don't like to talk about it much. I know you and your brothers, and your cousins too, all heard stories about me, mostly speculation about what I did in the war. Figure I'm some kind of Rambo or secret agent or some such nonsense. But I was just a grunt, a regular soldier. Did a stint in intelligence, so I guess that's where all those stories and speculation come from? But it was mostly reading maps, trying to guess what the enemy was up to and where they'd be heading next."

"But you did two tours. My dad told me you won some medals. Said you were wounded in action. More than once. That true?"

Frank turned his gaze back out the passenger-side window.

"If you don't want to talk about it Uncle Frank, I understand. It's none of my business. I don't want to make you feel uncomfortable. I was just curious, you know? That's all."

"Yeah, I know, Bill. It's just that it was a long time ago. I was a young man then, a boy really. I've got scars, but it's not the ones on my body that pain me the most. Every generation is the same, I guess. My dad fought in World War II. I heard a hundred stories from him when I was growing up, about him and his buddies in boot camp and being on leave and traveling in the troop ships and about the food and the girls and the beer.

14

Hell, how many times you hear your Grandpa tell those stories? But you never once heard him tell a war story, you know, like what you're asking around right now. My dad, he wasn't a drinking man, but one time when I was about nineteen or so, him and me started in on a bottle of scotch. Just that once I saw him drunk, and I mean shit-faced drunk. He told me some stories that night, not those fun stories about him in his tailored uniform chasing English ladies around. He told me about actually pissing his pants in fear lying in the mud and crying for his mommy like a child, about the sound that them old Panzer tanks made as they rumbled across a field that was different and more frightening than anything he'd ever heard before or since, said he often heard those Panzers in the middle of the night even there in bed with your grandmother and could actually feel the bed shaking. He told me about seeing his buddy, a guy from New Milford name of Al Kaspazack—Geez, I can't believe I still remember that poor soul's name—vaporized after taking a direct hit from a German 88. Said he saw him standing there one second, an instant later there was nothing left but two charred combat boots, each with a small, bloody stump sticking out of it."

"Jesus!" Bill was taken aback by the image. He knew that people died in war, but hearing this story about what his grandfather, the gentle, loving old man that he remembered from his youth, had gone through utterly shocked him.

"I saw your grandfather cry that night as he remembered those stories. I don't think it was so much that he couldn't hold his liquor, though that was certainly part of it. I think it was that those stories were suppressed for so long that all it took was a little booze to loosen his inhibitions enough to let all those memories and emotions come pouring out. And I mean, that's what happened. It was like he couldn't stop talking, one terrible memory after another. I was holding him in my arms, my own father, like he was a little baby. At the time, I'd never seen anything like it, a grown man crying like that. I've seen a lot more of it since then, but at the time I didn't know what to do. So, I made him stop after a while, dragged him off to bed. I stayed with him, watched him cry himself out and fall asleep. We never spoke about that night again. I never asked him to tell me another story about his time in the service. Not even about the girls in England. And he never asked me anything either after I came home. Just held me tight like I did him."

"Geez, Uncle Frank, I don't know what to say."

"It's okay, Billy. Truth is, I've seen some things and done some things I don't care to remember. Drank another bottle of scotch one night with your Aunt Sadie. That was shortly after I got back the second time. Wish I'd stayed away from it that night. I guess I blacked out because I don't remember much, just bits and pieces. But the little I do remember, I wish to God I had kept to myself. I asked her about it the next day, sort of casual, hoping I was mistaken, but she wouldn't say anything. So, I asked again the day after that. She wouldn't talk about it. We never spoke of it again. It's sort of like what happened between my dad and me. But after that night, for a few weeks at least, I could feel that something had come between us, something that wasn't there before. It was like she was afraid of me somehow, though I swear I never gave her cause to be. She never said so, you understand, but I could sense it. Believe me, I stayed away from the drink after that. Gave her some space, too."

"I guess she eventually got over it, whatever it was you told her."

"Well, I'm not sure I'd put it that way. She was young in age at that time, your Aunt Sadie, but she was wise beyond her years. I always believed she could see right inside my heart. I think she understood."

"Understood what?"

Uncle Frank didn't answer. He just turned away from Bill and stared out the window. After a minute or so he said so softly that Bill could hardly hear, "Lord, I miss that woman."

Neither Bill nor Frank said anything more for the rest of the drive home.

16

TWO

It was 4 a.m. when the bedroom window shattered.

Bill awoke with a start. He must have heard the glass shatter and the pieces begin to fall, followed almost immediately by a sharp smacking sound as something hit the wall, and suddenly he was sitting up. Then the other window shattered, and he heard that same loud, smacking sound as something hit the far bedroom wall hard. The concussion knocked down a framed photo of the kids, and again the sound of shattering glass interrupted the quiet night as the photo hit the top of the dresser and exploded into flying fragments. He wasn't sure what was happening, and he moved to get out of bed, but his wife, Samantha, was suddenly clinging to his arm whispering, "Billy, what's going on? What's going on?"

Bill grabbed his wife's arm and forcefully but gently dislodged it from his own. "Get on the floor," he whispered. "Under the bed."

"Why? What's going on? What's happening?"

"I don't know. Get under the bed. I'm going to check on the boys."

"Oh, my God!" She got up out of bed before Bill could grab her, and she rushed out the door, heedless of the broken glass strewn about the floor.

Bill followed her out and they ran to the boys' bedroom down the hall. The door was already open and they both rushed in. The two boys were huddled together in the far corner, away from the window. Uncle Frank was kneeling in front of them, his back to the window, his arms around their shoulders, whispering to them softly.

Samantha ran over and without thinking pushed Uncle Frank aside and hugged her children.

"Are you okay, are you all right?" she asked through tears, kissing each boy's head over and over again.

Uncle Frank stood and looked at Bill. "The boys are fine, Bill. Go call the police. Don't turn any lights on. Stay away from the windows. I'll stay with Sam and the kids until you get back."

Bill didn't move. He looked at his wife and children, then at the window that faced the side of his property. It wasn't broken. There was nothing amiss in the room at all.

"Bill." It was Uncle Frank, his voice a little more forceful. "The police, call them."

Bill walked toward the kitchen, peeking in each room as he went. He grabbed the cordless phone and dialed nine-one-one. He roamed the dark house as he waited for the operator to pick up. The big bay window in the living room that looked out onto his front yard was shattered.

"Hackensack nine-one-one. Where are you calling from?"

Bill gave the woman his address.

"And what is the nature of your emergency?"

"I'm not really sure what's going on. Somebody broke windows in my house. Two windows in my bedroom and one in the living room, maybe other rooms, too." Bill realized that he was whispering, so he raised his voice a bit. "I have a wife and two children here. They may still be outside."

"Your family is outside?"

"No, the people who did this."

"Okay, please stay in your home. Do not go outside. I am sending a patrol car right over to your house. Stay away from the windows. Is anyone hurt?"

"No, I don't think so. Wait, maybe. I'm going to go back and check again. Stay on the line. Please tell the police to hurry."

"The car is on the way. It should be there inside of three minutes. What is your name please?"

"Bill, Bill Thompson."

Bill walked back to the boys' room with the phone at his ear. As soon as he got there, Uncle Frank walked past him quickly and disappeared.

"Mr. Thompson, the police should be there inside of two minutes. They won't use sirens, but you should see the lights any minute now. Is everyone okay?"

Sam was looking up at him, fear and confusion on her face.

"I'm going to give the phone to my wife. Tell the police that my uncle may have gone outside to look around. Tell them I am going outside too."

"Mr. Thompson, don't..." He handed the phone to his wife and knelt down in front of his sons.

"Are you guys all right?" He tried a reassuring smile to little effect. Both boys nodded, frightened looks on their faces. "Probably just some neighborhood kids fooling around, nothing to worry about. The police are coming right over. Stay here with mom, okay? I'm going to go find Uncle Frank." He kissed each boy once on the head.

"Honey, the lady says to stay inside." Sam was looking at him, the phone tight to her ear.

"Frank's outside. I'm going to go find him. Tell her that. Tell her to let the cops know. Tell her it was probably just some neighborhood kids out on a bender causing trouble. Tell her I don't want anyone getting hurt." Then he got up and left the room.

He saw Uncle Frank down on one knee in the backyard. He had something in his hand, like a piece of paper or a candy wrapper. When he looked up and saw Bill heading his way, he got up slowly, almost painfully. He appeared to be palming the object, like he was trying to keep it from view.

"You find something Frank?"

"Naw, not really. Just some litter, it seems." He opened his hand and showed Bill the torn baseball card he had picked up. It looked old, like the cards Bill remembered as a child. He took it from Uncle Frank and looked at it. It showed a lefthanded batter, number eighteen, wearing a black hat with the letter P on the front. There was part of a blue sky in the background and the word "Pirates" was written in the top right-hand corner in all caps in white. He turned it over, and he could make out what looked to be player stats, but it was too dark for him to see anything clearly.

"Here, let me have that, Billy. I'll throw it in the trash." He reached for the card and took it gently from Bill's hand. "I see flashing lights; looks like the cops are here. Let's go out there and introduce ourselves before they mistake us for prowlers and throw our butts in the slammer." Frank slipped the card into the front hip pocket of his jeans, then put his hand on Bill's shoulder and gently steered him to the side of the house and towards the front yard. "Maybe you should put on a pair of pants, too. A bit chilly for you to be walking around in your skivvies."

There was one Hackensack patrol car in the street with its emergency lights going. Two police officers were getting out with flashlights already turned on.

As Bill approached, he raised his hand and said, "Hi, officers. Thanks for getting here so quickly. I'm Bill Thompson, the owner of this house. I'm the one who called. This is my uncle. He's staying with us a few days.

The policemen shined their flashlights up and down quickly over the two men, and then began playing the lights over the yard. One of the cops was a tall blond-haired young man somewhere in his early twenties. He had broad shoulders that at first glance made him look fit, but the hint of a spare tire was starting to grow around his middle. The other was shorter, thin and wiry with a deep voice and a thin mustache. He was the driver and seemed to be the one in charge.

"I'm Officer Breslow. We had a call about a broken window." The shorter of the two policemen shined his light over the big bay living room window, which now had a gaping hole right in its center. "I guess that's the one you called about?"

"That's one. They also broke windows in my bedroom; I mean the one that my wife and I share. I haven't checked the rest of the house yet."

"Shot out the window in the guest room, too. That's where I'm sleeping," said Uncle Frank.

The young cop looked at Uncle Frank and said, "Shot out? Did you hear gunshots?"

Uncle Frank shook his head. "No officer, I did not. But something small and fast came through my window. Not a rock or a brick. I took a quick look to see if I could tell what it was before I went in to check on Bill's kids. Didn't see anything, but there looks to be a deep pockmark in the wall. Maybe more than one."

"Is anyone hurt? Do we need an ambulance?" Officer Breslow, the shorter cop was taking charge again.

Bill looked at Uncle Frank, then turned back to the cop. "No, I don't think so. More scared than anything. My wife's inside with my two boys."

"Why don't we go inside, then, Mr. Thompson, check on the family? I'll have a look around, check out the rest of the house. Officer Stevens here will do a perimeter search, make sure who-ever did this isn't still lurking in one of the neighbor's yards." He looked at his partner. "Call it in, Rich. Tell them what we've got here, see if we can get another car to search the area. Then do a quick sweep. Just kids probably."

Officer Stevens headed around to the side of the house without saying a word. He shifted the flashlight from his right hand to his left and then reached up and keyed his shoulder mike and began speaking in a low voice. The beam of his flashlight played across the bushes of the neighbor's property as he headed around the house, out of sight and into the backyard.

"Shall we head in, Mr. Thompson?"

"Yes, of course. Follow me."

Bill and the policeman walked towards the house. The light came on over the front porch, the door opened, and Samantha appeared, now wearing a worn blue bathrobe over her night-clothes, the faces of her two children peeking around her backside. Uncle Frank began following the two men towards the house, and then stopped abruptly. The two men proceeded, Bill calling to his wife and telling her everything was okay.

Uncle Frank bent down and looked at something on the ground. Then he reached and picked up what appeared to be another piece of litter. He turned it over with his fingers. It was the top half of another torn baseball card. He could read the name and position of the Chicago Cubs player written in an orange circle in the top left-hand corner of the card. It was a name he remembered from long ago, Randy Hundley, catcher. He had already put a name to the face he had found earlier: Matty Alou, outfielder for the Pittsburgh Pirates.

He stood slowly and slipped the torn half of the baseball card into his hip pocket, where he already carried the one he had found earlier.

Matty Alou and Randy Hundley. Both of them players on the 1969 National League All Star team.

"Motherfucker!" He said it softly, yet fiercely to himself. It came out as almost a hiss.

He felt a bead of sweat form and slowly make its way down his right temple. He wiped at it with the back of his hand.

It's been almost forty-five years, he thought, his mind racing. I'm almost seventy fucking years old. He shook his head in disbelief.

"Frank, you okay?" It was Bill, calling from the front porch.

"Yeah, Billy, I'm fine. Go on in. I'm just getting some fresh air. I'll be along in a minute."

He looked up at the night sky. He could only make out one or two stars, ambient light from New York City and the surrounding towns obscuring the view. Nothing like the dazzling display of stars that he was used to seeing in the night sky of rural Maine.

He looked down at his feet, and then started toward the front porch.

Jesus fucking Christ, he thought, I'm too old to be back in the shit.

Sam and Frank sat at the kitchen table drinking coffee. Bill was with Officer Breslow going from room to room, surveying the damage and seeing if anything else was amiss.

Frank looked at the clock over the stove. Four-thirty in the morning. He shook his head.

"What's the matter, Frank?" asked Sam. She put a hand on his shoulder.

"I feel terrible. I wish I had just stayed up in Maine."

She smiled at him and rubbed her hand gently over his shoulder where she had placed it a second ago.

"Don't be silly, Frank. This is nothing. A little scary, I admit, but I'm sure Billy is right. Probably just some kids pulling a prank."

Frank didn't say anything, just looked down at the steam rising from his coffee.

"We love having you here. Really. And I want to thank you."

He looked up at her. "For what?"

She looked into his face with an intensity that took him a little by surprise. He noticed that her eyes were moist and glistening, like maybe she was about to cry.

"For going in to check on our boys. Billy and I were up as soon as the glass started flying. We rushed right in, and there you were already, with your arms around them, protecting them with—" A sob caught in her throat. She got up and threw her arms around Frank, and then she was sobbing into his shoulder. He didn't know what to do at first. Then he put one arm around her and patted her back.

Bill and Officer Breslow walked into the kitchen.

"Geez, Uncle Frank, I leave you alone with my wife for a few minutes, and I come back to find you practically making out with her."

"She's a little upset, Bill. How about you take over here for a while? My shirt's about soaked through."

Sam made a sound somewhere between a sob and a laugh and pulled away from Frank. Then she held his cheeks in both her hands, kissed him gently on the forehead and stepped away.

"Well," she said, "Uncle Frank and I have had our moment." She wiped at her eyes and tried a somewhat shaky smile, "How about I pour you guys some coffee?"

The four of them sat at the kitchen table. No one said anything for a minute or so until Uncle Frank broke the silence. "Well, Officer Breslow, any idea what broke the windows?"

The policeman pulled a small plastic bag out of his shirt pocket and laid it on the kitchen table.

"My name is Rudy. When my partner comes back in, maybe you should stick with Officer Breslow. He's still new on the job. We're supposed to keep it all official with you civilians when we're on a call."

Uncle Frank pulled the plastic bag a little closer with the index finger of his right hand and lowered his face close to the table to get a better look.

"What are they, ball bearings?"

"No, I don't think so. They're steel but look close. See that little flat part there? It's on each of them. If they were ball bearings, they'd be almost perfectly round. Use these as ball bearings, that flat surface would create friction, defeat the whole purpose."

Uncle Frank's nose hovered inches from the plastic bag.

"You want some glasses, Frank? I've got some readers right over here." Bill walked over to the refrigerator and reached into the dark space about an inch or two between the top of the fridge and bottom of the oak kitchen cabinets. When he pulled out his hand, he held a cheap pair of plastic reading glasses.

Frank leaned back from the bag, took the glasses, and put them on.

"Hate to admit it, but that sure makes a big difference." He bent back down and peered once again at the steel balls. "So, Rudy, what does that tell you? The flat surface."

"I'm pretty sure it's ammo, projectiles for a weapon. Remember you said you thought someone shot out the window? Well, I think you may be right. I pulled two of these out of the plasterboard, one in your room, one in theirs." He nodded to where Bill and Sam sat on the same side of the table. "The others were either lying on the floor or on a dresser. Left holes where they hit though. I suspect that we're missing one. Seems like the front window and the guest room each took two hits. The other bedroom had two windows shattered. From what you all said, I'd guess it was a simultaneous attack. Seems like all the windows blew out at approximately the same time. Also, from what Frank, I mean Mr. Thompson, said about getting outside relatively quickly, they probably synchronized their shots, planned in advance to each fire two and then run."

"What did they shoot these with, some sort of air gun? I didn't hear anything except the glass breaking." Now Bill leaned over the bag. Uncle Frank took off the cheap readers and handed them to Bill, who took them and put them on almost without thinking.

"I had to guess, I'd say they used a wrist rocket." Officer Breslow took a delicate, almost feminine sip of his coffee.

Sam had gotten up and walked over to the counter. She was walking back with the coffee pot in hand. "What's a wrist rocket?"

"It's like a sling shot, like kids make sometimes with rubber bands. Well, these are manufactured with surgical rubber tubing and high-density plastic or aluminum frames and have a wrist brace that adds stability and torque. They're actually pretty deadly. Some people hunt small game with them."

Officer Breslow picked up the plastic bag, opened it and peered inside. "These steel balls, they're not toys; these here look to be about .50 caliber. If this was kids playing some kind of prank, they're playing with fire."

There was a knock on the front door.

"That must be my partner."

"I'll let him in." Bill got up and headed out of the kitchen toward the front of the house. A few seconds later, Officer Stevens walked into the kitchen with Bill following behind.

"All clear outside, Rudy. I called it in. There's a car searching the area. It's Poncho and Frizz." He looked stricken for a moment, and then said, "I mean Officers Hernandez and Riley."

Officer Rudy Breslow smiled and shook his head. "Sorry folks, my partner here is still learning the ropes. We've got a patrol car out looking around. Officer Stevens and I will be in the area all night keeping an eye out on your home, but I don't imagine you'll have any more trouble. I'll pass the word along to the next shift as well. Rich and I will be on again tomorrow night. I'll file a report. If I hear any news or if we pick someone up, I'll be sure to update you. You may get a call from one of the detectives some time tomorrow. Here's a number that you can reach me on with any questions." He dropped a business card onto the kitchen table. "Thank you for the coffee, Mrs. Thompson."

He nodded to Frank and Bill, said, "Gentlemen," and then he and Officer Stevens exited the kitchen and walked through the house and out the front door. Bill followed them out onto the front porch and looked around to see almost every one of his neighbors looking out of their windows or standing on their front lawns or porches in pajamas or robes, entranced by the police car's red flashing strobe lights.

Later that morning Frank walked over to his truck, the ten-year-

26

old Ford F-150. He could see right away that one tire was flat. The right front side of the truck near the curb was angled slightly down. He walked over and knelt down to get a closer look at the tire.

Rusty Staub, National League All Star right fielder of the 1969 Montreal Expos, looked back at him from a torn baseball card with a 10-penny carpenter's nail stuck through his eye and right into the tire.

They decided to board up the windows until they could get someone to replace the glass. Afterwards, Frank asked Bill if he could use his computer for a while to check on his emails and touch base with a few friends back home. He also said he wanted to do a little shopping, find a mall not too far away so he could bring back a few things for the neighbor ladies.

"Everyone has been so nice to me," he said, "especially since your Aunt Sadie passed. Seems like someone is dropping by with food nearly every night. Must figure I can't cook for myself. Anyway, I'd like to see if I can't bring them back a little something, let them know I appreciate it."

Bill led him into his small home office and sat him down in front of the large screen of his iMac.

"You know how to use a Mac?"

"Actually, I've got one of these at home. Got an iPhone, too."

"Sorry. Go ahead and knock yourself out then. I'm going to go make some calls. Maybe leave a message with that contractor, check with the insurance people, maybe even leave a message with our buddy officer Rudy, see if there's any news. If you need directions to get anywhere, just let me know."

"Not to worry. Like I said, I'm high-tech. I've got a GPS in the truck, though it's getting so I can't even find my way to the bathroom anymore without her telling me how to go about it."

THREE

Around eleven-thirty Sunday morning, Jack Sprague was sipping from a mug of ice-cold Pabst Blue Ribbon beer at a corner table of the Morris Heights, New Jersey VFW hall. The table was in the back, away from the bar. A few other men sat around the bar nursing drinks and bullshitting. Two guys were shooting pool at a beat-up old billiard table. Sitting at the table with him were two men about his own age. One sipped from a can of Budweiser. The other rattled ice cubes in a now empty glass of rum and Coke.

"You hear from any of the others?" Jack wore a faded blue bandanna across his forehead and had on his mirrored aviator sunglasses, which he seldom took off. He had both feet on the floor, his right foot pushing rhythmically up and down at a fast and constant pace, causing his knee to bounce incessantly.

"Beezer called me,"—it was rum and Coke speaking—"told me he lost a leg a couple years back. Some kind of motorcycle accident in Florida. Said if he could be here, he would. Said his vote is to take him out. Said to bring him back an ear." He chuckled softly to himself. "Bring back an ear, you believe that guy? And you know what? I think he was serious."

"Pogo, what about you. You hear anything?" He looked at the man with the Bud can.

"Couple of emails, most guys drifting in the wind. Arizona said to let it alone. Tools and Spider don't give a shit what we do. Bunch of pussies. I'd say it's up to us three, right here. We can leave this be as it stands right now and let that motherfucker get away with what he did, or we can take it to the limit."

Nobody said anything for a while, just sat there, sipping beers and rattling ice.

"Well, we do this thing, we're under a black flag. You understand that, right? Disavowed, like *Mission: Impossible.*" Jack sipped his beer. His knee bounced faster, more intensely. "Plus, we don't know who, if anyone, Turd Man's got in his corner. He was a hard charger from recon, remember? After what he done, shit hit the fan, he still got out. Those agency spooks said he got sent home, just like that." He snapped his fingers. "You believe that? No reassignment, no brig time, no court martial, no bad conduct discharge. Must'a took some juice to get out clean."

"Shit, Jasper, I can't believe you ran into that motherfucker."

"Yeah, I can't believe it either. He knew I knew him, too, was scared shitless, I could tell. Took me a little while to piece it together. Hell, it's been a long fucking time. But I'm good with faces. Not so good with names. But even his name came to me: Turd Man. I remember everyone called him Bull at first. Like I said, he was a hard charger. But after what went down, even the gung-ho ass suckers knew he was a piece of shit. After that, he was just Turd Man."

That strange smile come to his face again, the one he had worn at the trap range the day before. "If either one of us had a knife, then I bet one or the other of us would be dead right now."

He took another sip of beer and wiped his mouth with the back of his hand.

"You would have sliced his bacon, Jasper." Pogo slapped Jasper's shoulder. "Remember that time you took that guy's head clean off? Right outside his hooch? We were planning to go in clean, silent and deadly, pull an All-Star Spectacular, do everyone in the hooch. Then our guy comes walking out, probably had to pee, almost bumped right into you. You grabbed that motherfucker and took him to the ground. He yelled, and you just started slicing. Streams of blood were shooting out every-where. You were covered, man, but you kept slicing. Next thing you know, there's dinks coming out of every hooch, dogs barking, kids crying. I tapped you on the shoulder, time to di di mau, but you kept hacking and whacking. I look up, there was a mob coming. I took off, man, made it to the trees. When I turn around, I see you holding his head in one hand, swinging it back and forth and, you had that bloody K-bar in the other. Those villagers stopped dead in their tracks like you was the devil himself. Then some dinks opened up out of nowhere. I was yelling, run motherfucker, run! I look around to see where the fuck the hunter team is, and when I turned back there you were hauling ass with that whole gook village screaming and cursing right behind you. And that fucking head was still swinging in your hand like a goddamn coconut."

All three men laughed. Jasper's face had turned slightly red. He started sweating and his other leg started in, now both legs going, up and down a mile a minute.

"I don't know as I would have took Turd Man's head, but I might have been tempted. Anyway, we put a scare into him this morning, that's for sure. Them little beanie slingers got some power, don't they? He'll get the message. We just have to wait him out, see what he does. I got this buddy with some connec-tions in the DMV; he's the one who got me the nephew's address from the license plate. Was also able to get me Turd Man's real name from his truck's plate and his address up in Maine, some podunk town in the middle of nowhere. That's good. Should make this easy. Well, easier. Three against one, that's better still. But understand, if we go through with this, we got to go asses and elbows and loaded for bear. Right now, he figures we're fooling with him. We left our calling card so he knows who he's dealing with. Knows we remember, that we don't never forget, nor forgive. Probably thinks we're just gonna run him out of town. That's good. We don't want him too scared. A man gets too scared, he prepares for the worst. And this guy was balls-out before he snapped. Got to remember that. The man was recon, and he was hardcore. Two tours. We get him from a distance, if at all possible. All those woods up there, we throw him in the trunk, drive the hell out and bury him miles away, they'll never find his body. He's a dangerous man. Well, he *was* a dangerous man. I know he's old now, but hell, look at us, we're old, and we're still dangerous." He smiled at his companions.

"Shit, I don't feel old." Pogo's eyes were shining and Jack saw a look on his face that he hadn't seen in over forty-five years. It was a look that he had seen in many of the faces of the All Stars when they were young and still in the shit. It chilled his soul and warmed his heart at the same time.

"I'm jazzed up, man." Pogo raised his voice. "I say we take this motherfucker out!"

"Pogo, shut the fuck up, man, keep your voice down." Jasper chuckled as he said this. He was feeling jazzed up, too.

"So, what say you, Birdman?"

"I say Chieu Hoi my ass. No free pass on this one, Turd Man." He held up his glass of ice cubes.

"Chieu Hoi? Listen to you, Birdie, talking like you're back in the shit!"

All three held up their drinks.

"Balls to the wall?" asked Jasper. The other men nodded. "Then lock and load, motherfuckers."

FOUR

Frank got into his truck and punched in the address of the trap range that he and his nephew had visited the day before. After driving for about a half hour, he pulled into the crowded lot, found a parking spot at the far end of the lot near the woods, and pulled into it. He shut off the engine and sat in the truck taking deep, slow breaths as he watched the crowd of shooters. The field house was packed with men, and some women, sitting or standing on the porch. It was like a picnic, people eating off paper plates, the smell of hamburgers and hot dogs mixing with the smell of burnt gunpowder from the shotgun rounds.

He walked casually and slowly, trying to keep what he hoped was a friendly smile on his face, scanning the crowd for anyone wearing a dark cap and mirrored aviator sunglasses or anyone else who might appear to recognize him. He didn't expect to find the short man he had run into yesterday here. He was sure the man would expect him to come back after what had happened this morning, but Frank decided to come by anyway, maybe leave a message of his own. He walked up the steps to the crowded front porch, leaned on the rail, and looked out over the trap fields. He stood there seemingly unnoticed for about five minutes.

"You thinking about joining?" A man stepped up beside Frank holding a hot dog wrapped in a napkin. He took a bite, and Frank watched as he chewed on his food, a dab of mustard stuck to his lip. The man was five-ten or so, in his late fifties or early sixties and portly. His hair was dyed black under a New York Yankees baseball cap and he had a thick mustache, dyed black as well.

"Looks like a mighty social club you have here. Always this crowded?"

"No, just on weekends. Most Sundays we have a barbeque. Then we get a little competition going amongst the members, shoot for a bottle of wine or a turkey or something. It's all in good fun. If you like to shoot, you should think about joining. There's a yearly membership fee, but you get to shoot half price and eat for free on Sundays." He smiled and shoved the last of his hot dog into his mouth, the dab of mustard on his lip disappearing with the bun.

Frank turned and surveyed the crowd on the porch. Some guys were sitting around a table playing cards, others eating or drinking soda or coffee and talking or telling jokes. In a far corner, one man passed around what looked like an AR-15 assault rifle, each person who handled the gun commenting on it in turn, though Frank was too far away to hear what they said.

"I came here yesterday with my nephew. Shot a few rounds. But I'm just visiting. Live up in Maine now, quite a drive for a weekly barbecue, though the food sure smells good."

"Would you like a dog or a burger? I can get you one, no problem."

"No, but thank you." Frank stuck out his hand, "Name's Frank. Frank Thompson."

The other man wiped his hands down the front of his shirt and then shook Frank's hand.

"Mike Belcher. No burp jokes, please. Been getting them my whole life. Think a man would get to an age where burp jokes aren't that funny anymore. But no, seems like every day someone comes up with a gem they think I might not have heard yet, you know? Even here. Been a member for ten years. Still hear the same witty comments."

"Must be tough, Mike. Some people just don't change. That smart aleck kid you knew in grade school is now that smart aleck old man. Well, in your case maybe not old yet. Sometimes even the jokes don't change."

"You got that right. Say, is your nephew a member? What's his name?"

"No, he's not a member. Only shoots trap once in while. Brought me here yesterday, and I really liked the club. Actually, saw a guy I might know. Been working at the back of my mind all night. That's why I'm back here today. Thought he might be here."

"What's his name? Maybe I know him."

"Well, that's just it. I'm afraid I don't recall his name. I grew up in Hackensack, but I moved out of there, geez, gotta be forty, forty-five years ago. Saw a guy yesterday I thought I remembered. Might be mistaken though. Actually, I probably am mistaken. I guess a person can change some in forty plus years, right?" He tried a slightly bigger smile.

"Yeah, that happens. What's this guy look like?"

"Well, he was a little on the short side, maybe five-six or so. Gotta be my age, late sixties anyway. Might have gone to my high school, something like that. He was wearing a camo vest and had these mirrored sunglasses on. Aviator glasses, I think they're called, like the pilots used to wear."

"Was he wearing a bandanna?"

"No, he had on a dark ball cap. Like yours, only not the Yankees. Nothing on the front."

"Well, I'm not sure, but that might have been Jack Sprague. He's a member here. Wears those sunglasses you mentioned. Actually, never seems to take them off. Usually wears a bandanna, too. He's not really a friend of mine, just a guy comes here to shoot. Doesn't really socialize much. I've never seen him at any of these barbecues that I can remember."

"Jack Sprague. That sounds familiar. Is he here today? Have you seen him? I'd love to introduce myself, see if he remembers me. I'm leaving for home tomorrow. Don't know when I'll get back down here. Guess I'll spend the next few days combing through my old high school yearbooks, that is if I can remember where the hell I put them."

"No, I haven't seen him. But I can ask around. Maybe one of these other guys has seen him."

They asked around and no one had, but Frank was sure that Jack Sprague was the man from yesterday. He went with Mike up to the front desk and tried to pry out a phone number or address from the guy there, but he wasn't cooperative. Said he couldn't go around giving out members' personal information. Frank said he understood, and he ended up leaving his cell number. Asked them to get a message to him from his old friend Bull. Tell Jack that they played on the all-star team together when they were young. Asked if they'd let him know that he was headed back home in the morning. Wasn't planning on coming down this way again. If he wanted to talk or to get together, to have him call that cell number. Then he thanked all the guys, told them again how much he liked their club, and promised to see if he could get his nephew to join, maybe talk him into bringing a few of his friends. Mike walked him to the edge of the parking lot.

"Mike, I'd really appreciate it if you could get Jack that message. Now that I went to all this trouble, be a shame to miss the opportunity to get reacquainted. Plus, I'm not getting any younger. Be nice to talk old times with someone I grew up with."

"I'll take care of it. Don't worry, Frank." The men shook hands one final time.

"Say, I heard you tell Keith that they called you Bull when you were a kid. That right?"

"Yeah, some did."

"Man, Bull, I like that. It sure is better than fucking Burpy."

"Well, Mike, to tell you the truth, at some point Bull turned into Bullshit, which somehow mutated into Turd Man. So, if you think on that progression, on the whole, maybe Burpy

35

wasn't so bad."

He turned and without another word headed over to his truck on the far side of the parking lot.

Bill was standing on the lawn next to a big green plastic barrel with a rake in one hand when Frank pulled up in front of the house around four-thirty that afternoon.

"You need some help there, Bill? Looks like you might almost break a sweat the way you're leaning on that rake."

"Well, it's pretty exhausting work standing here watching the cars drive by. So, tell you what, why don't we call it a day, go inside and have ourselves a beer?"

They took their beers outside to the backyard and sat at a table that was set up on a small concrete slab patio just off the kitchen. Frank had learned that Sam had run out with both boys to the local supermarket to shop for dinner. Frank had offered to take the family out for dinner, but they had decided to stay home and cook instead. Sam seemed a little nervous about leaving the house unoccupied with the windows boarded up, and Frank understood completely.

"You hear from the detectives?" asked Frank.

"Yes, I did. One of them stopped by this afternoon. Took a statement, looked around. I don't think they really have much to go on. Everyone seems to think it was some kids pulling a prank."

"Well, they're probably right. But still, if you have that detective's card, I'd like to give him a call. I thought that Officer Rudy was pretty much on the ball. Would like to hear what the detective thinks. Maybe I'll give Rudy a call, too. Couldn't hurt to press the issue a bit, make sure they keep on eye on things for the next few days."

"You think it could be something else?"

Frank picked up his beer and took a sip, thinking about what he should say, or not say. Finally, he put the beer down on the table. "No, I think it was probably just some local kids whooping it up a little. Still, I'd like to talk to the cops again. I'd just feel better making sure that someone is keeping an eye out for the next few days. It certainly can't hurt. Besides, it's probably better if a crazy old man is the one busting their balls and not you."

"Sure, Uncle Frank, if it will make you feel better. I'll give you the numbers when we go inside. I think you'd be the perfect old coot to bust the balls of local law enforcement."

Uncle Frank raised his beer in mock salute. "I appreciate your confidence in me, Bill.

A short while later, they both went back inside. Uncle Frank excused himself and said he was going to go to his room, make a few calls, and maybe lie down for a few minutes.

Later that evening, Sam cooked a dinner of roast beef with garlic mashed potatoes, corn on the cob, broccoli, carrots and a fresh garden salad. After dinner, Uncle Frank and Bill practically had to force Sam out of the kitchen and onto the couch in the living room while they cleared the table and loaded the dishwasher.

When they were done, the whole family sat around the TV in the living room, the adults talking comfortably while the kids watched the latest X-Men movie.

Around ten-thirty, Frank got up and said he was going out to his truck to get some eye drops that he had left in the glove box, and then he was going to turn in. He thanked Sam again for a wonderful dinner, said goodnight to Bill and the boys, and went to his bedroom to get his truck keys.

They heard him go out the side door. Then the truck door opened and a few seconds later it closed, and they heard Frank come back in the side door. He poked his head in before heading off to his room.

"Billy, I locked that side door, but do me a favor and double-check all the doors before you guys turn in, okay? That door heading in from the garage, too."

"Don't worry, Frank. I'll take care of it. You sleep well. We'll see you in the morning.

FIVE

Frank was lying on his back staring up at the ceiling when his cell phone went off at 3:40 a.m. He grabbed it off the little side table next the bed where he had placed it earlier, looked at the number, and then answered, talking softly.

"Hi, Jack. Glad you got my message."

"Hey, Frank. It's been a long time. I almost didn't recognize you the other day at the trap range. You look terrible, Frank, got real old-looking, getting fat around the middle, too, not like the old recon days when you were chiseled steel and sex appeal."

"No, Jack, those days are long gone."

"Gone, but not forgotten, Turd Man. I guess you got our little message the other night. Couple of All Stars back in action. Left you our calling cards, too, so you'd know who we are, just like the old days."

"Yeah, Jasper, I noticed that. Scaring women and children. Just like the old days. You were a pitiful bunch then, and I guess some things don't change. Takes three of you to bust a few windows in the middle of the night, come sneaking around to someone's house got nothing to do with anything. Cops stopped by after you and your boys hightailed it out of here. Said it looked like a couple of drunken teenagers were out playing with slingshots. Shit, Jasper, I laughed until I almost peed myself. You guys are a couple of royal fuck-ups, you know that? I didn't have the heart to give them your name and address and have them pick you up for being drunk and disorderly and stupid. Bet you got right on the phone to your boys after we ran into each other, got yourselves good and juiced up, get your courage up to come sneaking around when the ladies and the kiddies are all asleep. Geez, you guys are pathetic."

"Oh, it's good to hear you talking shit again, like the old Bull we used to know, not the fucking Turd Man you turned into. But I notice you're wide awake and bushy tailed. Not sleeping too well, I guess. Probably got yourself a piece tucked tight under your pillow."

Frank glanced at the Glock 9mm pistol on the side table. He had retrieved it earlier from its hiding place under the seat of his truck when he had told Bill and his wife that he was going out for his eye drops.

"What we did to that house was nothing, just a little warning is all, rattle your cage a bit. Want you to know that we know, that we remember, that we don't forget nor forgive. You're no better than the fucking VC, turn on your own man like you did. You're a rat motherfucker, that's what you are."

"Why don't you give it a rest there, Jasper boy? It was forty long years ago. Shit, it wasn't your mission, you weren't even there, and now here you are old and toothless talking shit. You have no idea what went down."

"Fuck you, Turd Man. We all know what went down. You killed Thumper, shot him in the back. What else we got to know? You get your ass gone, out of this town, out of this state, go on home. And watch your back, son, may be some All Stars going S&D on your ass."

"You mean the All-Star fuck-ups? You've got to be kidding. Hey, tell you what, Jasper. Why don't you and your boys come visit me? I'll make some sandwiches. We'll have us like a reunion. I'm heading home tomorrow, next day the latest. Maybe we can get together. I look forward to seeing you all. Or maybe better yet, I can come visit you boys. Maybe make a surprise visit one dark night, you know, like I was so good at back in the bad old days."

There was a moment of silence. All Frank could hear was Jasper breathing.

"You're pathetic, Jasper, you know that?" Frank said. "What happened there? You shit yourself? Why don't you go wash out your undies and tuck yourself back in for the night? You boys are just a waste of my time."

"It's been nice talking to you, Turd Man. Now why don't you to go on home to them green mountains of Vermont or wherever it is that you live? Maybe we'll see each other again someday. Maybe we'll have us that little reunion you mentioned."

"I'm looking forward to—" Frank stopped. The line had gone dead.

He reached over to put the phone down just as there was a gentle knock on the door. The doorknob turned, and the door opened slowly. Frank watched Bill's head appear, and then the rest of him entered the room. He wore boxer shorts and a white T-shirt, no socks or slippers, just bare feet. Bill closed the door and stood looking down at Frank, who was sitting on the edge of the bed.

"You want to tell me what's going on now, Uncle Frank? Want to tell me what that gun is doing on your nightstand?"

Frank pointed at a chair on the other side of the room.

"Why don't you slide that chair over a little closer? I guess I've got some explaining to do. But before we start, are Sam and the kids asleep? I don't want any more ears at my door. I guess it was the phone that woke you, right?"

Bill grabbed the back of the chair, dragged it closer to the bed, then sat down facing his uncle.

"I was awake already when the phone rang. Couldn't sleep, I guess I was still a little worried about what happened last night. It wasn't kids that broke my windows, was it?"

"No, Billy, it wasn't kids. It was a couple of old geezers that did it."

"It was whoever you were talking to, right?"

40

"His name is Jack Sprague. Everyone knew him as Jasper back in Nam. Seems everyone had a nickname. He was the man we ran into at the shooting club the other day. I went back there earlier today—well, I guess it was yesterday now—before I stopped at the mall. I poked around some, got to talking with some of the guys. It wasn't hard to get his name. After I heard it, then pieced it together, I remembered who he was. Geez, been over forty years I haven't had to think about any of those men. Wish I didn't have to now."

"Why'd he act that way towards you, so aggressive I mean? Why'd he break my windows?"

"It's over something I did a long time ago. Seems people can't let go of the past. You'd think people would forget what happened over there. But some people can't I guess, or just don't want to."

"What did you do?"

"I shot a man. His name was Jimmy Darrow. We called him Thumper."

"Thumper? Like the rabbit in that Bambi story?"

"Billy, you've got to lay off those kiddy videos. A Thumper is what we called the M79 grenade launcher. Also called it a Blooper, but we already had a guy named Blooper in the squad."

"Why'd you shoot this guy Thumper?"

"I wasn't thinking when I shot him. I just sort of reacted. His back was turned, and he was, um, I mean, he uh, he had jus—"

"Had just what?"

"I need a drink of water, Billy. Can you get me some water? Maybe you should get a drink, too. Maybe something a little stronger than water for yourself."

Billy looked at his uncle for a minute, then quietly got up and left the bedroom. He returned a few minutes later with a glass of ice water in one hand and beer in the other. He handed the water to Frank. When he did, he noticed that the gun had disappeared off the nightstand.

"I haven't talked about this in I don't know how long. Maybe the last time was that night I got soused with your Aunt Sadie. I think I told you about that. Scared her, bless her heart. It's scaring me, too, to think about it."

"You were saying that you shot Thumper. Shot him in the back. Why'd you shoot him? What was he doing?"

"He had just slit the throat of a Vietnamese child. A little girl, about five or six years old. His back was turned, but he had the kid by the hair, his arm out to the side, holding her head up. The blood was pumping out of her neck and down the front of her shirt. She was looking at me, making these gurgling sounds. I could see her eyes, the light of the moon and stars shining in them, big and scared. Anyway, that's how I remember it."

"Jesus! Why did he kill a little girl?"

"So, she wouldn't scream. You see, I had just done the same thing to her father. Cut his throat. Or maybe it was her grand-father. It's hard to remember now. I guess Thumper thought the kid was going to start screaming. He was right, of course, but, like I said, I just reacted."

"Jesus, Uncle Frank, what was a little kid doing there? This guy you killed was a VC soldier or something, right?"

Uncle Frank didn't say anything. He took a sip of water and looked at the floor.

"Come on, Uncle Frank, tell me the truth. He was a Viet Cong, right? He was the enemy." Bill's voice started to rise.

Uncle Frank picked his head up and put his finger to his lips.

"You wanted to hear some war stories Billy. It's like I told you, they're not pretty. Let me give you a little background. There was an operation during the war designed to carry out a strategy called counter-terrorism. You ever hear that term?"

Bill shook his head.

"Essentially it went that terrorism was okay so long as it was the good guys that carried out the strategy. Man, you put it in context to what's happening now, today, it makes your head spin. But it's nothing new. Been happening in every war since the Stone Age. This operation came under the auspices of the

Phoenix Program. You ever hear of that?"

Bill shook his head again.

"You should look it up online sometime. Your tax dollars at work. Anyway, it was an ungodly enterprise that was run jointly by the CIA and special ops under CIDEX, Counter Intelligence Deception and Exploitation Operations, got to be known as the CD Program; Counter Deception, but was also widely known as Count Dracula by us grunts in the field."

"You were involved in this?"

"I was. They started out using mostly South Vietnamese nationals, volunteers, to carry out operations. After a while, they looked for ARVN deserters, VC traitors, South Vietnamese criminals, anyone they could force or blackmail into carrying out these missions. They were known as Provisional Reconnaissance Units. But they also formed a few small squads made up of mostly US personnel. Was a mix of special operations forces along with a whole mess of unsavory characters they dug up to fill out the ranks. I started out as a recon marine, two tours combat duty, and I got assigned to the program. Simple as that."

"So, you were with special operations. What was this program about? I mean, what was the mission or the objective?"

"At the time, I wasn't even sure. Sometimes it was LRRPs, Long Range Reconnaissance Patrols. Sometimes we had orders to infiltrate mostly backwater enemy villages and abduct or kill specific individuals who were known enemy sympathizers or organizers. But there was more to it than that. We went out in small hunter/killer teams, usually six-man squads, four hunters to find the village or identify the individual target, then provide cover. Once we located him, then the killers would go in, two men to complete the mission."

"You were one of the killers?"

"Sometimes I was a killer, sometimes I was a hunter. Didn't matter, it was a dirty business all around. We'd often set ambushes, be out in the bush for days, no hunter/killer distinction then. We were all killers. Like I said, it was a dirty business."

Uncle Frank took another sip of his water. Bill opened his beer and took a big gulp.

"The thing about these operations was, the mission was never really clear, never totally defined. The intel was always sketchy. Part of this counter-terrorism strategy was to alter perceptions both in the South and here at home. This had been going on for years, almost since the beginning of the war. Some of these squads would be tasked with destroying whole villages and mutilating the bodies. The teams were given carte blanche. No rules of engagement, no repercussions to worry about. They wanted maximum destruction and terror. The point was to fabricate atrocities. Then the spooks or the guys in Psy-Ops would blame it all on the North, try and generate outrage toward the Viet Cong and sympathy with the cause of the South. Jesus, some of the shit that went down was unbelievable."

Uncle Frank took another sip of water. Bill noticed that Frank's hand had begun to tremble slightly.

"Okay, Frank, but what does all this have to do with us, I mean with us here and now? You shot a guy for killing a child. That's understandable. You weren't drummed out of the service for it, I saw your discharge papers hanging on the wall in your den up in Maine."

"We killed those people, me and Thumper, on a trail leading to a village. The village was deep in Indian territory, I mean VC-held ground. Once the shot rang out, my shot, the whole village came at us. I picked up Thumper, threw him over my shoulder, and ran like hell. Thankfully it was still dark, and the hunter team gave me cover fire, or I'd have been dead. We humped those hills for a couple of hours before we could get evacced. We stabilized Thumper in the field and took turns carrying him, but I shot him at close range, almost point blank with my .45. He was in bad shape. I heard later that he died. I didn't tell anyone in the team that it was me who shot him until we got back. Told the truth during my debriefing, though. Thought I was going to have to face a court-martial, but by then I'd had enough, I didn't give a damn. I wanted out of the squad, I wanted out of the war. But what's strange is, even after I told them what I'd done, they basically told me that they weren't going to do anything about it. I realized later that the guys in charge didn't really give a shit about us, our squad or our own casualties. Like I said, a lot of the guys were unsavory characters, but I'll talk more about that later. The spook in charge, the head guy at our firebase told me not to worry about it. Just like that. Said everything would be fine, just go back to my hut and lie down. I didn't know what to do. I was shaking. I guess it was that post-traumatic stress that people talk about now, but I don't know for sure. I decided right then and there that I was getting out; it was time to di di. I told this CIA guy I needed to get away, told him I'd been there long enough, did my duty. He told me to get some rest. I went back to my hut and grabbed a grenade, walked back to that spook's office, pulled the pin, grabbed that motherfucker by the throat and told the son of a bitch that if I wasn't on a chopper out of there in about thirty seconds, I was going to blow his and my ass to kingdom come. And I absolutely meant what I said. I was ready to blow us both to hell."

Billy took another big gulp of beer.

"About a half hour later, I was on a chopper out of there. Three days after that, I was heading home."

"Just like that?"

"Yeah, just like that. I heard later from a few friends, guys I had served with before, guys I knew well, that word had gotten out about what had happened. Probably that CIA guy I threatened. Word spread that I went crazy, killed Thumper and then tried to blame it on the VC. Said I was ratting out others in the squad about things that had happened, atrocities that went down on some of those raids, was trying to get the Dracula program shut down. That wasn't a stretch either. Some of those guys were facing life in prison before they got transferred into the squad. Given half a chance, I would have had some of them court-martialed, or even shot. Same for those goddamn spooks."

"What do you mean they were facing life in prison?"

"These weren't raids with military objectives against opposing forces that we were going on. We were assassination squads. Our assignment was to cause death and destruction. And our targets weren't always VC. Remember I told you that intel was sketchy? Well, turns out they were getting information from informants. And they didn't need any type of proof or verification of anything. And the informants knew that. Think about it: someone says so-and-so in the village is VC; we killed him. Usually, that's all it took."

"But that's crazy!"

"You asked me before, the man I killed, was he Vietcong? I honestly don't know. That man, the little girl, I see them sometimes at night. Them, and others, too. Most of the guys in the squad didn't care one way or the other. For some of these guys, it wasn't just an assignment, it was more of a game, like they enjoyed it. Remember I told you that Psy-Ops was involved? They had detailed jackets on everybody. I heard they screened guys, went looking for recruits in brigs and mental wards, looking for men that were unstable. Psychotic, I guess you'd say. Sick men, mentally ill, crazy. Had guys like me, from special ops, train them to kill. They'd give us these pills before operations, guys called them "blue bunnies" because they were long capsules, looked sort of like rabbit ears, I guess, said it was to keep us alert and sharp, but I don't know what they gave us. I heard later that they were feeding guys experimental, psychotic drugs, caused violent behavior. Some guys would hoard them, these pills, and then take them by the handful before contact with the enemy. You could see it working on them, their eyes light up and their faces turn red. It was scary what they became, what they were capable of doing. I didn't take anything they gave me. I knew better than to trust those spooks. But most of those guys, man, I'm surprised any of them came home. I really am. That stuff had to have done some real damage to their brains."

"And this guy, Jack Sprague, Jasper, he's one of those guys?"

"He was. Hung around with a small group of fuck-ups called themselves the All Stars. Thumper, the guy I killed, he was one of them, but not really one of the core guys. Thumper had a brain, though somewhat defective, I guess. Went to college and everything. Anyway, these guys thought of themselves as badasses, but they were just petty criminals and drug addicts. Crazy, though, every last one of them. And I helped train them, turned them into killers. Six months after I arrived in the States, I heard it was over for them. They shut it down. Not the whole program, they were still operating with Vietnamese nationals, just our little part of it. Well, that's what I heard, anyway."

"And you didn't think I should know about this? What the fuck is the matter with you, Frank? Why didn't you tell me? Why didn't you tell the police? For Christ's sake, I've got a wife and kids here."

"Easy, Bill. I didn't put it together until after the windows were already broken. I didn't know who that guy was until I went back to the trap range this afternoon. And I still wasn't one hundred percent sure it was Jasper who broke the windows until that phone call a few minutes ago."

Bill didn't say anything, just stared at this uncle, his face red and his eyes hard.

"Honestly, Billy, think about it. For all we knew it really could have been kids. Do you think I would put you and your family in danger, for even one second?"

"What about that gun? The one that was sitting on the nightstand a few minutes ago."

"That? Well, it's insurance, I guess. I already called Officer Rudy and that detective. Told them about Jasper, my suspicion that it was he and a few others that broke the windows. Rudy said him, and his partner would keep an eye on the house, make extra patrols, the detective is going to have a talk with Jasper, I guess tomorrow."

"You should have said something, Frank."

"Maybe, Billy, maybe. But what would come of it? Were you

going to move the family out of the house? You going to stand guard with your trap gun, maybe shoot some poor neighborhood kids tonight if they happen make some noise passing by your house? These guys, they're old men, like me. They weren't looking to hurt you. I don't believe they mean to hurt me, either. They were just making a point that they remember the past. Standing up for their friend. You heard the conversation; they want me to go home. And I'm leaving tomorrow. Like I told you, sometimes troubles can follow a man. I guess I brought mine here to your home, and I'm sorry, but I'm leaving tomorrow, and my troubles are leaving with me."

"What about that warning, to look over your shoulder? What does S&D mean?"

"It's all bullshit, stuff from the past. S&D, silent and deadly. It's what I taught them. But this was just an old vet talking out his ass. These guys were friends of a man I killed. I can't explain it. I don't feel guilty about what happened. Well, that's not really true, I do, but I guess it's just another horror story to come out of a war. That boy, Thumper, he was reacting, as I was. He killed that child, maybe without even thinking, to save us, the both of us. These guys, these old men, let them have their victory, chase me out of town, out of the state. It doesn't mean anything."

"And what did you mean when you said you might come visit them, make a surprise visit in the middle of the night? Were you threatening them? Is that what that was?"

"Like I said, just an old vet talking out his ass. Let's you and me take a ride down to the police station tomorrow. See what that detective has to say. If I have to, I'll file a complaint about the windows. Put everything in my name, leave you out of it. I believe this is all over with, I truly do. Still, maybe you should stay away from that trap range for a while, not provoke anything."

Bill stood up and dragged the chair back to its place on the other side of the room.

"Billy, I'm sorry for bringing this trouble to your doorstep."

Bill nodded. "Goodnight, Frank. I'll see you in the morning."

Uncle Frank lay back down on the bed and looked at the ceiling wishing he had a cigarette, though he hadn't smoked in over forty years.

Jasper put his cell phone down on his kitchen table and looked at it.

Things hadn't gone exactly as planned. Old Bull hadn't seemed as rattled as Jasper thought he should have been. And the thought of that old recon marine sneaking around his home at night put a scare into him. He hadn't seen that one coming; it had never even entered his mind. Jasper remembered the man in his prime. He was the real deal—tough, fearless and lethal. He never buddied up with any of the men in the squad, stayed mostly to himself or hung around with the other hard chargers, the Special Forces guys. Stuck-up assholes is what they were, all of them. Looked at the rest of us like we were shit on their shoes. He was also the one who had trained most of the squad, taught them how to move quietly through the jungle, taught them how to use a knife, taught them how to kill, silent and deadly.

He smiled to himself. We learned good, Turd Man. Served us well. And now we're coming for you.

There was a half-finished bottle of Wild Turkey on the table in front of him. He twisted off the cap and took a pull straight out of the bottle.

The man was dangerous, no doubt. On the phone, he had challenged him to come up there to Maine and get him, like he didn't have a care in the world. Jasper was glad he hadn't mentioned that he knew where old Bull lived. Turd Man, he corrected himself. He smiled again when he remembered telling him to go on home to the green mountains of Vermont. He had pulled that little gem out of his ass, a little spontaneous misdirection that could buy them some time. Wouldn't do to let the man know what they knew, let him know what they were up to, that they were coming for him and give him time to set up and get ready.

They had talked about it all afternoon, him and the boys. They were ready. Pogo had told him that he had a little surprise stashed away. Wouldn't say what it was, just that it would bring back some old memories. Wanted to surprise them. Surprise Turd Man as well. Birdie said he would borrow his cousin's pick-up truck for the trip, had an extended cab and an old Lance camper already attached. This way they could camp out, stay in the woods or at a campsite, be mobile and leave no trace that might come back to haunt them later.

He was glad to have Pogo and Birdie with him on this mission. He would probably have gone after him alone, but he wouldn't have liked his chances. Would have had to bide his time, wait a few weeks, months even, and then take him from a distance. Might still be the best way, but where's the sport in that? Three against one if we move fast, those are much better odds. Make us a hunter/killer team, just like in Nam. Maybe we'll wound him first, put him down, and then take him with a knife up close and personal.

His stomach gave a little twirl that he realized was half fear, half anticipation.

Then again, maybe it was just the Wild Turkey settling in.

SIX

Frank was packed, and all squared away, sitting in the kitchen drinking coffee when Bill got up. It was about 6 a.m. Frank hadn't slept much after the call from Jasper. He'd lain there staring at the ceiling thinking about the past, about his Sadie mostly, about how much he missed her. He was going to head back up to Maine today, just a matter of what time he could get on the road.

"Morning, Bill. I took the liberty of putting on a pot of coffee. I hope I didn't wake you, rustling around at this early hour."

Bill didn't say anything. Frank sipped his coffee and gave him room.

Bill poured himself a cup, added sugar and cream, and then sat down at the table and stared into his cup without saying anything.

"I know you're upset, Billy, and you've certainly got the right. But I don't see how this should have been handled any different. I'm sorry about the windows and I'm sorry about Jasper, but I feel like I was walking up hill and all this shit just started rolling down. You and me, we happened to be in the way. Like I said, I think the best thing for us to do is head on over to the police department and let them know what we know. Then I'll head on home. Once I'm gone, there's no reason for anyone to bother you and your family."

Bill took a sip of his coffee and finally looked up at his uncle.

"What about you? Do you think this nut case will follow

you up to Maine? Is there any chance there could be more trouble down the line?"

"I honestly don't think so, Bill. I'm betting that this guy remembered me from out of the fog of the past, then called up some of his buddies and they all got together over a bunch of beer in some dive bar and worked themselves up. I'm surprised, really, that they didn't get pulled over for DWI or run their car into a tree or something."

"How'd he find my house?"

"That I don't know. Maybe someone at the club knew who you were, or maybe he got the license plate of your truck and found out through that somehow. Can you find that information on the internet? I don't even know."

Bill took another sip of his coffee and thought back to the incident at the trap club. He remembered looking in his rearview mirror and seeing Jack Sprague writing in a notepad. Probably jotting down his car's license plate. It was the only thing that made sense. Bill didn't know anybody at the club. He only shot there on occasion and hadn't made any friends, hadn't really even introduced himself to anyone. That might be something he should mention to the cops later on, about the license plate.

"I don't know if you can find that out online. I don't think so. Let's ask that detective when we go see him later this morning."

After that both men seemed a bit more at ease with each other, and they sat drinking coffee until Sam and the kids go up about twenty minutes later.

Hackensack is a small city with a police force of just over one hundred officers. The headquarters are off the main street in the downtown section in a large, old municipal building. Frank and Bill entered through the front door and spoke with a uniformed officer through a glass partition. They told him that they had an appointment with Detective Tom Aletta. They waited until another officer came out and walked them up to the detective bureau on the third floor. Instead of a private office, the detective occupied a small, cluttered desk in a room full of small, cluttered desks. There were only two other people in the room, both in street clothes and wearing guns in holsters at the hip. One sat at a desk across the room talking on the phone. The other stood pouring coffee from a glass carafe next to a coffeemaker that stood on a counter in the far corner of the room.

Detective Aletta stood, shook hands with Frank and Bill, then offered them each a chair in front of his desk. He opened a manila folder that was sitting on the desk in front of him and began reading silently.

"Mr. Thompson, as you know, I've looked at the damage to your property and I spoke with the two responding officers, and I still believe that the windows were broken with some sort of sling shot. I had some officers canvass the area, talk to your neighbors to see if anyone saw or heard anything, but we found that most of them were sleeping soundly until they were awakened by the lights of the cruiser and the car doors opening and closing."

"My uncle told me that he spoke to you about this guy, Jack Sprague, that we ran into at the trap range."

"Yes, he did. He told me he felt that Mr. Sprague might have had something to do with this."

"Well, Detective," said Frank, "there's a bit more to the story now. Mr. Sprague called me last night, I mean this morning, about three-thirty or so, and told me it was he and a few of his buddies that broke the windows. Wanted to put a scare into me."

"Why does Mr. Sprague want to scare you, Mr. Thompson?"

"Well, this is going to sound crazy, but I believe it's over something that happened about forty or so years ago. Mr. Sprague and I were in the service together." He looked over at Bill, then continued. "He and some of his buddies were involved in some petty thefts, and I turned them in. Even though I haven't seen them since that time, it seems they still hold a grudge."

"Were they incarcerated or dishonorably discharged as a result?"

"No, nothing like that. Reprimanded is all. I think this guy just recognized me, got himself liquored up and then called some of his buddies and they went on a tear. It's not only teenagers that get drunk and do stupid things, Detective. Sometimes us old farts are guilty of the same behavior. Look, what I'd like, what we'd like, is if maybe you could talk to this guy, put a scare into him. I don't see him admitting to you that he broke those windows, and all we have here is my word against his as to what was said over the phone this morning. But I know I'd feel a whole lot better if he realized that the police know who he is and what he's done. We don't want my nephew Bill, or his family bothered again. Bill's got a wife and two small boys. Everyone was pretty shaken up with the window's being broken. This guy told me he wants me gone, and I'm happy to give him what he wants. In fact, I'm heading back home up to Maine this afternoon and I told him so over the phone, so I don't expect any more trouble. But like I said, we'd both sure feel better if you would speak to the man."

"Do you have his cell number? I'm guessing it's still on your phone. I can find it, but this will save some time."

Frank took out his phone, searched his incoming call log, and found the number.

Detective Aletta picked up his phone and dialed. After a few seconds, he mouthed the words "voice mail." A few seconds later he began speaking.

"Mr. Sprague, this is Detective Aletta from the Hackensack Police Department. We've had an incident here in town, and I'd like to ask you some questions. I'd appreciate it if you would call me back, save me the trouble of coming to your home to conduct a personal interview. You can reach me at 201-555-1923. The matter is urgent, and I thank you in advance for your cooperation." He then hung up the phone.

"I'll follow up with Mr. Sprague, but I'm afraid that like you already noted, Mr. Thompson, there's not much I can do unless he's willing to talk, admit to breaking the windows. I spoke with

Officers Breslow and Stevens, and I know that you've spoken with them as well. They will continue to keep an eye out on your house Mr. Thompson." He looked over at Bill when he said this. "In fact, we have several units patrolling the area, and each has been ordered to make frequent, random passes down your block. You can file a complaint against Mr. Sprague if you like, that's up to you. My feeling is that the incident is over, but like I said, I will have a talk with Mr. Sprague and maybe shake his tree a bit, let him know we're watching."

The detective stood, indicating that the meeting was over. Frank and Bill got up slowly, then shook the man's hand and made their way back downstairs and out the front door to where Frank's truck was parked on the street.

SEVEN

Jasper hadn't answered his phone when it rang earlier that morning. First off, he slept late. And second, he was slightly hung over and he didn't want to take any calls from numbers that he didn't recognize. Good thing, too, because it was a cop who had called him. He guessed that Turd Man had gone to the police, or maybe it was that young guy he was staying with, his nephew. Didn't matter; Jasper wasn't about to talk to any cops. They had nothing on him, couldn't prove that he'd been to the house in Hackensack and only had Turd Man's say-so that it was Jasper who had busted those windows. He didn't think that any detective would drive all the way from Hackensack to his house in Hibernia to talk about some broken windows, but he wanted to get gone just in case. They might have the local cops stop by, and he didn't want to talk to them either.

So, by eleven Monday morning Jasper was packed and ready to go. He packed like he packed for his hunting trips, which in fact, this was. It was early April, and up north it would still be real cold, especially at night. He also had his sleeping bag and pup tent, just in case. He didn't know how big the camper was and wasn't sure he wanted to be cooped up with Birdie and Pogo regardless of its size. He'd slept outdoors countless times and didn't mind at all sleeping under the stars as long as he had the proper equipment. Travel light, he told himself. When he was done packing, he went downstairs to his unfinished basement.

He walked over to a large wooden chest that was about knee-high off the ground, three feet wide and maybe five feet long. The box was held shut by a hinged hasp with a combination padlock. He bent down, dialed the combination, and then opened the box. Inside, the box was lined with green felt and had homemade brackets to hold his long guns—two rifles and three shotguns. It also had several small shelves built into the sides where he kept his handguns and assorted boxes of ammunition.

He reached in and grabbed his M16. He had bought it from a guy he met at a gun show in Nevada several years ago. The man had an arsenal in a shed out behind his home in the Nevada desert. This was the same type rifle he had used in the war, and this one had not been modified so it was illegal: it could be fired either semi-automatic or full automatic. He had two thirty-round clips full of cartridges, plus four extra boxes of ammo with twenty rounds in each box. He walked to a hat rack in the corner of the basement where an assortment of soft padded gun cases hung. He took one, put the M16 into it, zipped it closed, and then set it down on the floor. He didn't know what firepower the other guys had, so he also grabbed his favorite deer rifle and scope. It would be the perfect weapon if they decided to take him from a distance. He grabbed another soft case and slipped the rifle into it. We're loaded for bear, he said to himself. Or for Bull, he thought, and that made him smile. He reached into the box and grabbed his Smith & Wesson .38 caliber revolver. It was the handgun he was most comfortable with, the one he took with him on hunting trips to carry as an emergency sidearm. He then closed and locked the box and gathered all his firearms and extra ammunition boxes and headed upstairs.

First thing he did was carry the guns out to his Jeep Liberty and lay them in the back covered by a blanket. Then he locked the car doors and went back inside. Turd Man had said he was leaving today, tomorrow the latest. The plan was to meet at Birdie's house up in Suffern, New York. He said he'd have the camper all gassed up and ready to go. Pogo lived somewhere near Rahway, New Jersey. Since Birdie's house was north of the both of them, it made sense to meet there, as they'd already be heading in the right direction. They'd make the trip up north, scout out the area where Turd Man lived, and then see what developed. He loaded the rest of his gear into the car, did a quick walk through of the house, and then locked the doors and windows. Next, he was going to take a ride over to Mount Olive, pass by his son's house. His son was an electrical contractor and owned his own business. Jasper worked for him part time. He had already told him that he was going away for a few days and that he wanted him to take his cell phone, told him not to answer the phone but to make a few calls over the next few days. The kid was smart enough not to ask any questions. No point in leaving a phone record of where he was. Damn phones had GPS. This way, if he ever needed to, his phone would show that he never left the state. He would talk to the other guys about their phones as well. Maybe pick up a pay-as-you-go phone at one of those discount stores. He wanted to cover his tracks because as it stood right now, it was only his ass on the line. His was the only name that the cops had so far. Better for everybody if it stayed that way.

He arrived at Birdie's house around 1 p.m. Sure enough, sitting there in the driveway was a beat-up old Lance camper set atop a ten-year-old Chevy Silverado extended-cab pick-up truck. Jasper was glad that he had packed his camping gear. No way three men could spend the night comfortably in that camper. No way. He pulled up, and Birdie came walking out of his split-level home. His wife, Nancy, came out right after him.

Birdie was a tall man, about six-four. In his youth, he had been stick thin, but had since filled out, and now a bit of a beer gut hung slightly over his belt. His hair was mostly white, thick and neatly trimmed. His most distinguishing feature was his large beak nose. His wife was a handsome woman, thin and tall with hair dyed an unnatural red color. She was wearing a pretty yellow summer dress and a slightly awkward, uncertain smile.

"Hi, Jack, nice to see you again." She walked over and gave him a light hug.

"Hi yourself, Nancy. It's been a while. You're looking as beautiful as ever." Jasper smiled his crooked smile. She stepped away from him and grabbed hold of Birdie's arm, as if for protection. Jasper always got the feeling that Nancy didn't like him, that maybe she was afraid of him. He didn't mind.

"Well, what do you think, Jasper? Perfect vehicle for a turkey hunt or what?" He gently lifted his wife's hand off his arm. "Honey, I'm going to show old Jasper the camper. Why don't you go on inside, maybe make a few sandwiches for me and the boys, you know, for the ride." She turned and left without saying a word.

Birdie opened the back door of the camper and Jasper went to his Jeep and began grabbing his bags and weapons and handing them to Birdie, who placed them on the camper's floor. When everything was loaded, both men climbed into the camper and closed the door.

"Well, Jasper, what toys did you bring us to play with?" asked Birdie, rubbing his hands together like a child, a big smile on his face.

Jasper looked at him through his sunglasses and smiled back, then began unzipping one of the soft padded gun cases, teasing the zipper down like he was savoring the anticipation.

"Will you look at that! An M16, just like in the day! Man, this is fucking cool!" Birdie took the gun from Jasper and held it in his hands, then held it to his shoulder and sighted it toward the back door of the camper.

"Does it fire auto?"

"It does, and I got two full clips and a few spare boxes of ammo. Brought my Savage with a scope, too, just in case we need to get him from a distance. Wasn't sure what you boys had locked in your closet, so I figured I better bring both. What about you? Do you have anything to throw into the kitty, Birdman?"

"Well, hell, Jasper, I don't think I can beat this shit." He was sitting on a bunk and got up, then grabbed the edge and lifted it to reveal a storage area. Jasper got up and looked into dark box. "I got my shotgun. Told Nancy we were going turkey hunting. But I also got these new shells, they're called Hexolites, made in Latvia." He handed a box containing five of the tactical shells to Jasper. "Supposed to punch a hole the size of a bowling ball into any living thing it comes in contact with. And I got this."

He reached into the box and came out holding a dark handgun with an extended barrel. He handed the gun to Jasper.

"Man, Birdie, this is sweet!" Jasper turned the gun in his hand, admiring it, feeling its weight. "That a silencer on the end?"

"Sig Sauer 9mm with a suppressor. It's not totally silent like you see in the movies, but it cuts the noise down quite a bit. Maybe seventy percent or so."

"Damn, boy, you're full of surprises."

"Buddy of mine got it out in Arizona. I didn't even know you could get a silencer unless you were some sort of secret agent or something. But this guy told me they're legal out west. Said he bought it off of some guy that he met out there while traveling cross-country. Maybe at one of those gun shows, though he didn't have any paperwork for it. His wife found it after they got back home and freaked out. Guy said she thought he was a hit man for the mob or something. I thought it was cool as hell, so he sold it to me."

He took the pistol back and placed it in the storage bin, then began loading Jasper's weapons in as well.

"I'm thinking, if we can sneak up close, we can use a knife or pop him with the Sig. He knows you now, Jasper, but I'm sure he won't remember Pogo or me, least not right away. Just got to get him alone, someplace quiet. I looked up his address and scoped out his house on Google Earth. You can see it's pretty desolate where he lives, real rural. It looks like a small town, not much to it, and he lives on the outskirts, big piece of property, several acres, anyway. I only saw one or two other houses on his street, then nothing but woods. We just have to do a little recon. Wish we had a night scope. You bring a night scope?"

"Don't own one. But truth is, I didn't even think about that. A fucking night scope, that's what we need."

Pogo arrived about a half hour later. He was driving a dusty old lime-green 2000 Toyota Rav4. He got out of his car, and when he saw Jasper and Birdie, he lifted both arms high and whooped like an Indian in an old western movie. He was wearing green paratrooper pants that had large pockets running down the outsides of both legs, well-worn work boots and a black T-shirt. He hadn't shaved in a day or two, and gray stubble covered his face. He was reed thin, but his hard, knotty, muscular arms and defined chest and stomach seemed out of place on a man in his mid-sixties. He had a stud earring in his left ear and wore his long, salt-and-pepper colored hair hanging down the sides of his head in two tight braids. He looked a lot like the Willie Nelson of a few years ago.

"My brothers in arms." His voice boomed as he walked up to the two men taking long strides and bear hugged each of them in turn.

"Pogo, you crazy motherfucker," said Birdie. "How goes the war with the Indians?"

"The renegades are on the warpath, my friend, and them renegades is us!" He was smiling broadly, his eyes shining and just a little off somehow, like he was seeing everything from a distance. The smell of cannabis and some other burnt substance drifted off his clothes and hair.

"Looks like you started the party a little early," said Jasper.

"Well, shit, Jasper, as far as I'm concerned, every party calls for a little celebrating. I don't care if it's three old buddies going to a kiddy birthday party or the second coming of the All Stars putting together a fucking war party. I brought the chemicals to help see us through it." He clapped Jasper on the shoulder and smiled at him with his shining eyes.

"Amen to that, brother!" said Birdie.

"What say you, brother Jasper?" asked Pogo.

Jasper looked back at this friend and smiled his crooked smile. "I say let's put on the war paint and fire up the hash pipe. We've got some unfinished business to attend to."

"That's the spirit!" Pogo raised his hands again and let out another Indian war whoop. All three men burst into laughter.

"Now I promised you boys I was going to bring a little surprise. Why don't you climb into the back of that camper and I'll go fetch what I brought?"

As Pogo turned and started walking back to his car, Jasper saw Birdman's wife peeking at them from behind a curtain in the living room window. She saw him look over, and she stepped back. Maybe this wasn't such a good place to leave from, Jasper thought. Maybe that woman was smart to be afraid of him. Then Birdie opened the camper door again, and both men stepped inside.

They were sitting side by side on the bunk when Pogo entered carrying a rifle wrapped in a big SpongeBob SquarePants beach towel. He leaned against a small shelf and pulled back the towel to reveal what looked like an assault rifle.

"Hot damn, Pogo, is that an AK-47? Where in the hell did you get that?" Birdie stood and bonked his head on the cabinet. He grabbed his head and sat back down slowly.

"Easy there, Birdie. Guy your size ain't meant for a camper this size. And to answer your questions, first, this is not an AK-47. But it is another marvel of mayhem from those wonderful commie bastards. This is a Kalashnikov RPK light machine gun. A bit longer and heavier than the AK. Came with a bipod mount and a seventy-five-round drum magazine."

"Lord Almighty, that is some serious firepower, Pogo. What the hell you planning to do with it?" asked Birdie.

"I'm not really sure yet, Birdman. I bought it from a kid I know runs in one of those Mexican gangs, lives right nearby where I do down in Rahway. Those guys, man, they've got all

kinds of shit, you just wouldn't believe it. I help them out sometimes, do some favors for them."

"What else they got?" asked Jasper.

"Hell, son, you name it, they got it. Or can get it. Kid told
me he could get me an RPG if the money was right. I believe
him too."

"This is just one guy we're after here, Pogo," said Birdie,
looking at one man, then the other. "You guys really think
we're going to need a fucking machine gun?"

"Better to have it and not need it then the other way
around," said Jasper. "You fire this thing yet, Pogo?"

Pogo beamed, "You bet your ass I did. Look at this baby!
How could I not? Guy, I did some work for owns land way
upstate New York. I went up there and shot about four of
those drums' worth, just to get the feel of her. Had me a fucking
boner the whole time, too!"

"Seems like overkill to me," said Birdie. "Hell, we've got
enough firepower in here to take on a whole NVA regiment."

"Birdie, right now we're three little Indians hunting us one
solitary cowboy. But suppose he calls in the cavalry, what then?
We don't really know what we're facing, do we? Us three, we're
still together. Suppose he calls in some of his hard charger
buddies, got himself a little army full of old special forces guys.
What are we gonna do then? This ain't like the old days when
we had a hunter squad there to give us cover, blow the shit out of
anything trying to creep down our drawers. But with this baby
right here," he said, patting the RPK, "no matter how many
fucking special ops traitors we got on our ass, any one of us
becomes a hunter squad all by his lonesome."

Jasper reached over and ran his index finger gently down the
long barrel. "Damn, Pogo, I do believe this thing is giving me a
woody, too, and I ain't even fired her yet."

EIGHT

Frank lived outside a town called Boland in Cumberland County, Maine, near the New Hampshire border. His house was on an unmarked road off US Route 201. The area where he lived was semi-rural, about two miles south of town out in the woods and about three miles from a body of water called Altman's Pond. Altman's was bigger than a pond, but not as large as some of the lakes in the area. There were only about twelve-hundred full-time residents in Boland, but since the area was renowned for its hunting, fishing and hiking, there were also a good number of tourists visiting on and off year-round to enjoy all that the seasons had to offer.

The air was cold, and the road was dark with about an inch of fresh snow blanketing the ground as Frank pulled off Route 201 and onto the road where he lived. He passed both his neighbors' homes and saw lights on in some of the windows along with the bluish glow of TV screens. The houses were set back, maybe a hundred or so yards from the road. What Frank liked about where he lived was that he couldn't see his neighbors' homes from his own, the houses separated by at least a quarter mile, but he could walk to either in minutes if need be. He and Sadie had liked the privacy and solitude that their home afforded them, but they were also glad they weren't living in total isolation.

It was nearly 11 p.m. when he pulled into the long driveway that led to the house he and Sadie had shared for nearly thirty years. His was the last house at the end of the street. Only one light was on in the house as Frank pulled into the driveway, a table lamp that Frank had attached to a timer that turned on at 5 p.m. and off at midnight. His truck crunched over the light coating of frozen snow as he pulled up to a large, detached, two-car garage. He got out of the truck, leaving his lights on, and lifted the garage door by hand, then got back in and drove the truck slowly into its spot next to his wife's Subaru Forester.

He got out of his truck and looked at his wife's car, and his heart warmed at the thought of his Sadie waiting inside. Then reality hit him like a sledgehammer, and his head spun, and he thought he might fall over right there in his garage, and he put his hand on the SUV for support, and suddenly he felt a cold, hollow ache inside and thought he might throw up. He stood like that, his head down, his hand on the roof of the car, waiting. He hoped that maybe he was having a heart attack. Maybe he'd slide to the floor and close his eyes and just not wake up. But the dizziness passed, and he took a few deep breaths to steady himself. He opened the door to the truck and removed his travel bag and then reached under the front seat and grabbed his Glock. He shoved the gun into the front waistband of his pants, shut the garage door and walked toward the front porch feeling tired and worn down and old.

The house was cold. He had set the temperature at fifty-two degrees before he left, and now he turned on a few lights and walked over to the thermostat that hung on the dining room wall and turned it up to sixty. He walked into the kitchen and turned on the Keurig coffeemaker that Sadie had gotten for him last Christmas and then carried his bag to the spare bedroom that he now called his own. He found that he no longer felt comfortable sleeping in the room he had shared with his wife for so long, not without her sleeping next him. The house was quiet, and he flipped on the TV in the den just for the noise and went back to the kitchen and made himself a cup of coffee and then put an English muffin into the toaster. He pulled the 9mm out of his waistband and laid it on the kitchen table. When his toast popped up, he tossed both pieces on a paper plate, got butter out of the fridge and then sat there, drinking coffee and eating his toasted muffin. After he was finished eating, he sat for a long while staring at the gun, trying hard not to think about anything at all.

NINE

Birdie drove the truck with Jasper as copilot sitting next to him. Pogo sat in the back seat of the extended cab rolling an occasional joint, which they passed around. Birdie had stashed a pint bottle of Jim Beam in the glove compartment, and that got passed around as well. They were trying not to overindulge, since they didn't want a state trooper to pull them over and end their party before it started. But traffic had been light, and Birdie was a slow and cautious driver, so they saw no reason not to enjoy themselves a little.

Jasper had a road map of the East Coast and another of Maine. He had warned his two friends about bringing any electronic devices like GPSes and especially their cell phones, but Birdie had decided to bring his daughter's old iPad, explaining that it might come in handy if they got lost or if they needed to get any information off the internet. They decided to bring it, but to use it only if absolutely necessary.

Pogo talked almost non-stop the entire drive through New York, Connecticut and Massachusetts. His stories seemed to get funnier as the drive wore on and the joints and the Beam got passed around, and they all laughed a lot, enjoying each other's company.

When they had passed through Boston, Pogo seemed to be running out of stories and the truck got quiet for a while. Then Pogo came alive again.

"Hey, Jasper, what ever happened to your wife?" he asked. He was lying across the back seat now, his hands laced behind his head, feet propped up against the passenger-side door, head leaning against the opposite door.

"Deena? She was never really my wife. We just lived together off and on for like thirty years. She moved out for good about five or six years ago. Haven't really talked to her since the front door hit her ass on the way out. She still talks to our boy once in a while, but he don't see her much either, or so he says."

"No, not Deena," Pogo said, "that other one, the one with the big titties. She was a stripper or something, wasn't she? When you first met her, I mean. I can picture her, but I can't remember her name."

"I bet what you're picturing is them big knockers bouncing around, Pogo." Birdie started laughing, by himself at first, and then the others joined in, Pogo once again whooping like an Indian in the back seat.

When the laughing fit had died down, Jasper reached into the glove box and took out the now half empty bottle of Beam and took a pull.

"That was Roxy, my first wife. Well, my only wife, really. And yeah, she used to dance. Had a set of tits on her like I never seen. And they were real, too, not those silicone jobs most of the girls sport these days. Had a nice can, too."

"Yeah, I remember," said Pogo with a smile in his voice, "but in a brotherly sort of way, you understand. She had some fine friends, too, as I recall."

"I bet you remember *them* in a not so brotherly way, ain't that right partner?" Birdie adjusted the rearview mirror with his right hand, so he could better see Pogo in back.

"Yeah, Birdie, you got that right. Those were some wild times back then. All you'd need is a little coke, and you could take them bitches two, three at a time. They'd line up to suck your dick."

"You mean you were bribing them to suck your dick with

coke? Man, Pogo, I'm disillusioned and disappointed. Here I always thought it was your good looks and charm got them girls to line up."

"Well, Birdman, good looks and charm is one thing and being hung like an ox is another, but a baggie full of coke sure don't hurt your chances none."

All three men laughed again.

"Something I always wanted to ask you, Jasper. Why in the hell did you marry that girl? I mean, she was a looker, all right, and she seemed nice enough, but why'd you decide to actually tie the knot? Just don't seem like something you'd do."

"Well, looking back on it, I don't really have a good answer. I guess it was because she liked to fuck every which way, couldn't get enough. Sweet ride, too, best I ever had. And she was a looker, that's for sure. I'd walk down the street with that girl on my arm, man, I'd have to watch where I'd step, guys' tongues hanging out all over the place. Took her to Vegas one time, came back married, simple as that."

"How long were you with her? Married, I mean?"

"I don't really recall. Maybe a year, something like that, anyway."

"What happened? She run off? You kick her ass out on the street?"

"Sort of. It ended for the same reason it started; because she liked to fuck every which way, only turns out it wasn't just me going for that ride, you know?"

"Even after you married her? That lowlife bitch!"

"How'd you find out she was cheating on you, Jasper?" asked Birdie.

"It was a bunch of things, you know? She'd get a phone call and then drag the phone into the next room, so I couldn't hear. When I asked who it was she was talking to, it was always some friend of hers. I'd call or come home unexpected, and she wouldn't be there. Or I'd be home, and the phone would ring, and I'd pick it up, and soon as I answered, the line would go dead. Still pains me to think about it."

"You ever catch the son of a bitch?" asked Pogo.

"No, I never found out who he was. I would have fixed his ass good, I can tell you that. I had my suspicions, though."

"I bet old Pogo here was number one on your list!" said Birdie, and all three laughed again. "So, what'd you do, divorce that cunt and throw her out on her ass? You should have made her tell you who that fucker was."

"Believe me, I tried. She never would admit it. Right until the end she kept saying she wasn't cheating on me. Lying piece of shit. Woman who looks like that, sneaking around all the time, I ain't stupid."

"So, what'd you do, get divorced?" Birdie asked again.

"No, not officially anyway. I guess we separated is the best way to put it. She left one day and never came back. I never heard from her again. In fact, no one I know ever heard from her again. She just up and disappeared."

Nobody said anything for a second and then Pogo said, "Holy shit, you motherfucker!" and started laughing hysterically.

"What's so funny, Pogo?" Birdie took the bottle of Beam from Jasper and took a short pull.

Pogo was howling with laughter in the back, tears rolling down his face.

Jasper turned in his seat and looked at his friend. "What the hell are you laughing at, Pogo?"

Pogo reached behind his head and down behind his neck. Then he slowly pulled a K-bar combat knife from the sheath he had strapped to the middle of his back. He laid the knife on his chest, its gleaming tip pointed up toward his throat.

"I had some of the same type troubles in my day, Jasper boy, with several different women. And goddamn if the same thing didn't happen. One day each of them poor girls just up and left and never came back. Disappeared."

Jasper didn't say anything for a minute. Then he smiled his crooked smile. "Disappeared, eh?"

"Yeah, Jasper, ain't that something? Just up and left one day and never been heard from since. By nobody." Pogo picked up his K-bar by the blade tip, flipped it in the air once and caught it by the handle. Then he raised himself slightly and reached back over his head and slipped the knife back into its sheath.

"Crazy bitches," said Jasper. "Unfortunately for them, they didn't know what kind of crazy they were dealing with."

"Amen to that, brother. What about you, Birdie?" asked Pogo. "You ever have some woman disappear from your life like that? Just leave and no one ever hears from her ever again?"

"No, I can honestly say that never happened to me," said Birdie. "I've been married thirty-three years, and she's still with me."

"Hell, boy, either she's a fucking saint or she's dinky dau," Pogo said.

Birdie reached back without looking and handed the bottle of Beam to Pogo, who took it and then took a long pull.

"I guess she's pretty much both, depending on the day. But on the subject of strange disappearances, I did have a former boss who used to like to get in my shit. Biggest douchebag you ever met. He finally got my ass fired. Three years later I found out that motherfucker had a sales meeting at some hotel right near where I work now over in White Plains. It was one of those two- or three-day seminar things, supposed to get you all pumped up to go out and sell shit. Usually run by a bunch of rah-rah, suck-up assholes. I had to go to them a few times, sit there with a fake smile on my face thinking about fragging the whole fucking bunch of them. Anyway, funny thing is, about a week or two later, I heard from some guy I know that my ex-boss, the douchebag, he never showed up for work after that. He just quit showing up, and no one knows where he went or what ever happened to him. Seems he ain't been heard from since."

"Disappeared," said Jasper.

"Yeah," said Birdie, "disappeared. Like as if someone slit his throat one day and dumped him in a pre-dug hole in the woods near a rest stop off the Taconic Parkway."

"Just like that," said Jasper.

"Yeah, just like that," replied Birdie, looking straight ahead at the road.

"Damn," said Pogo, "I've missed you boys!"

"Well, son," said Jasper reaching over the seat to take back the bottle of Beam, "if you really feel that way, why don't you show us some love and roll another one of them Bong Son Bombers?"

It took almost seven hours to get from Suffern to the Portland area of Maine. They had stopped several times for gas, piss breaks, and to load up on hamburgers, fried chicken and other junk food. Now Birdie had to pee again, so he got off I-95 at one of the Riverton exits and jumped onto Route 302 heading north. He also had a powerful craving for a Snickers bar and decided to look for some place where he could piss, buy candy and maybe pick up another bottle of Jim Beam. Pogo and Jasper were involved in a deep discussion about the many strip clubs each had visited, ranking them in terms of the quality of the dancers, the nationality of the women, location of the club, the availability and cost of sex and how far you could take your fun until you got thrown out on your ass.

It wasn't until about forty-five minutes later that Jasper looked out into the dark night and realized that they were no longer on the highway.

"Birdie, where the hell are we?"

I'm not really sure. I got off 95 a ways back to pee and maybe get us another bottle of Beam. I think we're on 302. I know we're past Portland."

"Shit, Birdie, I hope you don't pee your pants," said Pogo from the back seat.

"Well, I sort of lost the urge, but now that we're talking about it, I just might."

Jasper got the map spread out on his lap and he grabbed a

small flashlight from the glove compartment. He put his finger on Portland and found Route 302 and began following it with his finger.

"Did we get to a town called Naples yet?"

"Fuck if I know. I haven't seen anything but woods or farms for miles. We may have passed a town back there, if you can even call it that. I didn't see a 7-Eleven or liquor store, not even a fucking McDonald's."

"We're in the wilds now, son. A whole lot of nothing is what you get up here in the North Country. Gotta start watching out for fucking moose crossing the roads," said Pogo, now propping his chin on the back of Birdie's seat.

"You're shitting me."

"I shit you not, Birdman. Big bull can get up to fifteen-hundred pounds. Hit one of those suckers, and chances are you'll total the truck and maybe only manage to piss him off."

"Hell, I'd love to see a moose."

"Should be a town called Bridgton up the road," said Jasper. "Looks like it might be something. Maybe there's a store sells something besides farm implements and chainsaws."

"Well, Birdman, if we see one, I sure hope it's in the daylight and not at night going down one of these dark roads. Because if we run into one up close and personal like, then this trip is over."

"Pogo, I've seen moose that look a whole lot better than some of the women you've stuck your pecker into over the years," said Jasper.

"It's my libido that gets me going, Jasper. I can't help myself. Shit, there's times I get so horny I'd probably fuck a snake if you'd hold it."

"I believe you would, brother, I believe you would."

"Hey, there's a sign up ahead. It says 'Bridgton, 2 miles.'" Birdie cracked his window and let out a loud fart. "I hope they have a grocery store, I'd give just about anything for a fucking Snickers bar."

"Hell, I hope they have a pharmacy, Birdman," said Pogo,

"I'd give just about anything to get you a box of Gas-X."

They rolled into Bridgton a few minutes later. Birdie looked at the clock on the dash and saw that it was a little before 10 p.m. The town seemed nearly deserted, just a few cars on the street, most of the local stores along the main strip of the small downtown already closed for the night.

"Jesus," said Birdie, "can you imagine living around here? I'd go fucking nuts. What the hell do these people do at night? I don't see a movie theater, a restaurant, not even a fucking bar."

"Not everyone is as cosmopolitan as we are, Birdman. Place is probably rocking and rolling at 5 a.m., all those farmers, early risers, milking the chickens and butt fucking the hogs. Where do you think your bacon and eggs come from?"

"Wow, Pogo, you must stay up late watching a lot of those nature shows, learning all about farming and living off the land. And here I always thought my breakfast came directly from the ShopRite."

"Keep driving," said Jasper, as he looked out the window searching for signs of life. "There's got to be somewhere these shit kickers get their hooch, probably near the edge of town. Place closed down like this as early as it is, people probably sitting in front of the TV watching *Dancing with the Stars* and getting stewed."

They drove about a quarter of a mile to the end of the main drag, and when the stores and businesses started thinning out, they came upon what looked like a small convenience store with the lights on and a neon Miller Lite sign in the window and Jasper said, "Bingo."

The store was a small, stand-alone building at the very end of town. The large front windows were covered with posters advertising different beers. All the posters seemed to feature beautiful young women in skimpy cheerleader outfits or bikinis. There were also several bright orange signs with the word SALE prominently displayed and the names and prices of different brands of beer and wine and liquor hand lettered using a thick black marker.

The entrance to the parking lot was to the right of the store, and the small lot had parking spaces on the side and also around behind the building. Birdie pulled the truck to the back lot and parked next to the only other car there, a slightly beat up older Toyota Corolla.

All three men got out and Birdie said, "You guys go on ahead in. I've got to pee like a racehorse. I'm going to walk back there by those trees and take a leak. I'll see you inside."

There was a sidewalk that led around to the front entrance, but there was also a door right in back that had an OPEN sign hanging from a hook attached to the glass with a suction cup right next to where they had parked the truck, and so they entered through that door. A bell chimed as they walked into a small storeroom loaded with stacked cases of beer and wine and assorted liquor. There was also a broom and a mop in a bucket next to a pile of flattened cardboard boxes. Off to the left was a small desk with a computer monitor on it and what looked like an old Dell tower sitting underneath. Beyond that was a small bathroom, the door was ajar, and you could just make out the toilet in the dark. They followed a winding path through the boxes and past a large glass refrigerated cooler loaded with assorted beers in six-packs, twelve-packs and thirty-packs. Just past the coolers, they entered the main store, which also had boxes of assorted alcoholic beverages down the middle, creating two aisles that led to the front door, which was to their left. There was a thin young man behind the counter with stringy brown hair that hung down past his shoulders and looked like it could use a wash. He wore a thick knit sweater and a dark blue insulated vest, and he seemed to be sitting on a stool.

"Where the hell is everybody in this town?" asked Jasper loudly. He had put his aviator sunglasses back on, that strange crooked smile returning to his face.

"Good question, mister. I'm afraid there's not much happening in town during the week. Truth is, there's not much happening in town ever, unless it's deer season."

"Yeah, I noticed that coming in. Seems like the whole place is deserted. We just drove down this main drag right outside here, didn't see anybody. Not even a car with its lights on. Kind of spooky, like that old show, *The Twilight Zone*. You ever see that show?"

"Wasn't that like some old movie where one of the actors got his head chopped off by a helicopter?"

Jasper looked at the kid for a second and said, "What the fuck are you talking about?"

"Never mind, mister. Yeah, it is kind of spooky sometimes, but you get used to it."

"I don't know how you can stand it out here," said Pogo. "You've got to be a moron to live here. I mean, most people need some kind of mental stimulation for their brains, you know. What the hell do you do for fun? Tip cows?"

"Tip cows? Jesus, Pogo, what the fuck are you talking about? This kid's telling me about actors getting decapitated, and now you're going on about tipping cows." Jasper was walking down the aisle looking at the booze that lined the wall. "Okay, I know I shouldn't, but I'll bite. What the fuck does tipping cows mean?"

"You never heard of tipping cows? It's what these yahoos do for fun. Seems cows sleep standing up, or at least maybe they're dozing, you know. I'm not really sure; I never actually looked into their eyes to see if they were asleep or awake. Anyway, if ya sneak up on 'em at night, real quiet, you can push 'em right on over. Must be a laugh a minute, ain't that right, Gomer?"

The young man behind the counter didn't say anything. Pogo looked over at him, and the kid wasn't smiling at all. Then Pogo stole a glance at Jasper and winked at him.

Jasper grabbed a bottle of Jim Beam off a shelf, then thought for a second and grabbed another. "This one we'll open on the

76

ride home, after we take care of the business we came for."

He walked toward the counter carrying a bottle in each hand to where the young man was now standing, no longer sitting on the stool.

The young man cleared his throat and said, "I'm sorry guys, but I can't sell you any alcohol. You'll have to put those bottles back on the shelf."

Pogo walked up and stood next to Jasper. "What do you mean you can't sell us alcohol?"

"I'm not allowed to sell alcohol to someone who shows signs of intoxication. And I'm afraid you guys fit that bill to a tee. I can't sell you anything except maybe a pop or a candy bar. I guess I can sell you cigarettes if you want. Geez, I can smell the booze and reefer reeking off you from here. I'm sorry, really, but I can't sell alcohol to someone who's already loaded. That's the law. I already got caught last week, and my boss reamed me out good for it, too. Would have fired me except it was his damn brother-in-law came in and bought the bottle. But he said if it happens again, it's my ass."

"Fuck your boss, sonny. Show some backbone here and ring us up so we can get the fuck outa here," said Jasper.

"Sorry mister, but I can't do it. I don't want any trouble, but I can't sell you any alcohol. Like I said, it's against the law. Besides, I need this job."

Pogo smiled at the man behind the counter.

"Look, I was just kidding about that cow-tipping shit. I didn't mean anything by it. Just teasing a little is all. How about you ring us up and we'll get gone and out of your hair?"

The young man shook his head. "No can do."

"I'm trying to be reasonable with you, kid. How about this? I'll put down forty bucks right here on the counter, and you just tell your boss two crazy-ass Mexicans came walking in here and shoplifted those bottles. That way you can put the money in your pocket, screw your boss, and we'll be on our way. Everybody's a winner."

Again, the young man shook his head.

"Jesus, kid, what's with you? You some kind of Boy Scout or something? This is no way to treat strangers come visiting your nice little town. How would you like it if I jump over this counter here and teach you some manners before we get gone?"

The young man reached down behind the counter and came up with a snub-nosed revolver. He pointed it at the two men and said, "How about you just get gone? Then maybe I won't have to call the cops and tell them about you two fucked-up old geezers driving around stoned out of your mind pissing off us local folk."

"Holy shit, Jasper, you believe the balls on this kid? And look at him, I bet he don't even shave yet." Pogo reached his hand up to his head and slid it across the top as if smoothing his hair and then reached down his neck to where the K-bar rested in the sheath strapped to his back. He brought the knife slowly over his head and then held it flat against his chest.

"There was no call to pull out that revolver, boy. You've changed a friendly disagreement into something more. What's your plan now, son? You gonna shoot us just because me and my friend here are trying to buy us a drink?" He edged away from Jasper to the right very slowly. The kid's face had lost some of its color when the big knife appeared. Beads of sweat appeared on his brow and above his lip just under his nose.

"You ever face death, son? Me and him,"—he nodded toward Jasper whose expression hadn't changed at all since they entered the store, that same crooked smile pasted on his lips—"we sure have. Ain't that right, Jasper?"

"Lots of times."

"The Grim Reaper, son, he comes in all shapes and sizes. I seen him dressed every which way, in black pajamas and motorcycle leathers and sometimes in one of those Mexican shirts, you know the ones I mean? I think they're called guayaberas."

Now Jasper turned and looked over at Pogo and said, "Are you fucking kidding me?" Then he started laughing.

"Let me finish talking to the young man here, Jasper, before you go interrupting. Now, where was I? Oh yeah, guayaberas. Anyway, I'm looking at you now, and you know what? I don't see death staring at me. No sir, not even close. Just some pimple-faced Gomer thinks he's a man 'cause he's got a gun pointed at my face. But shit, son, I've had lots of guns pointed at my face, ain't that right, Jasper?"

"Lots." Jasper laid both bottles on the counter. The smile never left his face. "He's not lying to you, friend. I've seen old Mr. Death come sneaking around lots of times, too. And you know what, sometimes he looks like a fucking monster gonna eat your guts out and then other times, hell, other times he looks a lot like old Willie Nelson."

Then a bell chimed, and the front door opened. Neither Pogo nor Jasper moved a muscle. The young kid stole a glance over their shoulders and looked relieved. "Hey, mister, you got a phone?"

"What the hell's going on here?" said a voice behind them.

"It's a robbery. This guy's got a knife. Call nine-one-one. Tell them to get to Murphy's right away."

"A robbery? Holy shit!"

"Call the fucking cops, will ya! I got a gun on 'em. Tell the cops that."

"I left my phone in the car," said the voice behind them.

"Then go get your goddamn phone and call somebody! And hurry up, goddamn it!" yelled the kid, his voice cracking a bit.

The bell chimed as the door closed and then it was just the three of them again.

"You guys better get out of here," said the kid. "Take the damn bottles and go. I'll do like he said, tell the cops two Mexicans came in here and robbed me. Just get the hell out of here."

Pogo looked over at Jasper. "Hey, you know what's funny, Jasper? I've been told on more than one occasion that I look a lot like Willie Nelson. What do you think of that kid? You think I look like Willie Nelson?"

"Just get out of here, mister. I'm not kidding. Get out before

I blow your fucking brains all over the place."

The bell chimed again, and a voice was talking as someone entered the store.

"Yeah, officer, that's right, I'm at Murphy's, a liquor store. There are two guys in here, and some kid's got a gun on them. Yes, yes, a gun. Can you believe it? Some pimple-faced fucking teenager has two mad dog killers pissing in their pants."

Then a strange sound erupted from the front of the store, like a firecracker muffled under a steel pot, and suddenly the young man behind the counter went flying back into the wall, his gun dropping from his hand. Pogo turned around and smiled at Birdie, who was holding the silenced Sig Sauer P226, his right hand straight out in front of him. A small coil of smoke wafted up from the end of the barrel.

"Birdie, that was fucking awesome! What the hell you got there? Is that a Sig?"

Birdie turned and closed the store's front door of the store. Then he flipped the sign around so that it read CLOSED from the outside. He locked the door, turned back around and began scanning the floor. He bent down on one knee and picked up the spent brass casing, stood back up, and put it into his pants pocket.

"One of you boys want to check on that guy, see if he's still breathing?"

Pogo walked to the end of the counter and knelt next to the young man. He had been shot in the chest and blood had stained his thick knit sweater. His eyes were wide, and he took deep, heaving breaths, like he couldn't get enough air.

"Take it easy there, son. I think you took one in the lung." Pogo leaned down over the kid, his knife in his right hand. He put his face right in front of the kid's, eye-to-eye, and whispered to him. "I bet this is a big surprise, huh? Just another lonely night, then Mr. Death comes walking into your store. You start to realize that the Grim Reaper can come in many guises, just like I told you, and then you think, wow, I can't believe he looks a lot like old Willie Nelson. Suddenly things take a sudden turn, and shit, death starts to look like that Big Bird on *Sesame Street*. Then, wham, here you are again looking old Willie right in the eye."

He placed the tip of his K-bar on the kid's sternum and pushed slowly. The kid's eyes widened even more. He began to struggle, but Pogo held him down hard, his arm on the kid's throat as the knife worked its way through his sweater and into his chest and then up into his heart. Blood gurgled up into the kid's throat and oozed out the side of his mouth as Pogo twisted the knife.

"Pogo, what the fuck are you doing?"

Pogo looked up and saw Jasper's head hovering over the counter, his own image reflected back at him in Jasper's mirrored lenses. Then he looked back down at the kid, looked into his lifeless eyes, and slowly pulled the bloody K-bar out of the kid's chest.

He looked back up at Jasper and smiled. "I think the best part is watching the lights go out, don't you?"

TEN

Bill Thompson was worried. He couldn't help it. Deep down he was still angry with his uncle for bringing this trouble to his home, for not warning him about this fellow Jasper. But when he thought about it, he also saw the logic of his uncle's reasons for not saying anything until after that early-morning phone call. After all, he, and even the cops, had all thought that it was probably neighborhood kids causing mischief. And Frank was right. If he had known about Jasper, he probably would have kept that shotgun by his bed just in case, even if it was just loaded with those light target loads. Not a good idea. He was jumpy enough thinking it was neighborhood kids who had broken the windows. Now Frank was gone, off on his own back home to his empty house in that desolate part of Maine. He had left just after noon and now, at 9 p.m., he should be getting pretty close to home.

Something else that worried him was that Frank had forgotten to take his shotgun, the old Fox. They had removed it from the Jeep when they came home and locked both guns in Bill's bedroom closet, intending to clean them later that evening. But then things had gotten away from them and Bill had found the gun in his closet a few hours after Frank left. He wished Frank had taken the gun. It might not be a great weapon for long distances, but for home defense, it was perfect. The report was loud, and those double barrels could spread quite a pattern. Even if he didn't hit anything, it would probably be enough to scare the shit out of anyone lurking in the shadows.

Shit, he thought, what he'd learned about his uncle this morning should be enough to scare anybody, shotgun or no.

Frank, his uncle, also known as Bull, the special ops soldier, the deadly killer, cutting someone's throat—he just couldn't picture it. Frank may have been a little intense sometimes, but on the whole the man seemed calm and friendly and level-headed. He was a sweet man, gentle with kids and a loving husband.

It was hard to get his mind around that, what he had heard firsthand from the man himself. All those theories, all those stories that he and his cousins had made up or imagined as kids about their reclusive uncle, some of them, the wildest ones they could have ever come up with, had been true.

Now he wished he had never found out the truth about Uncle Frank. Or about that band of psychos he served with in Vietnam. Maybe Frank was right, and those guys had only wanted to scare him out of New Jersey. But what if they wanted more? What if they wanted retribution? Jasper just didn't look normal. Who would carry a grudge like that for such a long time? And that demented smile that never seemed to leave the guy's face, that was downright spooky.

Bill decided he would give those two cops a call in the morning and see if they had gotten the opportunity to talk with this guy Jasper. Officer Rudy had said that maybe he would take a ride to Hibernia even if the detective couldn't make it. He'd feel a lot better if one or both of them had a face to face with this guy.

But Bill didn't have a good feeling about any of this.

Not a good feeling at all.

ELEVEN

They decided to take the kid's body with them and bury it out in the woods someplace. The kid's thick knit sweater absorbed most of the blood and Pogo buttoned the insulated vest to cover the wound and catch any drips that might fall when they carried him out to the camper. He went through the kid's pockets and found a beat-up old wallet with all of eleven dollars in it and the keys to the old Toyota Corolla that was parked out back. Then he and Birdie carried the body through the storage area in back and out the door. Jasper had gathered a few flattened cardboard boxes and carried them as he held the door open. Then he got in the camper, laid the boxes on the floor, and dragged the body all the way in once the other two guys had gotten the head and shoulders through the small door.

That done, all three men went back into the store. Birdie took the mop out of the bucket in the back room and swabbed the floor where the kid had lain to be sure that there would be no obvious bloodstains after they left. Jasper said he was going to set up outside and cover the front. He went back out through the storage room and into the camper, climbed over the body, and opened the storage bin. Then he grabbed the M16, slammed a clip home, and chambered a round. He squatted at the corner of the building and watched the road for any signs of activity. He hadn't seen any people or cars moving, but he also didn't want to get caught unaware by someone stopping in for a late-night six-pack or by a cop cruising the outskirts of town looking for something to investigate to keep from going stir crazy.

After a few minutes, Pogo and Birdie came out. Jasper walked over to his two friends and said, "We ready to boogie?"

"I'm going to take the car," said Pogo, nodding toward the Corolla, "make it look like the kid got sick of working in this dump and went home. I won't touch the register. We don't want the cops thinking he robbed the place and go out looking for him. You guys take the truck and keep heading up this road. Just stay on 302, and I'll catch up. I'm going back inside. I'll wait a minute or two, give you guys a chance to get out of town a ways, then I'll shut the lights, lock the door, and catch up with you."

Birdie handed Pogo the silenced Sig. "You take this; Jasper's got the rifle. We shouldn't have any trouble. If something happens, you got someone on your ass, don't slow down, just start flashing your brights. We see those lights flashing behind us, we'll pull over and blow the shit out of anything behind you."

Pogo took the gun and aimed it two-handed towards the woods, testing the weight, a big smile on his face. "Man, I almost hope someone comes snooping around so I get a chance to try this bad boy out tonight."

Jasper clapped him once and the shoulder and said, "Let's rock." Then he and Birdie got into the truck and Pogo headed back into the liquor store.

Once inside, Pogo took a quick look behind the counter to see if he could spot any bloodstains. The floor was wet but looked clean. He looked up in all the corners of the store for cameras, but the place was old and didn't get much traffic, and there were no cameras visible and no little mirrored boxes they could be hiding behind. Nor were there any monitors in the back. He walked to the front window and looked out at the quiet street, then walked back to the counter and went around behind it. He found a fat magic marker and one of those orange sale signs on a shelf under the counter right next to the snub-nosed revolver that he had replaced there. He wrote, "This job sucks, I quit!" in fat black letters and left the sign on the counter right next to the cash register. He shut the lights and headed out the back. He turned the sign over so that the CLOSED side was facing outside and locked the door with the kid's keys and got into the old Corolla.

Just as he was about to start the engine, he stopped, got out of the car, ran back to the door, unlocked it and went inside. Once inside, he walked to the front of the counter where they had some gum and candy bars on display. He reached into one of his pockets and pulled out a thin stack of baseball cards. They were held together with a dirty red rubber band. He removed the rubber band and spread the cards out in his hand like he was playing poker, looking at each in turn. They were all 1969 National League All Stars. He grabbed Denis Menke of the Houston Astros and tore the card in half. Then, using his T-shirt, he wiped his fingerprints off one of the torn halves and put it on the counter next to the register. They were, after all, on a mission. The other piece went back into the stack of cards, which he re-banded and then slid into his pocket.

He grabbed a Snickers bar from the display rack for his buddy Birdie, and then the two bottles of Jim Beam that Jasper had left on the counter and headed back out to the car.

As he turned the key in the ignition and the engine caught, he noticed the clock on the dash. It read 10:35 p.m. Geez, it was getting late. Good thing he remembered to grab those bottles of Beam. Hell, he couldn't think of anything worse than being stuck out here in the middle of nowhere with no more hooch.

And what were the chances of finding another liquor store open at this late hour?

TWELVE
RECKONING

Maine

Frank was up and showered by six the next morning. He hadn't slept well. He still wasn't used to sleeping in the spare room, and he probably shouldn't have had coffee that late at night. He thought the exhaustion from the long drive would have put him out like a light no matter how much caffeine he ingested, but he spent most of the night awake and staring at the ceiling, his mind racing in uncontrollable directions.

He made a cup of coffee and brought it over to the computer he had set up in his den. He liked to read the morning paper with his coffee and, weather permitting, he usually drove into town to buy the *New York Times* and several of the local Maine papers. But he wasn't in the mood to drive this morning and so decided to surf some news outlets on the internet and then check his email.

After scanning the morning's major headlines and then reading some of the stories that caught his eye, he logged into his email program and began looking down the long list of mail that had accumulated in his in box while he was away. He had done a per-functory check of his email back at Billy's, but hadn't bothered to open anything, most of it being obvious spam and other junk.

Not that he was expecting anything. Frank had been co-manager of a lumberyard for over twenty-five years. A cousin of Sadie's by the name of Nelson Stahl, who had taken a liking to him, owned the place. Nelson talked him into leaving the paving company where he had been working until then to take the job at the yard, and Frank had never regretted the decision. Not that he made a lot of money, but he liked the work, and the truth was he and Sadie didn't need a whole lot. Besides, his wife's parents had been relatively well-off and when they passed, Sadie and her brother had each inherited a nice stock portfolio, which provided a supplemental income. So he stayed at the lumberyard and then retired two years ago, but had since returned to work part time simply because he didn't like being retired and Nelson had told him that he could use the help. So, no pressing emails from the lumberyard. He did have some friends and family that he communicated with via email and he found that he pretty much preferred sending short notes over the computer as opposed to having to talk with people over the phone, but that correspondence, too, was infrequent.

He was going through his email, deleting most of it, when he came across a subject line that stopped him cold. It said, "All-Star Warning."

He hesitated for a second before opening the email.

It said, *Heavy hitters coming your way. Advise you stay loose and vamoose. This is no bull, Bull. Ha ha!*

There was no indication who had sent the email. The return address was a long list of letters and numbers at Yahoo. It was obvious that the sender had registered the address with the intention of staying anonymous and sending just this one email. He couldn't think of anyone from his past who would have his email address, but that didn't matter. The message had been delivered, and he was glad to have received it.

A warning. At least one of those crazy bastards from back then had regained some measure of sanity.

He looked at the time. Almost 7 a.m. Stay loose and vamoose.

He got up and walked back to the spare room where he had left his 9mm on the nightstand next to his bed. He checked the load and slipped it into his belt. He'd have to make sure that he had a weapon within easy reach from now on. The email had said that heavy hitters were coming his way but hadn't said when. He had to assume they'd be on their way soon. Or maybe they were already here, maybe getting set up outside this very minute. He was tempted to peek out one of his windows but thought better of it. They would have had to move pretty quickly to be here by now. And he was sure they wouldn't try to take him at his home in daylight. If they were already here, they would have tried last night. Or maybe they'll wait until tonight.

He went back to the den and opened one of the closets. Taking up the whole inside was a low-end Liberty Centurion gun safe.

Goddamn fucking war, he thought, as he dialed the combination.

THIRTEEN

Bill was up by 7 a.m. Normally he was up by six, but he had trouble sleeping last night, getting up frequently to check on his two boys and then double and triple checking the locks on all the doors and windows. Around 5 a.m., just as the sun was starting to come up, he had fallen into a deep, sound sleep. At 7 a.m. he woke up with a start and realized that he could hear his kids arguing somewhere in the house, and he decided to get out of bed. His wife was already up and out of the room.

Normally, Bill would be on his way to the office by this time. He was a civil engineer and worked for a construction management company out of an office in Westfield. It was about a forty-minute drive from Hackensack to Westfield with no traffic, but most mornings it took him well over an hour to get to the office. But he had decided to take a few days off, thinking Uncle Frank would be staying for the week. Then, with the broken windows and Frank leaving and the contractor coming, he decided that since he had already told them at the office that he was taking the time off, it might be a good idea to stick around the house for a day or two before returning to work.

Sam had the coffee going, and the kids were eating their cereal, getting ready to walk down the block and catch the bus that would take them to school. He said good morning and kissed each child and his wife, then sat down at the table and had his coffee and scanned the morning paper.

When the kids were finished with breakfast and they'd brushed their teeth and gathered their backpacks, Bill slipped on a pair of jeans and a sweatshirt and walked them to the bus stop. When he saw the bus down the block heading his way, he waved good-bye and headed back to the house, not wanting to embarrass the boys by letting their friends see him waiting with them at the bus stop. He hadn't felt the need to walk them to the bus stop for protection, but that unease from the night before was still with him, and he had decided to take the walk.

The bus passed, and he waved, though he didn't see either boy looking out the window at him. As he walked back toward his house, a Hackensack patrol car pulled up alongside him, stopped, and Officer Rudy opened the driver's-side door and stepped out. The younger cop, Officer Stevens, waved and stayed in the car.

"Good morning, Mr. Thompson."

"Morning, Officer Breslow."

"Nice the way you eased on out of there before the bus got to the stop, so the kids don't have to explain to their pals why their old man is waiting for the bus with them. You're a good dad."

"Rudy, I can't tell you how impressed I am to see you here this early watching my kids get on the bus. You are one fine police officer and a damn fine human being. Can you and your partner come on inside for some breakfast, or maybe a cup of coffee?"

"No, but thanks. For the compliment as well as the offer. I figured as long as I caught you out here, I'd fill you in on what's happening. Did Frank get off okay?

"Yes, he left yesterday afternoon. I haven't heard from him, but I was planning to give him a call this morning, make sure he got home okay. Did you and that detective get a chance to speak with our Mr. Sprague?"

"That's what I came over to tell you. The answer is no. Detective Aletta called him several times yesterday. He also called the local police department in Hibernia, where the guy lives, had an officer swing by the house yesterday afternoon. Then he and I took a ride out there in the early evening, around six or so, but there was nobody there. Tom slipped a card under the door to let him know that we'd stopped by, just in case he figured we wouldn't take a ride out so far on what may seem like a trivial matter. I don't think Tom has the time to head out that way again, unless of course you have more trouble here. But I honestly don't think you will. I called and got a cell phone number for the officer on patrol up there this morning. I just got off the phone with him. Said he passed by the house every hour from 4 a.m. to now. Said it looked like nobody had been home. No lights, no car or truck in the driveway, nothing."

"Shit, Rudy, I don't like the sound of this. I guess old Jasper could have stayed with a friend, or maybe he's got a girlfriend or something. But I don't have a good feeling."

"Well, I thought you guys should know. Anyway, you need me, just call. Tell Frank that, too." Then Rudy turned and walked around to the driver's side of the patrol car, opened the door, and got in.

Bill waved as the patrol car passed, but he didn't see Rudy or Officer Stevens turn their heads as they drove by.

Just like the damn school bus, he thought.

It was right after 9 a.m. when the phone rang, his house phone, not his cell. Frank picked it up on the third ring.

"Hello?"

"Uncle Frank? It's Bill."

"Hey, Billy Boy, long time, no see. How are things way down south in the tropics?"

"I take it you made it home all right. How was the drive?"

"Not bad. Well, it was long, and dark once I got off the main roads. But hell, I live in Boland, Maine, not Manhattan, so it wasn't entirely unexpected. Look, Billy, I want to thank you and Sam again for having me come down for a visit. And I'm sorry again for what happened. I'm hoping you haven't had any more problems since I left yesterday."

"No, no problems. I walked the kids to the school bus stop this morning, not that I expected anything to happen. It was just that I took off from work and was up and all. Anyway, there was Officer Rudy and his partner in their patrol car parked at the corner watching the kids get on the bus. Sure made me feel good to see him there."

"He's a good man, that Rudy. I feel better knowing he's there too. I don't expect that you'll have any more problems from Jasper and his boys, but it's nice knowing that someone is watching out."

"I had a chance to talk with Rudy. He told me that he and that detective took a ride over to Hibernia to pay a surprise visit to Mr. Sprague."

"And what did old Jasper have to say for himself?"

"Well, they didn't find him at home. They even had one of the local cops watch the house, drive by every so often throughout the night. Seems Jasper has not been home for the past day or two. They don't know where he is."

"He's probably out on a drunk with his buddies."

"Maybe. I'm worried Jasper and his buddies might decide to take a road trip, maybe up north somewhere."

"Like Boland, Maine? I wouldn't worry about that too much, Bill. Like I said, I bet those boys are out on a drunk, probably holed up in one of their houses celebrating the big victory. They're not going to drive all the way up here into the freezing cold to try and scare me some more."

"That's what's worrying me. What if they're not trying to scare you?"

Frank didn't say anything for a second. "I guess that's a possibility, though I daresay it's a long shot. But you know where I live Bill, small town where I know everybody, and everybody knows me. I'll let folks in town know to be on the lookout for strangers. Jasper's kind of hard to miss. I'll let my neighbors know too. You've been to my house, you know there's only one way in and one way out. Be hard to miss anyone driving down the lane."

"Uncle Frank, do you know anyone who can stay with you, you know, for a few days? I could come up. You left your shotgun here, the old Fox. I could bring it with me, maybe bring my gun, too, just in case."

"Look, Bill, let's not get paranoid. First off, we don't know that anyone is coming up this way. Second, I don't think that old Fox shotgun would do me much good unless they come after me with some trained killer rabbits. Why don't we wait a few days and see what happens? My good friend Noah is a state trooper, lives right here in town. I'll let him know what's going on. I'm sure that like Officer Rudy, he'll keep a good watch out for me. If I hear of anything or of anyone suspicious coming to town, I'll make myself scarce. I got lots of friends I can go visit, or better yet, I may spend a few days up at hunting camp and enjoy the great outdoors. I just might do that anyway, get out of the house and check on the cabin. There's really nothing to worry about. Do me a favor Billy, tell Rudy I said thanks."

"Will do, Frank. And you do something for me, okay? Give us a call here every day for the next few days. I know I'm being a pain in the ass, but I'll feel a whole lot better if you let us know you're doing fine up there. I just don't need anything else to worry about, you know?"

"You are indeed a pain in the ass, Bill, but I'll stay in touch."

"What do have going on today, Uncle Frank? Are you doing anything fun?"

"Not really. I understand there may be a storm heading this way. I'm gonna hunker down and get ready."

They talked for a few more minutes and then said good-bye. Frank hung up the phone and went back into the living room, where he had the shades closed and all his handguns and rifles laid out on the floor. He sat down on the couch and started breaking down his .45 caliber pistol. He took good care of his guns, always had. He hummed softly as he began cleaning, oiling and loading his weapons.

FOURTEEN

It was around 9 a.m. when Pogo woke up. He was lying on the bunk that covered the storage bin containing their guns. His face was to the wall, and for a few seconds, he couldn't remember where he was. His head hurt, his mouth was dry, his stomach was unsettled, and he had to pee. He heard loud snores from somewhere behind him.

He rolled over, his bleary eyes slowly getting accustomed to the low light. The snores were coming from above. He swung his legs out of the bunk to stand, and they hit someone lying in the small aisle. He nudged softly with his foot, and nothing happened. Then things began to come into focus in his mind.

I'm in the camper, and we're up in Maine. Jasper and Birdie are around here someplace. We drank a bottle of Jim Beam. Wait, maybe more than one bottle. The guy on the floor is dead. It's the body of the kid from the liquor store.

He placed his legs carefully on either side of the body and stood. Two feet hung in the air, sticking out of the bunk space in the front of the camper that protruded over the pickup truck's cab. The snoring came from there. The size of those feet could only mean that was Birdie.

Pogo made his way carefully toward the back door and stepped out of the camper to a crisp, sunny morning. Over to his right was Jasper, sitting on log next to a small campfire drinking coffee from a tin mug. The M16 rested across his lap.

95

He had a small gas camping stove set up next to him with a coffee pot on it. Pogo could hear the gas from the stove hissing, the odor of fresh coffee wafting toward him.

"Good morning, Sunshine," said Jasper, his eyes never leaving the campfire.

"Good morning, my ass. My head feels like it's about ready to fucking explode."

"Grab a seat, have a cup of coffee, maybe help clear out some of the cobwebs."

"Gotta take care of some important business first." He walked away from the campsite, past where the Corolla was parked, and urinated against a tree. When he was finished, he stayed for a few seconds trying to decide whether it would be worth it to try to make himself vomit, get the worst of the hangover out of his system. He decided against it and headed back to where Jasper was sitting next to the fire.

Jasper had already poured Pogo a steaming cup and handed it to him.

"We ought to get that body buried first thing," said Jasper.

"Where the hell are we?" asked Pogo. He took a hesitant sip of his hot coffee, wrapping his hands around the warm tin cup to take edge off the chilly morning air.

"Damned if I know. I remember Birdie saw this turn-off, an unmarked dirt road right off that road we were on, 302. Don't know how he could even see, it was so damned dark last night. But we turned off and followed it for a while, maybe a mile, mile and a half, then pulled off to this spot right here. You were right behind us the whole way driving the kid's car. We didn't see any lights following you out of town. We didn't see another damn car after we left that liquor store, just dark woods. When we stopped, we all got out, then I walked back down the way we came along this dirt road a ways with this here—" he patted the M16 on his lap, "—and stood watch in case we missed something. You boys lit a small fire and set us up nice and cozy. After a while, I realized I was wasting my time out there and came back. We passed one of those bottles of Beam around till it was finished, then you and Birdie went into the camper and passed out. I slept in the cab of the truck. And here we are."

"We got any drinking water?" asked Pogo.

"Cooler in the truck. Got a few bottles of Poland Spring and some sandwiches that Birdie's old lady made, in case you think you can keep anything down."

Pogo got up slowly, "Water's fine for right now."

"Yeah, me, too."

About fifteen minutes later, the camper's springs squeaked and a few seconds after that, Birdie emerged from the back of the camper.

He looked at the two men by the fire drinking coffee.

"Geez, for a second there I thought I dreamed that whole thing and it was one of you two boys lying there sound asleep on the floor in that camper."

Pogo smiled. "That kid's still in there? For Christ's sake, the way you were snoring, I figured it was loud enough to wake the dead."

Birdie walked over and accepted a cup of coffee from Jasper.

"We got to get that body buried first thing," said Birdie.

"Yeah, well, let's have a cup of coffee first and enjoy a little bit of this beautiful morning before we begin another busy day," said Pogo. "That kid's not going anywhere."

So, they all three sat around the campfire and talked about what had gone down the previous evening, Pogo praising Birdie for his fast thinking and precision shooting.

"I still can't believe that kid pulled a gun on you boys. I about shit my pants when I opened that door and saw him standing at the counter holding that snub-nosed .38."

"Yeah, stupid little shit. Got himself killed over two damn bottles of hooch," said Pogo. "Wouldn't listen to reason."

"Listen to reason?" Jasper chuckled. "You should'a heard this asshole, Birdie. Kid was holding a gun on him, and he starts telling him how the Grim fucking Reaper sometimes shows up wearing a Mexican hat, a sombrero or some such shit. Can you believe this guy?"

"Not a hat, a shirt, dumbass."

"What did you call it Pogo? That shirt thing?"

"A guayabera."

"Yeah, that's it, a guayabera. I almost peed myself right then and there I was laughing so hard. Here's this kid about ready to blow his fucking brains out, and old Pogo starts talking about a fucking Mexican shirt."

Birdie smiled and clapped Pogo on the back. "A guayabera! Goddamn, Pogo, you are a fucking multicultural wonderment."

"Aw, geez boys, I was just killing time until old Birdie here could show up with his secret agent gun and save our asses."

"And save our asses he did," said Jasper.

"Birdie, you're a fucking hero, son. You deserve a medal. I sure hope you enjoyed that Snickers bar I gave you last night as a reward for saving our sorry butts."

"Well, that Snickers bar sure hit the spot Pogo. But it probably wasn't all that smart killing that kid last night," said Birdie, "even though I didn't see as I had much choice at the time."

"It was me that killed him, Birdman, with the knife. You nicked him is all."

"What's done is done," said Jasper. "Nobody's going to find him now. And Pogo, that was damn smart thinking, taking the kid's car. We can keep that for a while, use it to recon the area when we get near Turd Man's place. No way we're going to be sneaking around unnoticed in that fucking camper. May as well wear a sign that says 'All Star War Party' and blow a siren."

"You think he knows we're coming for him?" It was Birdie who asked.

No one said anything for a minute, and then Jasper said, "Yeah, I believe he does, at least that I'm coming for him. Probably figures I ain't coming alone. He just doesn't know when. That's our advantage."

"Yeah," said Pogo, "that and a silenced Sig and an M16 and

that motherfucking machine gun and three dedicated and determined military combat veterans with a hard-on to see his ass sliced and diced and fed to the hogs."

After they had finished their coffee and Birdie had eaten one of the sandwiches, Pogo and Jasper walked into the woods carrying a shovel and began looking for a good spot to bury the body. There was a crunchy coating of snow about three inches deep, and they left a trail of footprints as they walked. They found a small clearing about seventy-five yards into the woods. There was nothing that looked like any type of hiking or game trail nearby, so Jasper started digging while Pogo went back to the truck.

The ground was hard, frozen under the snow, and the digging went slowly. About twenty minutes later, Pogo and Birdie came back carrying the kid's stiff body between them. Jasper had a hole roughed out about five feet long, three feet wide and about a foot deep. They took turns digging until the hole was about three and a half feet deep. They argued a bit about whether they should keep digging, afraid some animal would pull the body out. Pogo reminded everybody that they were in the wild here, that animals like bears prowled these woods and if one of them got a whiff of what was buried here, he'd dig it up for sure. So, they each took one more turn at the shovel, digging hard until the hole went down another six or seven inches, and then they dragged the body into it. Pogo reached into the kid's pants pocket and pulled out his wallet. He opened it and saw the photo on the driver's license. Geez, he thought, kid looks better dead in the pit than he does in the photo. He looked at the kid's name, Warren Hicks, and then at his date of birth. He did the math in his head. The kid was twenty-five. He removed the eleven dollars and stuffed that back into his own pocket, then threw the wallet into the hole with the body, and they again took turns with the shovel, piling dirt and any rocks or stones they could find on top until the body was covered. They then did their best to tamp everything down until the dirt was level with the surrounding terrain.

They didn't worry about footprints, figuring nobody would be walking through this exact spot any time soon and it would probably snow or rain within the next night or two, and that would obscure any trace that anyone had ever been there.

Back at camp, they burned the bloody cardboard they had placed under the body. Then Pogo and Jasper managed to choke down a sandwich each and Birdie ate another for good measure and after all the exertion and the coffee and the food, each man admitted that he felt pretty darn good and not nearly as hung over as he had every right to feel.

FIFTEEN

After all his weapons were cleaned, oiled and loaded, Frank arrayed them on the floor. He didn't want to leave guns all over the house since, number one, that was dangerous, and number two, if he had to crawl around looking for a gun, he'd probably be as good as dead anyway.

He grabbed the Colt .45 and put that on the coffee table. He grabbed his Glock 9mm and put that on the coffee table as well. He had a few other handguns, but he gathered those up and returned them to the shelves in his gun safe. He went back into the living room and looked over his long guns. He picked up his Mossberg 930 tactical shotgun. If he found himself inside his house or some other building or if someone attacked him at close range out in the field, he could fire this autoloader as fast as he could pull the trigger. As a last resort, it made a good fighting club.

He put the shotgun on the couch. Next, he picked up his old M40 sniper rifle, along with a box of cartridges. He had an extra clip for the M40 that he had bought at a gun show but had never used. Might come in handy. The M40 had a new scope he had bought online that was better than the original they used in Nam. His neighbor had told him about a night vision attachment that he had bought for varmint hunting. Said it could be attached to just about any scope. Frank decided he'd pass by his neighbor's house on his way into town, see if he could borrow it for a few days. Night vision would be good to have.

He put the rest of his rifles back in the safe and locked it. He reached onto a shelf high in the closet and patted around until he found his old SOG Bowie knife. This was the knife he had worn when he was in the service. The knife he had used to kill enemy soldiers.

And others, he thought with a pang of guilt.

He slipped the knife and sheath under his belt. He reached up again took down a box of 9mm shells, a box of .45s and some extra clips. He balanced the boxes in one hand, shoved the two extra clips into his hip pocket, and then reached up one last time and grabbed a box of double ought buckshot for the Mossberg. He closed the closet door with his elbow and headed back into the living room.

He put everything down on the coffee table. Then he took the two extra clips out of his pocket. He loaded each with the appropriate ammunition and set them down next to the handguns. He left the boxes with the leftover shells on the coffee table. He had more boxes of shells in the closet. He was going to keep extra rounds in whatever vehicle he was using and also place a few full boxes around the house, just in case. He didn't want to have to worry about running out of ammo.

He looked at the guns on the table and the couch and thought, geez, I'm glad Sadie's not here to see this.

Then he remembered why she wasn't, and his heart squeezed tight.

But another thought made him smile.

Keep a seat warm for me Sadie, honey. I may be coming to join you shortly.

Frank removed the scope from his rifle, then carried it with him to his truck and drove down to his neighbor's house. His neighbor, Matt, a good friend to Frank and his wife as well as an old hunting buddy, invited him in, showed him his night vision setup, and demonstrated how to fit it onto his scope.

"Works best at relatively short distances. I'd say out to about a hundred to a hundred and twenty-five yards. It's not much good once you get past that. What are you hunting for?"

"I'm not really hunting anything. I've been having a problem with my garbage cans," said Frank. "Got them fenced in, but something's getting at them. Don't know if it's skunks, raccoons or something else. Don't plan on shooting anything unless I have to, but I'd sure like to get a look at what's making all the racket."

Frank made small talk for a few minutes and then Matt's wife, Barbara, came out and they talked for a few minutes more. Barbara invited Frank over to dinner and he thanked her but said that he wasn't very good company yet and would certainly take her up on her offer just as soon as he was feeling up to it.

He left with the night vision attachment and a small tuna casserole that Barbara had been meaning to drop off and then drove the truck into town. He pulled into Roy Sutherland's gas and service station, where he told Roy about the flat he'd had back in New Jersey and asked him to replace the tire. He also asked him to give the truck the once over, change the oil, check the hoses and belts, etc. Roy told him he'd need the truck for a day or two as he was busy, and Frank said that was fine, he'd leave it there with him right now so long as Roy or his boy could give him a ride back to his house a little later to pick up his, uh, late wife's car. He said he might need to head out of town for a few days and if it was all right with Roy, he might leave the truck until he got back.

Frank left the service station and walked down Henry Street, Boland's main drag. The town was small, a few shops, small supermarket, hardware store, a diner, post office, service station and a small municipal building. There was no police station. The town was just too small to warrant its own force. Policing duties were shared between the Cumberland County Sheriff's Department and the State Police, but crime was relatively low, most problems just drunk drivers or bored, mischievous kids.

Waving to people he passed by on the street, people he'd known for years, he walked into Udder Heaven, the town's only diner/coffee shop, and sat at the counter.

Kate Henshaw, who'd been working behind the counter since Frank first moved to town forty or so years earlier, stepped over with a cup of coffee already poured and set it down in front of him.

"How's things, Frank?"

"Hey, Kate. Things are coming along. Just got back from New Jersey. My nephew and his wife had me down for a few days. Wasn't going to go, but then I figured I better show my face down there, see some family. Couldn't put it off much longer. If I did, I was afraid there might be a parade of loudmouth, obnoxious relatives invading this town, you know what I mean?"

She smiled and patted his shoulder. "Maybe some company is just what you need, Frank."

He looked into her eyes and saw the unspoken invitation. She looked back at him, and then dropped her gaze. Her face reddened.

"Well, funny you should say that, Kate, about having some company, I mean. But before I start talking your ear off, think I can order some breakfast?"

"Sure, hon, what'll it be?" She looked at him, her face still flushed. She sounded almost relieved.

"How about some of your corned beef hash with a slice of American cheese and two fried eggs sitting right on top?"

"Coming right up, Frank."

Udder Heaven was the social center of Boland. There was no bar or other restaurant in town, so most of the old timers gathered in the diner for breakfast or lunch and gossiped about neighbors or chatted about world events or sports or whatever came up.

Sitting to Frank's left, two stools over, was Jimmy McAllister. Jimmy Mac, as he was known to his friends in town, was a dairy farmer who lived a few miles outside of Boland. Frank looked over at Jimmy just as Jimmy turned in Frank's direction.

"Hey, Jimmy Mac."

"Hey, Frank. Was hoping to run into you. Wanted to say how sorry I am about your missus. Sadie was a fine woman. There's many around these parts will mourn her loss."

"I appreciate that, Jimmy Mac. She was the finest woman I ever knew. No one will mourn her loss more than me."

Jimmy Mac raised his coffee cup and nodded, a solemn expression on his face. "If you need anything, Frank, just ask, eh."

"I will, Jimmy Mac."

Frank's breakfast arrived a few minutes later. Kate put his plate in front of him, plopped her elbows on the counter, laid her chin in her hands, and watched Frank eat.

"You were gonna talk to me about company, Frank. Who are you expecting?"

"Well, I'm not sure that I'm actually expecting anybody, Kate. It's just that when I was in Jersey, I ran into a guy I used to know. Way back when I was a kid. Anyway, turns out that he's in touch with a few other people that I used to know."

"Isn't that something? And he remembered you after all these years?"

"What, you think a guy really changes all that much in fifty or so years?"

"Geez, sorry, Frank. I didn't mean to imply that you're getting old or anything."

"I should hope not, Katie girl," said Jimmy Mac from two stools over. "Frank here is a few years younger than I am. If you're saying he's old, what's that say about me, eh?"

"Jimmy Mac, you were born old. And Frank here, well, let's just say he's a man that's slid nicely into the prime of his life. I mean, look at him, with those pretty-boy good looks and still got his girlish figure."

Jimmy coughed into his cup. He had to grab a napkin to keep himself from spewing coffee all over the counter.

Kate burst out laughing, and Frank smiled, and Jimmy Mac

chuckled while wiping his mouth and the front of his shirt where some of his coffee had ended up.

"I think she's right, Jimmy Mac. I mean about the pretty-boy good looks. Though I'm not too sure I can agree with the girlish figure."

"Not too sure you'd want to, eh, Frank?"

"Okay, enough fooling around," said Kate. "So, Frank, who's coming up?"

"Well, like I said, I'm not really sure anyone is. But my nephew has been fielding a few phone calls. Told me some of these old friends of mine were hinting around coming up on a surprise visit—you know, well intentioned I guess, hoping to make me feel better. But lately I'm not really in the mood to host any surprise guests."

"Surprise guests? What in the hell is the matter with these people? Don't they know you just lost your—I mean, well…"

Jimmy Mac touched Kate's arm and said to Frank, "What she means is, don't they know you're still in mourning? Intruding on a man at a time like this is, well, it's unconscionable."

"Like I said, I believe they mean right, but the truth is, I'd just as soon avoid company right now."

"Don't blame ya, not one bit."

"So, I wanted to ask if maybe you guys see any strangers, anybody asking around about me, maybe you could let me know. This way at least I'll know they're in town. Maybe I'll go find them, or maybe I'll make myself scarce for a day or two and contact them after they return home, pretend like I just missed them."

Kate patted Frank's hand. "Don't you worry. I'll spread the word to all my regulars. Get the whole town keeping an eye out for ya. I can't believe the nerve of some people, so dang inconsiderate of someone else's feelings."

"Well, Kate, don't be too hard on 'em. Like I said, I truly believe they're well intentioned and if, well, if circumstances were different, I'm sure I'd have been glad to see them. But I appreciate your help, I truly do. You too, Jimmy Mac."

Frank got up and walked with Kate over to the register, where he paid his check. Then he walked back and slipped a five-dollar bill under his empty coffee cup.

"See you around, Jimmy Mac."

"Take care, Frank. And don't forget, you need anything, anything at all, just ask."

"Appreciate that, partner."

Frank smiled at Kate and she smiled back. Then he turned around and walked out the door.

He walked up Henry Street to the hardware store. He cupped his hands to the window and looked in, then stepped to the front door and entered. A bell chimed as the door shut gently behind him.

"Howdy, Frank," said a voice from the back of the small store.

"Tom." Frank turned to make sure that the front door had shut securely. The store was warm and smelled of power tools and machine oil and pesticide and sawdust like a real hardware store should.

"Something I can help you with?" The voice got louder. Frank turned back and saw Tom Stubbleman approaching. Tom wore an off-white canvas apron with large pockets and *Ace Hardware* across the front over a red, green and yellow checked flannel work shirt.

"Not sure yet, Tom. How are you?" The two men shook hands. "Haven't been by in a while, Tom. To be honest, I've been kinda occupied these last few weeks."

"Yeah, I sort of figured you would be. Sorry about your loss, Frank. Sadie was, well, she was a special person and dearly loved by all of us here in town. I hope you got our card, the one the wife and me sent. I was gonna call, but, truth is, I don't handle these things too well. Plus, I figured you'd have your hands full talking to friends and family."

"I did get the card, Tom, thanks. I'm afraid I don't handle these things too well myself, and in all honesty, the phone calls were a bit much after a while. Please tell Janice how much I appreciated her thoughtfulness. And yours, too."

"If there's anything we can do, Frank, me and Janice, please, just let us know. Maybe you could stop by for dinner one night. Janice makes a mean tuna casserole."

"That's awful nice of you, Tom, and I'd love to, really, but I think I'm gonna need a little time alone first, to sort of get used to things. People have been so nice to me, bringing me food and inviting me over. I must have gained about ten pounds over the last few weeks. But, well, when I'm ready I'll take you up on that dinner. Anyway, I'm gonna look around a bit."

"Sure, Frank. If there's anything you can't find, just let me know."

Tom clapped Frank on the shoulder, then turned and walked back to the counter and began fussing with one of his pneumatic paint-shaking machines.

Frank wandered the store thinking of things he might need or be able to use later. He was thinking of devising some type of trip-wire alarm, something he could set up around a perimeter to warn him of intruders. Back in the service, they had made simple booby traps using spring-loaded rat traps to set off shotgun shells, but he didn't want anything lethal. He thought of maybe removing the powder and pellets from the shells and setting off the primer caps when he spied a display of personal key chain security alarms. He picked up one and read the small bulleted features printed on the back:

Personal security key chain alarm
Handy alarm goes everywhere with you
Built-in key light makes it easy to find door locks
Low-battery indicator
120 decibel alarm sounds when pin is removed

* * *

Frank smiled. One hundred and twenty decibels sounded about right. And just about four bucks apiece. There were twelve alarms on the small display, and Frank took them all. He went over to where Tom was working on the paint shaker, put the key chain alarms on the counter, and then leaned over and grabbed a can of dark green spray paint.

"I guess you found what you were looking for there, Frank. Think you got enough of these?"

Frank smiled at Tom.

"I just got back from visiting my nephew down in New Jersey. His wife joined one of those self-defense classes, you know, for women. I guess to learn how to protect themselves against muggers and such. Anyway, I met some of the gals from her class, real nice women, actually joined them for lunch one day. Thought I might send these down, maybe my nephew's wife can hand them out next time she goes, show my appreciation for their kindness. Besides, might save some poor mugger from getting his balls kicked up into his tonsils."

"Gee, that's awful nice of you Frank, thinking about the well-being of those poor muggers down there in New Jersey trying to make a living."

"Well, what many people don't realize, Tom, is that behind this rough exterior, I have some saintly tendencies. Say, you carry monofilament fishing line?"

SIXTEEN

Bill was having a hard time not using his cell phone.

He wanted to call his uncle again, check up on him. He had a bad feeling about this whole Jasper business. He wanted to call Officer Rudy, too, see if he had any further news on the whereabouts of Jasper. He wanted to call Detective Aletta and find out what could be done or what was being done to track this guy down, find out who his accomplices might have been.

But he ended up sitting and staring at his phone knowing that becoming a pain in the ass to any or all of these men would just cut him out of the loop. He hoped he was just being paranoid, but deep down he felt that something bad was coming, not for him so much as for Uncle Frank.

And he felt guilty, too. He had let Uncle Frank leave. He hadn't insisted that he stay until this Jasper fellow was found and interrogated. Hadn't even tried too hard to keep him here. He knew that he had a right to be worried about his family, his wife and children, but Uncle Frank, he was family, too. And families stick together.

He walked into his bedroom and then over to the closet and opened the door. The old Fox was in there leaning against the wall barrel up. He pulled it out, opened the breech to make sure again that it wasn't loaded, and then set it back down. He wished Uncle Frank had taken it with him. He knew his uncle had more guns at home, all sorts of guns, but still, he wished he'd taken this gun as well.

Uncle Frank, recon marine, Special Forces hunter/killer. He remembered Frank saying that he wasn't some kind of Rambo, just a grunt marine during his time in Vietnam. Grunt marine my ass, thought Bill. He had a hard time reconciling the thought of his mild-mannered uncle with his soft voice and easy smile creeping through the jungle at night with a hunting knife and slitting the throats of enemy soldiers.

Maybe not just enemy soldiers he thought. The image of a fragile old man and a five-year-old child with blood-soaked shirts and vacant eyes came to him unexpectedly, and he shuddered.

Then he remembered the stories Uncle Frank had told him about getting drunk and telling his wife some things about the war, how afterward she had seemed afraid; afraid of him.

Maybe that was why he had let him go back home without so much as an argument.

Stupid.

And he thought about his grandfather, how he had heard the sound of German tanks rumbling in the night outside his window in Hackensack and had cried himself to sleep.

Then he pictured is uncle, old and cold and alone in his house up in Maine. A man who refused to even hunt because he had lost his taste for killing. And no wonder, he thought, him having to live with those memories.

Memories relived because of the nutcase psychopath at the gun club. Why did he have to take Uncle Frank to that fucking shooting range? Why did old Jasper have to pick that day to be there?

He grabbed the old Fox out of the closet again and carried it to the bed, where he sat down and laid the gun across his lap. He took the cell phone out of his pocket, set it on the bed, and stared at it.

Goddamn fucking war, he thought.

SEVENTEEN

He owned over five acres, about two of them cleared land that bordered a state park. His backyard led to the base of a hill with thick woods that stretched for miles. His driveway was paved and ran in a straight line out from his detached garage to the street. The front yard was a grass lawn, at least in the summer, save for one chestnut crabapple tree that Frank had planted when he and Sadie had first bought the property. To his amazement, the tree had thrived and was now maybe eighteen feet high. In the spring, the tree produced large white flowers and its fruit— small, yellowish apples—was crisp and had a sweet, nut-like flavor. Every year, Frank would pick apples and Sadie would make jams and jellies for family, friends and neighbors.

The street in front of the house dead-ended about thirty yards past his driveway. A white wooden barrier with red and yellow plastic reflectors let people know they had reached the end of the road. But there was not much need for the barrier since few people used this road. Unless you lived in the area and knew where the turnoff was, there was a pretty good chance you wouldn't see it even if you were looking. Besides, thirty or forty yards past the barrier were thick woods that not even a bulldozer could penetrate.

It was mid-afternoon as Frank surveyed his property from the deep woods about seventy-five yards up the hill behind his house. After his trip into town, he had had his mechanic, Roy

Sutherland, drive him back to his house. He went into his bedroom and pulled on flannel-lined jeans and a waterproof camo outer shell that he used when hiking in deep snow. Then he grabbed his Sorel winter boots, warmest winter jacket, gloves and hat, and carried them all into the living room, where he bundled up for his walk. He traded his 9mm handgun for the .45 and put that into his jacket pocket along with a full extra clip. Into his other pocket he placed an unopened box of .45 shells, just in case. He wasn't expecting any trouble, not in daylight, but he had decided to err on the side of caution and keep himself well-armed at all times. He also grabbed a small backpack with several bottles of water and few energy bars. He took his cell phone out of his pocket, was going to set it on vibrate, then thought better of it and turned it off completely. Sound carries in the wind at night, and he didn't want to take any chances. He put the phone into a pouch on the pack where he could reach it easily. Then he grabbed the Redfield scope and headed out the door.

He walked down the driveway, then turned left and walked past the barrier at the end of his road. He hiked straight into the woods for a few minutes, then began an arcing turn that took him up the hill directly behind his house. He stopped every so often, checking angles and looking at the natural cover. After about forty-five minutes, he found a spot that afforded a good view of his house. He could see the entire driveway, from the street to the garage doors. He could also see the front and back of the house. Just the one far side of the house was not visible, but that was okay. He was standing next to a tall pine tree, its boughs thick and long and snow-covered. He pushed aside a few branches and watched the loose snow cascade down. Then he got down on his hands and knees and crawled inside. The boughs draped over and around him like the walls of small cave. He unstrapped his knife from his leg and cut some dead twigs and undergrowth until he had a small space suitable for a comfy hideaway. He turned away from the tree trunk and lay down on a bed of dried pine needles, pushing leaves and twigs and dead growth back and out of the way with his feet until he could lie prone comfortably. He raised the Redfield to his eye and surveyed the property through the boughs. A few bushes and tree branches in the near distance obscured some of his sight lines, but that couldn't be helped. For his purposes, this was fine. He was sure he couldn't be seen, even by someone walking right past this tree in daylight and most certainly not by anyone anywhere near his house at night. Even lying flat, he could see most of the property right to the road. If someone were to come looking for him, chances are they would come on foot and follow the road, staying to the side near the trees. There were no streetlights, and that would give them confidence that they wouldn't be spotted, he thought. As long as the night was even partially clear, he should be able to see well with his night scope attachment.

He adjusted the scope, sighting the crosshairs first on his front door, then on one of the side windows.

Confidence was good. He wanted them to feel confident.

He sighted down the driveway and then moved the crosshairs slowly down the street toward his neighbor's house, adjusting the power up to see as far as he could, then crawled out of his blind. He decided to leave the pack with the water and power bars there in the tree for later. He stood and started following the path in the snow he had made back to his house.

EIGHTEEN

They drove through town in the old Camry. Birdie was behind the wheel, Pogo riding shotgun, and Jasper slouched in the back seat wearing his mirrored sunglasses, a black knit watch cap pulled low over his brow.

"Geez," said Pogo, "what a godforsaken shit hole. How can people live like this? I mean, look around. There's absolutely nothing here. Nothing—not a fucking thing. Is the whole state like this? We're in the goddamn U.S. of A., for Christ's sake. Where are the bars and the mini-malls and the chain restaurants? Where is the fucking Walmart? This reminds me of some of the dumps I been through in Mexico."

"Yeah," said Birdie, "just like Mexico, only it's thirty degrees out and there's snow on the ground."

"What, you think it doesn't get cold in Mexico? You ever been to Mexico, Birdman?"

"No, but I've watched all them old westerns on TV, and all I've ever see are deserts and cactus and pretty women in white dresses and small Mexican dudes wearing sandals and sombreros, and I don't ever see snow on the ground. Not ever."

"He's right, Pogo, and them funny Mexican shirts, what do you call them again? Kind of shirts old Mr. Grim Reaper seems partial to."

"I can't believe you fucking guys. I'm driving around in a dead guy's stolen car on some serious fucking business, and I'm stuck with two comedians, ass and hole."

"You ain't driving, Pogo. I'm the one that's driving, and speaking of which, we're almost through town," said Birdie. "What do you want to do?"

"Jasper?" said Pogo.

"Keep going. Let's find his street and drive past. I want get a feel for the area, see if we can find a place to leave the car later where it can't be seen." Jasper sat up a little in the back seat and peered out the side window, looking closely at people strolling down the sidewalks and getting in and out of parked cars. "After that, we'll drive through town again, see what we can see. Then you boys take me back to the truck. You leave me and come back to town, get a cup of coffee, pick up some food and poke around some. I don't want to take a chance on him seeing me, or maybe someone ringing his phone that can describe me. Tonight, late, we'll pay old Turd Man a visit, recon his house. If we can, we take him out, simple as that. Best to make sure first we know what we're dealing with. I don't think he's expecting us, but I also don't want to get surprised, find out he's got some buddies watching his six. If he does, I'm sure it'll just be some locals, farmers or maybe town cops, but better to know first. We don't want to walk into anything crazy, and we don't want a massacre. We get him, and then we get the hell out."

"Hell, I don't mind a massacre, long as we come out on the right side of it," said Pogo good-naturedly.

"Yeah, well, I'm thinking about afterward. If he's alone, we do like we talked about, throw him in the trunk and bury him in the woods like we did that kid, nice and quiet. If we get into a major firefight, we'll have local cops, state police, hell, probably even the National Guard, all trying to hunt us down."

"He got an old lady?" asked Birdie.

"Don't know," said Jasper.

"He do, we'll have to do something about her," said Pogo.

"Yeah, I guess we will," said Jasper, that crazy smile of his forming slowly on his weathered face.

"Yes, indeedy," said Pogo rubbing his hands together. "We'll surely have to do something about her."

NINETEEN

Frank was filling a small thermos with strong black coffee when his cell phone rang. He looked at this phone and didn't recognize the number. But it was a local number, so he picked up.

"Hello?"

"Frank, it's Kate. Kate Henshaw."

"Hi, Kate."

"Sorry to bother you, Frank. I hope you're not eating dinner or busy with something."

"No, not at all, Kate. Is everything all right?"

"Oh, yes. Everything is fine. I just wanted to let you know, well, I'm not real sure, but I might have met some of your old friends from New Jersey earlier."

"Really?"

"Like I said, I'm not sure. I didn't ask if they knew you, and they didn't mention your name or anything, but, well, they had that accent, you know, and that attitude."

"You mean they were loud, obnoxious assholes?"

"I might not have put it that way exactly, but, ah, yes. At least one of them was. The other one was quieter."

"Gee, they already sound like a lot of people I know in New Jersey. Maybe even relatives. What'd they look like, Kate?"

"Sort of a Mutt and Jeff pair. The loud one was a wiry little fella, long hair gone mostly gray, had it hanging in two braids down the sides of his head. Gave him a strong resemblance to one of my favorite all-time singers, Willie Nelson. Don't know if you like country music or not. I love it, especially Willie and Waylon Jennings and Merle Haggard. Hank Junior, too. Not too crazy about some of the newer stuff. Anyway, the other guy was tall and lanky. Had a big honker on him. Both in their sixties, I'd say."

"The little guy was he wearing a hat or bandanna, maybe mirrored sunglasses?"

"No, not that I recall. They looked like a pair of old hippies. Smelled like it too. They must have been partying some in the car before they came in, you know? I could smell the reefer. It was coming off their clothes. Must've had the munchies, too, because they ate like it was their last meal at the counter, then took a pile of food to go."

"Anything else you can tell me about them, Kate? Did you see what type of car they were driving? I don't know if they're who my nephew told me was planning to come up here or not, but if they are, I'd sure like to avoid them. I don't think I can handle a couple of old stoners on a road trip, think they're going to cheer up a friend they haven't seen in a whole bunch of years."

"Sorry, Frank. They came in, made a bit of a ruckus, ate, and left."

"Did you hear any names? Maybe when they were talking to each other?"

"I'm not sure, but the tall guy with the nose might have called the little guy Pogo, you know, like the old comic strip. You remember that?"

"Sure."

"Well, I think he might have called him that when he was trying to get him to keep his voice down. If he'd have called him Willie, I don't know what I would have done. I mean, he looks just like him, he really does. Well, younger obviously. When they first walked in, I swear, I almost asked him for an autograph."

"To be honest, Kate, I really don't think I know those boys, but I sure appreciate you calling to let me know. And Kate, you make sure to stay away from them, you hear. They sound like they could be trouble."

"I don't know, Frank, it's probably like you said, just a couple of old boys out on a road trip happy to get away from their wives, right? Wait, geez, I didn't mean...oh hell, Frank, I'm sorry. Sometimes my mouth goes faster than my brain."

"I'm the same way, Kate. Don't worry. I think you're probably right about those two, but do me a favor and stay away from them anyway, okay? They may be harmless old hippies, but if they're smoking dope and driving around, that still spells trouble. Might not be a bad idea to call nine-one-one and tell the police, let them know to be on the lookout. Wouldn't want anyone getting hurt, maybe getting into an accident or something."

"Okay, Frank. Maybe I'll give Noah a call, see what he says. I'd just hate to get anyone in trouble, you know?"

"Sure, I understand, but it would probably be better for everybody if they weren't driving around. Best for them, too, I imagine."

"Yeah, I guess you're right. I'll try and reach Noah, see if he's working today. If he is, he might be out on the road already and can keep an eye out for them. Are you planning on coming in tomorrow? Meatloaf and gravy's the special."

"Just so long as it's not tuna casserole. Got a bunch of them in my freezer already."

"Courtesy of the good ladies in town, I imagine. I'll tell the chef to keep it off the menu for a while," she said with a chuckle and then hung up.

Frank finished pouring the coffee into the thermos and then screwed the cap on good and tight. He walked out to the living room where he had his winter gear laid out, the M40 sniper rifle with the scope and night vision already mounted. He decided to spend the night in the woods watching the house. The call from Kate confirmed what he already knew, that the All Stars were in town and they would be coming soon. There had to be at least three of them since it didn't sound like Jasper was one of the two in the diner—maybe more than three. He knew he couldn't fight from the house, as there were too many points of entry to cover. Also, he would be trapped with no means of escape. If one or two of them set up on the hill and he tried to make a run for it out a window or back door, they'd be able to pick him off easy. There was just too much open land to cover before he could make it to the woods. And the snow would slow him down. Better that he was the one up on the hill. He grabbed the M40 along with the shotgun and his two handguns, walked them out to his wife's car, and laid them in the back. He picked up the Colt, checked to make sure there was a round in the chamber, and carried it with him in his right hand back to the house. Next, he gathered several boxes of shells for each weapon and carried them back out to the car, then locked the car and returned to the house.

He put the thermos in a daypack along with some snacks, nuts, granola bars and a few energy drinks.

He figured he would be up all night tonight.

That is, if he lived through the night.

TWENTY

They had dinner early. By five-thirty they were finished eating, the boys were in front of the TV, and Bill was stacking the dishes that his wife handed to him as she finished unloading the dishwasher. Dinner had been quiet; at least Bill and Sam had been quiet. The boys had carried the conversation with talk about school and sports and video games, but Bill had been distracted and Sam, sensing this, had given him his space.

"It's Frank, isn't it," she said without looking at him. It wasn't a question.

"What? Oh, I'm sorry, babe. I guess I'm off in my own little world tonight. And yes, it is Frank. I can't stop thinking about him. I'm worried. I don't like thinking about him all alone up there. I should have kept him here, at least for a few more days. At least until they find this Jasper fellow. You know, I can't believe I let him leave, that I let him walk right out of here."

Sam grabbed the last plate, handed it to Bill, and then took a dishtowel off the rack by the oven and dried her hands.

"Did you call him today?"

"Yeah, I spoke with him this morning, after I walked the kids to the bus."

"How did he sound?"

"Heck, he sounded fine, but you know Frank. He always sounds fine. Guy seems to live his life on an even, steady keel. You saw the way he was that night the windows got broken. He didn't seem rattled. Not even a little shaken up. And this whole thing with his wife; Aunt Sadie dies, and he doesn't even call us until a week later. A whole week, for Christ's sake! He's married to the woman over forty years, you'd think he'd have enough sense to call and tell his family about it, right?"

Sam put the towel down and then laid an arm on Bill's shoulder, squeezing gently.

"Take it easy, honey. You're getting yourself worked up. Everybody handles grief in his or her own way. I can understand Frank not wanting to tell us about Sadie right away. Think about it: if he did, what would we have done? We'd have been in the car on our way up there inside of an hour. You know it, I know it, and he knows it. I'm sure he had plenty of company up there in Maine as it was with her family and all their friends and neighbors. Don't forget, it's an awfully small town they live in. People in small towns are usually pretty close. Everybody knows everybody else. It must have been pretty hard on Frank having to deal with all those people, having to make arrangements to bury his wife and keep listening to people say how sorry they are over and over. I think he didn't want to feel pressured into talking about it anymore than he already had to. Probably felt he couldn't handle seeing anybody else, not even family— especially not family. Maybe he needed some time alone. I think that's all it was, don't you? He just needed some time alone."

Bill didn't say anything. He finished drying the last dish and put it away in the cabinet over the sink.

"Yeah, I guess you're right. When I think about it like that, I can totally understand. Especially with him being the way he is. I'm just worried, that's all. I can't help thinking that I shouldn't have let him leave. Like he needs me, or us, you know. Like he needs family right now."

"I don't think there was anything you could do, hon. He was ready to go. I think he felt that what happened with the windows was his fault. And I think that leaving like he did is just his way of, you know, trying to protect us. Like he did with the boys, you remember?"

"Yeah, well, I'm afraid that I may not have entirely dissuaded him from that notion."

"What do you mean?"

"I was a little upset with him about not telling me about his past association with this Jasper guy earlier. If he knew this guy was a psycho, he should have told me."

"Did he know? After what, forty years? Do you think he knew, I mean actually knew for sure, that this guy would do something like this? How could he?"

She cupped his face in her hands, holding it like a child's and speaking softly. "I'm pretty sure this is all over, Billy, I mean with that whacko Jasper. It's some male macho bullshit that happened all those years ago. This whole thing reminds me of some petty high school feud. I think men, they never grow up, not really. They grow old, but they never grow up."

"All men?"

She poked him in the ribs. "Yep, every last one of 'em."

He put his arms around his wife and held her close.

"Maybe you're right, babe. But I still don't feel right about this, about letting him leave. He's my uncle, and he doesn't really have anybody else, not anymore. I'm it—I mean, we're it. You, me, the boys, we're his family."

"So, you're feeling guilty and you're heading up there, to Maine, aren't you?"

"Well, I'm thinking about it. I haven't decided yet. But if I do decide to go, I'll only do it if you and the boys can stay with your folks while I'm up there. I won't leave you here in the house without me, not until this guy Jasper is picked up and things settle down. I'm sure you're right and there's nothing to worry about, but still, I'd feel better if you stayed with Phil and Sharon. Do you think your folks would mind?"

"Mind? Are you kidding? Mom and Dad would love to have the boys around for a few days, especially if I'm there to referee. Besides, it would just be at night really, with the boys in school and me at work."

"You'll have to drive the kids to school and pick them up, too. Or your parents will."

"Not a problem. I'll tell Fiona what happened. She probably knows already anyway. Seems like everybody in town knows about our windows. I'll go in an hour or so late and leave a little early. It'll only be for a few days, she won't mind. Besides, the store has been slow lately, so cutting a few of my hours isn't going to bother her all that much."

"Before we do anything, let me call Frank tomorrow and see how he sounds. Maybe I'm making more out of this than I should."

"And maybe you just want a few days away from the old ball and chain, so you can go out drinking with that handsome old coot and pick up women."

"Well, yeah, there's always that, too."

TWENTY-ONE

It was about four-thirty when Pogo and Birdie drove back up the dirt lane to where they had dropped off Jasper at the truck earlier in the afternoon. Jasper must have heard the car because he was just climbing out the back of the camper when they pulled up.

Birdie pulled up next to the truck, turned off the engine, and got out of the driver's-side door carrying a paper bag. Pogo got out the passenger side. He was carrying a bag as well.

"Howdy, boys. I sure hope you brought some food with you. I can't even look at them soggy sandwiches Birdman's old lady packed for us anymore."

Birdie tossed him a grease-stained brown paper bag.

Jasper caught the bag, opened it delicately, and took a quick peek. Inside he saw what looked like a couple of burgers wrapped in wax paper and a large tinfoil platter that he assumed was filled with warm, soggy French fries from the diner. He stuck his nose into the bag and breathed deep.

"Burgers and fries. I see you covered all the major food groups." He then reached in and with one hand removed the paper from one of the burgers, pulled the burger out, and took a big bite.

"Damn, that's good. I don't suppose you thought to bring me a milkshake," he said, talking around a mouth still full of half chewed burger.

126

"Think again, my friend." Birdie leaned back into the car and came out with a large plastic cup with a cover on top. "Vanilla. I watched her make it right there in front of me, like when I was a kid. Forgot to grab you a straw."

"Birdman, I could kiss you right on the lips for bringing me that shake."

"Well, if you really feel you have to, I guess it'd be okay, Jasper, so long as you swallow that mess in your mouth first. But no tongue." He handed the cup to Jasper and walked past him over to where they had built the campfire earlier. He began hunting around for dry twigs and branches that he could use to start the fire again.

"We stopped at one of the stores in town and picked these up, too." Pogo opened a plastic bag that he was carrying and took out a package of three Motorola walkie-talkies.

"Two-way radios. Folks around here use them for hunting, I guess. Supposed to have good range, couple of miles anyway, waterproof, can run on AA batteries, which I also bought, and they come with ear buds."

"Damn, Pogo, you must have been in the military or something."

"Regular hard charger," said Pogo with a smile. "I figure whichever one of us is designated hunter can set up and keep watch. He'll do all the talking. The other two just listen. I'm going to put the batteries in. We'll each take one, and then I'll walk out in the woods and we can test them out."

Jasper took another big bite of his burger.

"Say, I got an idea, Jasper. Why don't you stand there like a fucking moron chewing on them burgers while I go help Birdie get us a fire going?"

He walked past Jasper to where Birdman was just sparking a Zippo lighter to a small pile of kindling.

Jasper sat on a log finishing off the last of his burgers and fries, staring at the fire. Pogo used his knife to slice into the radio's molded plastic packaging. He wrestled the radios out and worked at inserting three AA batteries into each, turning them on and off to be sure each was working. He then set each radio to the same channel, inserted the metal jacks of the ear bud wires into the proper hole, and carefully unraveled the wires, letting the ear buds dangle. Once that was done, he handed a radio to each of his two compatriots.

"I believe these radios are ready to rock and roll. What's say we give 'em a test run? I'll head out that away, you guys separate some, and let's see how they sound."

With that, Pogo headed off into the woods.

After throwing the wrappers of his meal into the fire, Jasper stood holding the cup with the last of his milkshake.

"I'll head back down the road in that direction. Why don't you walk up that way?" he said to Birdie, gesturing with his paper cup in the opposite direction. Then he turned and began the quarter-mile hike back down the old dirt road. Birdie saw no reason to get up, so he stayed seated on a folding canvas chair he had found in one of the small storage bins in the camper and warmed his hands by the fire.

"Red Fox one to Red Fox leader, come in. Over." Pogo's voice came in over the ear buds.

"Goldilocks, this is Papa Bear, right back at ya," responded Birdie.

There was silence for a few seconds.

"Anyone else out there on this channel?" Pogo again.

"Jesus Christ, but you guys are couple of fucking asswipes."

Silence again for a few beats.

"Well, I heard that loud and clear," said Birdie.

"Like a fart in church," said Pogo. "I'd say this commo gear is in fine working order. When we get back to camp, let's discuss plans for this evening's festivities. Make sure you turn these things off. I don't want to take a chance on one of you sitting on the transmit button so anyone playing with a scanner can pick up this channel while we're planning our little party."

"One of us should have reconned his house. We could have driven down the lane and made like we were lost; got a look at the road, the house, the property." Birdie was talking, still seated in the folding camp chair. Jasper sat on a log, Pogo next to him with his legs crossed Indian-style.

"No, Birdman, what we've got going for us now is the element of surprise. If Turd Man happened to be home and saw a car he didn't recognize, what do you think he would have thought? Tourists? Besides, I figure tonight might end up just being recon anyway."

"Jasper's right. We got the general idea of the property from what you told us you saw on the computer. We park the car in that spot we found, go in on foot in the dark, nice and quiet, stay off the road. Hunter will set up in the woods right outside the driveway with the RPK. This way he can cover the house and the driveway. From there, he should be able to see the front and both side yards, plus the street. There's only one road in. Should have a good field of fire all around. That machine gun will tear the ass out of anything tries to get in the way. We'll spread out and check the woods, then watch and listen for a while, see what we see. If it looks good, killer team goes in for a closer look. We get a shot, we take it. If it don't smell right, we back on out. Killer team stays silent the whole operation. Hunter is the commo, he sees anything, he'll let killer team know and provide cover if needed."

"Okay, sounds good to me," said Birdie. "Who does what?"

They looked at one another in silence. Finally, Jasper spoke up.

"I think it's best if me and Pogo are killer team. We got to squeeze in through a window or, if comes down to it, didi out in a pinch, we're better suited to it. Guy your size is liable to get his ass stuck, plus you're slow as shit. We'll take the M16 and that silenced Sig with us. Be best if we can do this without waking the neighbors. Birdman, you set up with the machine gun, and maybe we'll bring the Savage along, too. It's got a good scope, and if we get some moon tonight, it should help you keep a good watch. Plus, he tries to make a run for it, you can pick him off no problem."

"All right, I'm good with that. Long as I don't have to hump both the RPK and the Savage all the way to his house and back."

"Hell, Birdman, you're hunter team. Of course, you got to hump your shit." Pogo clapped Birdie on the shoulder. "But don't you worry none, my friend, I plan to do my part. I'll carry in the Sig."

"I think we should saddle up around midnight or so," said Jasper. "It won't be so late as to look suspicious should anyone notice us driving down the road, and it will give us a good half hour to find that place you guys found to stash the car. Figure another hour to work our way up the road to the house, and that should have us set up by one-thirty or two. I'm not sure what time first light is, but we should plan to be out of there, one way or the other, I'm figuring by five, five-thirty the latest. If he's down, one of us can hustle back, get the car, and we'll load him and our gear into the trunk and then get the hell out of Dodge. Otherwise, we backtrack out nice and quiet, drive back here, and figure out our next move."

Pogo reached into his pocket, pulled out a joint, and put it between his lips. He leaned over, grabbed a twig that was lying near him in the dirt and poked it into the fire. Once it caught, he brought it up near his face and lit the end of the joint.

"Maybe you should go easy on the weed, Pogo. Need to be sharp tonight," said Jasper.

Pogo inhaled deeply, holding the smoke in and then exhaling slowly and watching it dissipate. Then he handed the joint to Birdie.

"Don't worry, Jasper, this is just to help us relax, get a little shut-eye before we head out later. I also brought us something to wake our asses up, get us hardwired for the fun we got planned tonight."

Birdie took a hit off the joint and then held it out to Jasper.

Jasper took it, looked over at Pogo, and nodded.

He brought the joint to his lips and took a long, deep drag.

TWENTY-TWO

Frank scooped some tuna casserole onto a plate and put it into the microwave oven to heat. Tuna casserole was not one of his favorites, but he figured he'd better eat a warm meal while he could.

He was going to watch the house from the hill tonight. He was sure they would come. It would be either a recon mission to get the lay of the land, or maybe a killer team to try their hand at finishing him off quickly. He had thought to set up some booby traps, some lethal surprises near and in the house, but then thought better of it. What if someone stopped by to see him, maybe a neighbor with another casserole?

Better to see what he was up against. If he could take them out quickly with a few well-placed shots, he could hide the bodies and explain the shots to his neighbor as scaring a bear away from his garbage. But he knew that was a long shot. He was old, his eyes weren't what they used to be, it would be night, and he'd never used this night scope attachment before—not to mention that he would be shooting at moving targets. Plus, he didn't have a flash suppressor, so they'd target his location pretty quickly.

When he was done eating, he washed his plate and set it in the dish rack. Then he went into his den and opened the top drawer of his desk. Inside was a cheap tin cash box with a lock on it. He opened the box with a small key that was in a plastic dish filled with paperclips, pushpins and pocket change right there on the desk. Hidden in plain sight for security. That's what Sadie had always told him, and he remembered it with a sad smile. Inside the box was about five hundred dollars, mostly in fifties. It was their emergency money. Well, he was sure this counted as an emergency, and he slipped the money into his pocket. He was going to be away for a few days at least, and this money was enough to buy any supplies he might need. He'd have his wallet with credit and debit cards, too, but better to have cash for now.

His plan was to drive the Subaru out his road and turn right towards town. There was a turnoff a few hundred yards down that road with a small parking area. In the back was an old logging road that ran up into the hills. People used this old road for riding snowmobiles and ATVs. The road ran up the into the hills and followed the ridge that ran behind his neighbor's property before turning north right before his own property line. The snow was usually packed down pretty well from all the recreational traffic. He'd put the Subaru in four-wheel drive and see how far up the ridge he could take it. He hoped he could make it all the way to where the road snaked north. Then he would leave the car and walk into the woods along the ridge that bordered his property and find the blind that he'd scouted earlier. If the road looked slick or treacherous, then he'd leave the car in the parking area and hike the road, but he hoped to keep the car relatively close in case he needed to didi out in a hurry.

He went through his closet picking out jeans and shirts and sweaters and socks and underwear and packed a bag. Then he went into his storage closet and took out his camping gear: cold-weather sleeping bag, gas cooking stove, and some propane canisters. He made a few trips out to the garage, carrying the last of his gear to the car, then came back in and walked the house quickly, making sure the windows and back door were locked. He double checked his gun safe to make sure that was secure as well, turned the heat down to fifty-five degrees, set the timer for the living room lamp, then stepped outside and locked the front door. He looked up to the ridge where he was going to set up and then stopped and looked back at the house. He turned around, unlocked the front door, went into the spare room, and looked out the window. He had a clear view up to where he would be watching from. He unlocked that window and walked back through the house and out the front door. He relocked the door and headed toward the car.

He was losing daylight quickly. He wanted to be up on the ridge before full dark. He was confident that he could find the blind, even at night, but it would be better to get situated and comfortable as soon as possible.

He got into the Subaru and took a last look at the house. Then started the engine, set the Colt .45 down on the passenger seat next to him, and started down the driveway.

The drive up the old logging road had been precarious. The snow was packed down, and with the sun having already gone down over ridge, the road had iced. The Subaru's four-wheel drive had muscled its way up the road, but the going had been slow and uphill most of the way. He slipped and slid a bit, but the road was wide enough that he had room to maneuver, so he was able to keep the car on track. Once Frank reached the bend that turned away from his property, he made a three-point turn and parked the car facing the way he had come. He figured that if things went to shit and he had to make a run for it, he wanted the car facing downhill, so he could get going in a hurry. He was going to leave the door unlocked, then remembered that he had all his weapons and ammo and other gear in the back and decided he had better lock the car. If someone happened by and found the door unlocked, they might just find his stash too tempting to pass up. But someone had to be intent on robbery to break a window to get in, and he thought the chances of that were pretty slim.

He disabled the interior lights, grabbed his rifle, a daypack and blanket roll out of the back, and then headed into the trees. He took his time hiking across the top of the ridge through his neighbor's property and then onto his own. The transition from dusk to dark came quickly, but he found the blind without any problems. His blanket roll contained a small tarp and an old fleece blanket. When he got to the blind, he moved aside the low-hanging boughs of the pine tree and laid the canvas tarp on some dried-up pine needles. Then he backed his way into the tree feet first. He extended the rifle barrel and adjusted the bipod mount until the gun felt comfortable. He looked through the scope, then turned on his night vision attachment. His property glowed green, and he could make out details that had not been visible with his day scope. He unfurled the old fleece blanket over himself, making sure it covered his head and hooded his rifle, so no moon or starlight would reflect off the scope. It was going to be a long, cold night, but he was dressed for the weather. His only real worry was that he might now be able to stay awake. He had decided to leave the thermos with hot coffee in the car, feeling it was too cumbersome to pour in the blind, but he had several bottled energy drinks and snacks to fortify him.

All that was left to do was wait and watch.

TWENTY-THREE

It was 11:45 p.m. when Jasper walked to the back of the camper and knocked on the door. A minute or so later, the door opened and Pogo came out carrying the RPK in one hand and the drum magazine in the other. Birdie followed carrying his Mossberg and the M16. The handle of the silenced Sig stuck out of his pants just above his crotch.

They walked over to where Jasper was seated on his log watching the fire.

"I do believe we're ready to get this party started," said Pogo cheerily. "Birdman, since you're hunter on this mission, why don't you step over here and let me give you a quick refresher on how to use this thing?"

Birdie leaned the shotgun and the M16 carefully against the camp chair and walked over to where Pogo was standing.

"Drum's loaded with seventy-five rounds. Got a spring mechanism inside, and it's that tension that feeds 'em. So, we got to wind her up like a clock." He turned a key on the back of the drum and ratcheted up the tension, and said, "Then insert that sucker right here." He pointed to a slot on the stock just past the trigger guard where the drum would go. "Pull the bolt back to chamber the first round, and you're ready to rock and roll." Pogo handed the gun to Birdie.

"Easy enough. I'll wait till I'm set up before I lock and load."

They both walked back to the fire where Jasper still sat staring.

"Why don't you take the M16, Jasper? It's your gun, and you're more used to it. I'll take Birdie's Mossberg. I don't think we'll need the Savage. Hell, we got more guns than we got hands. He does a runner, you can get him, or Birdie can splatter him with that machine gun. Even Birdie can't miss him with all those fucking bullets. You take the Sig, too. Be best if we can get him with that and keep things quiet. That'll be the plan anyway. But he hears us coming, it will be a firefight for sure. You cool with that?"

"Yeah, it all sounds good."

"Wish we had night vision," said Birdie.

"Well, we got a moon tonight, or partial moon, so it shouldn't be too bad. Pogo, we got to watch for motion sensor lights when we get near the house. Don't see any reason why he'd have those living way out here, but we got to be aware. We trigger one, we'll be blinded, and he'll know someone's coming for him. You cover the windows Birdman. Anyone fires out one of them, you rake it good. If this goes beyond just a recon, then we got to finish it tonight no matter what. We'll have to storm the walls, burn the village, and take no prisoners. It goes that way, we won't be able to sneak out of Maine once it gets started, and even if we do, we'll have to deal with old Turd Man somewhere down the line. He'll turn the tables on us, and we'll have to wait and watch that he don't come sneaking around our back doors late one night."

"Hell, son, this is what we came here for," said Pogo. "Don't go getting all paranoid on us. He's in that house, we kill that son of a bitch, simple as that. Or die trying. It's three against one. But even if it ain't, so what? We got Birdie manning the equalizer. I guarantee no one else is bringing a fucking machine gun to this party. One of us gets it, then so be it. Nobody lives forever."

It was quiet for a full minute, each man looking into the fire with his own thoughts.

Finally, Jasper looked up. "We ready to roll?"

"Yep. I mean no, just a minute. You boys wait here, and I'll be right back." Pogo walked back to the camper, opened the door, and disappeared into the back.

Birdie took the Sig out of his waistband and handed it to Jasper.

"You see him, Jasper, you put a bullet in his brain. You're right. I don't want to even think about that motherfucker coming after me and mine after this."

Jasper took the gun and slipped it into his own waistband.

The camper door opened and Pogo came out carrying what looked like a small glass bottle.

"We got to take our meds, boys. Get ourselves a little cranked up. I told you I brought us something to get us wired." Pogo held up a glass tube with a bulb at the end and dropped some crystals into it, then began heating the tube with his Zippo.

"That crystal meth?" asked Birdie.

"Yep. Dusted. Got a secret formula that sets you right."

Pogo sucked the smoke out of the glass tube, blew the stream straight up into the air, and then let out his Indian war cry. His eyes were wide and shining when he handed the glass pipe to Birdie.

Birdie held the pipe while Pogo waved his lighter under the bulbous end, and they both watched as the crystals began to vaporize.

"What do you mean dusted? What's your secret formula? I don't want to burn out the last few brain cells I got left," said Birdie.

"Are you shitting me, Birdman? Them last few brain cells of yours gotta be on a respirator as it is. Stop being a chicken shit and toke up!"

So, Birdie did, and then handed the glass pipe to Jasper.

TWENTY-FOUR

Frank was startled awake by the sound of snow sliding off a branch, and then a second later felt a light impact on top of his head. For a second he didn't know where he was, his eyes heavy with sleep and wet from tearing in the cold. He took a breath to steady himself and then saw the gun with the scope set up right in front of his face, and he remembered where he was.

Dumb shit, he thought. Fell asleep. You're getting old and soft and stupid. Body heat rising must have loosened some of the snow on the boughs overhead and caused the snow to fall.

He rubbed his eyes and looked down at the vista in front of him. Soft light from the moon reflected off the white snow, and he could make out his front door and the windows and the dark ribbon that was his driveway leading all the way to the road. He put his eye to the scope and flicked on the switch that powered the night vision attachment. The landscape glowed a soft green, and suddenly everything came more clearly into focus. Trees and bushes that before were mere shadows now took shape with amazing clarity.

He took his eye from the scope and checked to make sure the blanket was lying properly, hooding any reflection that might bounce off the lens. Then he tightened the rifle stock against his shoulder and peered through the scope again, moving the crosshairs all around the house. Nothing looked amiss. No lights were on, so he knew it was past midnight. He had set the timer in the living room to shut the light off at twelve. He wanted to check the time, but his watch didn't have a lighted dial and he didn't want to chance turning on his phone. The time didn't matter anyway. He scanned the perimeter of his property, and then sighted slowly down the long driveway all the way to the street. He looked first to the left toward the dead-end barrier, and then began a slow pan down the street as far toward his neighbor's house as he could see.

After a few minutes, he turned off the power to the night vision attachment. His neighbor had told him that the scope ate through batteries. He had bought a package containing spare lithium batteries just to be safe, but there was no need to waste them. He would check the area periodically and conserve juice. He didn't want to have to try to change batteries in the dark.

He eased the rifle off his shoulder and reached behind him and rummaged in one of the daypacks with his hand until he found one of the five-hour energy drinks he had brought with him. He bought these because they were small (he didn't want to drink a lot of fluid and have to pee), and they had twist-off caps, which would come off silently. He worked himself up onto his elbows, careful not to disturb the boughs and branches overhead, twisted off the cap, and drank one down. He left the bottle on the ground, figuring he would clean up when he left in the morning, then eased the rifle back into his shoulder and peered through the scope, this time with the night vision off.

He brought the crosshairs back to his front door, and then began scanning the property as he had before, slowly and carefully, looking for any movement or anything that looked out of place. He worked the scope back down the driveway to the road, looked left, and then began working his way back down the road. About a hundred yards from his driveway, he detected what he thought might have been movement along the side of the road. He felt a sudden chill and then a queasiness and an ever so slight tingling in his testicles. He steadied the rifle and pushed it a bit harder into his shoulder and flipped the night vision adapter on.

The green light came on, and he saw nothing for a fraction of a second. Then the scope came back into focus with the same sharpness and clarity it had had before.

He hoped to see a deer or a raccoon or even a bear.

Instead, he saw three men working their way slowly along the side of the road near the tree line. All were armed. Two carried assault rifles. The one in the lead had what looked like an old M16. The next guy looked to be carrying a shotgun, but he couldn't see clearly enough from this distance to be sure.

One guy, the one bringing up the rear, was much taller than the other two. Had to be one of the Mutt and Jeff team that Katie had told him about that had come into the diner earlier. That meant that one of the other two was Jasper, no doubt about it.

They moved slowly in single file. When they got within about fifty yards of the driveway, the guy in front put a hand up, and all three stopped and knelt on one knee, the trail guy with one of the assault rifles turning to watch their rear. He watched as the tall guy in back raised his rifle with the barrel pointing up and leaned the stock on his thigh to take some of the weight off. Frank saw the big drum magazine. Looked like either an AK47 or an RPK, either of which was some serious firepower. Those drum magazines could hold about seventy rounds.

Shit.

Frank sighted the scope in the direction they had come from, looking down the road for more men. Are you hunter or killer team, he was thinking, but he detected no movement.

When he brought the scope back to the men, they were working their way off the road and into the woods. Frank watched them make their way the remaining fifty or so yards until they were almost directly opposite the entrance to his driveway.

There was no movement for several minutes. Then two of

the men darted across the road, hunched over as they ran. Each took up a position on one side of his driveway, staying low and keeping their weapons trained on his house.

The third guy, the tall one, stationed himself in the woods behind a downed tree. From there he could easily cover the house, front and side yards, and the road. That AK47 with all those rounds could hold off an army. It could certainly take out a fleeing car. He was glad he had decided not to stay and fight from the house. He wouldn't have stood a chance.

Now he knew there were only three men in this hit squad. The tall guy, he was hunter team all by himself. The other two were killer team, and one of them was surely Jasper.

He began thinking about his shots. His rifle was sighted in, but he hadn't fired it in a while, and he didn't know what effect the night vision attachment would have on his scope. He was about one hundred yards from the house, another fifty or so to the end of the driveway and the street. No easy shot, much less so at night from an angle. Plus, he couldn't really judge the wind. The cleared area that was his property would have gusts coming down off the ridge. He should have set up a flag in the yard, which would have helped.

He sighted back to the tall guy in the woods. That shot would be a waste of lead. He was situated behind a log with only the barrel of his gun and a portion of his head visible. It would take a perfect shot to get him. And Frank's confidence was low. He went back to the killer team, each man now slowly making his way up one side of the driveway toward the house.

Keeping his sight's crosshairs on one of the creeping men, he lifted the bolt of his rifle, pulled it back, then slid it slowly forward and down again, chambering one of the high-velocity NATO rounds.

Locked and loaded. He kept his finger off the trigger as he followed the men's progress.

He was pretty sure he could hit one of them, though he wouldn't even try for a head shot. He would aim for center of mass, put him down. But without a suppressor, he would give his position away from both the muzzle flash and the noise, and then the guy with the AK would open up on him. From his position across from the end of the driveway, he'd have a good line of sight to cover most of the ridge. Probably wouldn't hit him unless he got real lucky, but with seventy or more rounds ready and available, he could cover a lot of area and keep him pinned down. Plus, if any of these guys had night vision, and they probably did, he'd have to stay put or try to crawl out, stay on his belly and hopefully out of sight.

He moved the crosshairs to the other member of the killer team. He hoped to figure out which guy was Jasper. If he decided to shoot, he'd want to hit Jasper first, then make a run for it. Maybe he could make it out if he moved fast.

He wished desperately that he had set some booby traps. He could have rigged something using shotgun shells, maybe kill or maim one of the two men. All he would have had to do was wait for one to set something off, and then shoot the other. Simple. Even if the trap didn't get one of them, the noise would have created enough of a diversion that he probably could have gotten a shot off without giving away his position. At the very least, they'd think they were facing more than just him.

Shit.

He hadn't thought things through. He worried about a neighbor or a delivery, but he could have watched the house and then warned any friendlies away.

I'm a man with no plan, he thought, and that's not good.

Both men followed the driveway all the way to the detached garage. The guy with the M16 crouched in one corner and covered the house. The other guy took his shotgun and went around the garage, looking in windows. He found the side door, which was unlocked, opened it, and disappeared inside. Then he came back out and crouched next to the first guy.

Frank's finger unconsciously went to the trigger of his rifle. His mind was working quickly, and he thought he should shoot when they were close together. Sweat beaded on his forehead. A drop threaded its way down over his brow and into his eye, the salt stinging and ruining the shot. He leaned away from the sight, wiped his eye on his shoulder, then went back to it, but it was too late. The two men were on the move again, each in a low crouch and heading to the front of the house.

Shit.

Frank's breathing came faster, and he tried to slow it down, taking long, deep breaths. He knew he was getting nervous, that he had to get hold of himself.

This is surreal, he thought. What the fuck is happening? Almost seventy years old, and I'm taking a bead on two men I haven't seen in nearly fifty years.

TWENTY-FIVE

Jasper and Pogo crept along the front of the house, careful to stay below the sight lines of any windows.

Birdie's voice whispered in their ear buds: "No movement in any of the windows. Yard looks clear. Nothing coming down the road."

Jasper and Pogo got to the front porch and climbed the stairs, careful to make no sound. Pogo stepped back and aimed the shotgun at the door while Jasper stood to one side, quietly opened the glass storm door, and tried the knob. Locked.

He let the storm close without a sound, then backed away from the porch while Pogo held his aim on the door. When Jasper was clear, Pogo stepped back while Jasper covered the door and windows. They made their way carefully around the house, peeking in windows and trying each one. Everything was quiet and locked tight. They continued around the house until they came to a side window of a bedroom. A quick peek showed the bedroom to be empty, but the window was unlocked, and Jasper raised it an inch to test it. He looked at Pogo and nodded. Pogo stuck the Mossberg's barrel in while Jasper raised the window as far as it would go, then hoisted himself up and into the house. He did a quick check of the small room, opening the closet and checking under the bed. He positioned himself in a corner covering the door with his M16 while Pogo eased himself in. Pogo closed the window behind him, not wanting a sudden gust to give them away.

Jasper laid the M16 on the bed and pulled the silenced Sig out of his waistband, then made his way to the bedroom door. He opened it silently and looked down the hall. The house was quiet and had that empty feel to it. He crept into the hallway, then made his way down the hall to the next bedroom. The door was open, and he could see the bed was made. He went in carefully and searched the room, again looking in the closet and under the bed. He checked the master bath, even looking behind the shower curtain and in the tub. When he came out of the bedroom, he heard a refrigerator door open and a can being opened. He moved toward the sound, his gun at the ready. He poked his head into the kitchen and saw Pogo at the kitchen table with a beer in his hand.

"He ain't home," Pogo said smiling up at Jasper. Then he took a sip of his beer.

Then they heard Birdie's excited voice in their ear buds: "I saw a flash in one of the windows! Jasper, you pop him? Is he down?"

Jasper keyed the mike on his radio. "No, Birdie, that was just dickhead here grabbing himself a beer out of the fridge. Turd Man took a powder. Nobody home."

"Roger that," replied Birdie.

"Roger that? Is that what that shit bird said? You believe this guy? Thinks he's Dick fucking Tracy."

Jasper walked out of the kitchen and back to the bedroom where they had entered and retrieved his rifle. Then he walked back to the kitchen and sat at the table with the rifle between his knees and watched Pogo drink his beer.

Finally, he said, "What do you think, Pogo? He gone for a while, or do you think maybe he stopped someplace overnight on the drive up here and he just ain't arrived yet?"

"Well, Jasper, no car in the garage. House is fairly cool, so nobody put the heat up. I guess that means it's one or the other. I suggest I finish my beer, maybe use the potty and take myself a leak whilst you unlock the back door and all them other windows in case we got to leave quick or get back in later. We'll leave the front door locked. Don't want him to suspect anything if he comes home anytime soon. We're here already and Birdie's set up. You and me can wait in the living room until morning. If he shows up, we'll take him as he comes in the front door. If he doesn't show up, we'll withdraw like we planned. Tomorrow we can set up surveillance on that main road leading into here, so we'll see him coming. We can probably park the camper where we left the car tonight. We do that, one of us can watch the road from the front seat of the truck or from the car while the others take turns getting some shut-eye."

"What's the plan, boys? It's getting a bit chilly out here." Birdie, coming through the ear buds again.

Pogo keyed his radio. "Birdman, you keep a sharp lookout on the road. You see lights, you let us know right away. We're counting on you son, so stay sharp, you hear?"

"Okay. What are you guys going to do?"

"We got plenty of shit to do in here. Me, I'm going to finish my beer and maybe have me another while Jasper takes a little nap on the couch. You got that, good buddy? Hope that's a big ten four. Roger dodger over and out." He winked at Jasper, and then took another pull on his beer.

"He won't be arriving before late morning if he does show up," said Jasper. "I can't see him popping in before eight or nine. Otherwise why would he have stopped in the first place? We should be outta here by first light."

Pogo took another sip of his beer. "Unless we stay. We could park our asses right here and wait him out. Be the last thing he expects, walking in that door and seeing our handsome faces."

Jasper sat quietly for a minute looking at the floor. Finally, he looked up at Pogo and said, "Something to think about. Maybe just for a day or so. If he don't show up, then he probably lit out for parts unknown. Maybe figured we were coming. Them Hackensack cops are probably looking for me right now.

No doubt he's talked to them or to his nephew, the guy's house we visited the other night. They can't find me, where do you think he thinks I'm headed? On the flip side, he thinks we're up here already, he might bring a posse home with him. Maybe some local cops or some buddies he trusts to back him up. I wouldn't want to be caught here in this house if that happens. We get in a firefight like that, we're toast. Even if we make it out of the house, we'll never make it out of the state. Best way to take care of this business is like we planned, silent and deadly."

Pogo stood and walked over to the fridge. "You want a beer? This sorry motherfucker only got two more in here. Shows what kind of asshole we're dealing with." He grabbed both beers without waiting for a reply and brought them back to the kitchen table.

"Let's wait here until late morning, see if he shows. We'll take turns outside, so we won't have to listen to old Birdman piss and moan. He doesn't show up, let's do like I said earlier and set up in that car park, watch the road. We can give it a day or two more. After that, hell, let's head home. We can come back in a couple of weeks when the weather warms up, play war party all over again."

Jasper took the beer that Pogo handed him.

"You wanna tell Birdman the plan, or you want me to?" he asked Pogo.

"Aw, geez. That's a tough question, Jasper. Why don't we work on finishing these beers first and let's think about it a little?"

TWENTY-SIX

Frank watched the two men climb in through the bedroom window. He had left the window open, figuring whoever came for him would do that, and doing so, give him a clear shot. But he didn't pull the trigger. As he lay there watching these two men invade his house, the home he had shared with his lovely Sadie for all these years, he realized that he wasn't going to kill anyone. He just didn't have it in him anymore. He had done his share in the war, maybe more than his share, and had been proud of his service up until his last assignment. But that was long ago. He was old now, he knew, but it wasn't just that. He had changed. He had told his nephew Billy that he had lost his taste for killing. But it was more. He knew these men were here to murder him. That they were hoping to find him sleeping in his bed, maybe hoping he wasn't alone, and they were going to kill him and anyone else they found. He would be justified in killing them, simple self-defense. He knew, too, that if he didn't end this now, it might not end until he himself was dead. He would be doing the world a favor by ridding it of these two; these three if he got real lucky and could get off another good shot. It shouldn't have any effect on him at all, like squashing a bug, he thought, but he couldn't do it. Instead he watched through his scope, the crosshairs perfectly aligned on his targets as they climbed in through the window. Once inside, one of them turned and slid the window shut behind him.

He watched the house for several more minutes. He could make out no movement inside until a light went on briefly in the kitchen, and then off again. He swung his scope to the woods and could just make out the head and the barrel of the rifle sticking up behind the downed tree.

Time to boogie, he thought. Clear out slow and easy, take his time and make sure he wasn't seen or heard. He would make his way back to the car past his neighbor's property on the other side of ridge. He was glad he had thought to turn the car around. The car was parked pointing slightly downhill. It couldn't be seen from here, and certainly not from below, but he had some electrical tape in the car, and he would cover his brake lights anyway. He was pretty sure he could push the car until it started rolling, and then coast a good part of the way down the other side of the ridge in neutral. He'd rather not start the car unless absolutely necessary. He knew the sound would carry in these hills. Even if they couldn't place where the sound of the engine was coming from, they'd most probably figure out who was up here. Better to let them wait, scope out the house until they got tired or bored. Give it a week or so, then come back up the ridge behind the house and see what was what. He was sure they wouldn't be able to wait that long, but better safe than sorry. He'd have to be careful going in. They'd probably set up a few little surprises for him, but he wasn't too worried about that. After all, he was the one who had trained them. Even though the materials will have changed, he was sure he could defeat anything these numbnuts could come up with. Geez, look how well their little mission had gone so far. If he was, well, of a different mindset, he could have killed two of them already, and quite easily. He smiled, took his eye away from the scope, and shook his head. No wonder we lost the fucking war. No, he would go up to hunting camp. There was a cabin there with a wood-burning stove, working compost toilet and water tank, and it was even wired for lights and electricity. There was a small generator in back, and all he'd need was a few gallons of gas, though he probably wouldn't use the generator at all. They'd never find him there, not in a million years. But if by some dreadful miracle they did, then the choice would be taken out of his hands, and he would give them the fight they were looking for. And he wouldn't have to worry about any civilian casualties.

"We'll let God decide this for us boys. His will be done," he said, speaking softly to himself as he eased out from under the boughs of the big pine tree, careful not move any branches or dislodge any more snow.

TWENTY-SEVEN

Around 4:30 a.m. Pogo made his way slowly and carefully out the back door and then around the house and back down the driveway to where Birdie sat shivering behind a tree.

"It's about fucking time, Pogo. My feet are all but frozen, and I can't hardly feel my fingers anymore."

"It's good to see you too, Birdie." Pogo clapped him on the shoulder, then crouched next to him. "See anything?"

"Yeah, I've been watching my fingers turn an interesting shade of blue from the frostbite." He handed Pogo the RPK and took the shotgun.

"Jasper made a pot of coffee after the beer ran out. Why don't you go get yourself warmed up? We should do a commo check every fifteen minutes or so. I don't know how fast these radios eat up batteries, but I just put in a fresh set. Jasper's got some more up at the house."

"Coffee sounds good. My brain is frozen along with the rest of me."

Pogo reached into his jacket pocket and came out with the small glass pipe.

"Here, Birdman, take this with you. It's already loaded. You and Jasper fire it up and put a little sass in your ass, get you feeling top-notch in no time."

Birdie smiled and put the pipe into his own jacket pocket. "I think I'm taking a liking to that secret recipe of yours."

"Yeah, well, don't take too much of a liking to it. Remember them last few brain cells you still got left ain't doing so hot as it is."

Birdie got up and stretched his legs, then made his way across the road and up the driveway in an awkward crouching gait.

Jasper watched Birdie shuffle up the driveway. Even though the moon was still out, the sky was beginning to show just the faintest hint of dawn. He keyed his radio. "Pogo, you all set?"

"Roger that," replied Pogo.

Then Birdie's voice came over the radio, somewhat breathless from the exertion of running up the driveway: "Fuck you, asshole."

"I'll Roger that, too," said Jasper. Then he walked into the kitchen in time to see Birdie coming in through the back door.

"How's the weather out there, Birdman?" Jasper was pouring a cup of hot coffee.

"And you can go fuck yourself, too, Jasper. I hope that cup's for me. I don't think I can bend my fingers around that coffeepot handle enough to pour."

Birdie made it to the table, sat on one of the chairs, and leaned the Mossberg against the wall. Jasper slid the cup toward him and watched as he wrapped both hands around the steaming cup and breathed in the smell of hot coffee.

The room was dark, but soft moonlight came in through the window, and the green glow from the digital numerals of the clock on the small microwave oven over the stove provided enough light so the two men could see each other fairly well.

"I don't ever remember being so fucking cold," said Birdie.

"That's what you get for coming up to Maine dressed for a lovely spring day in New York City," said Jasper. "You should of planned ahead."

"I should of planned to get my ass in the house and have you set up outside in the fucking cold with that machine gun all night."

"Yeah, that would probably have been a smart plan on your part too, Birdman. I don't think he's going to show up here anytime soon, do you?"

Birdie brought the hot coffee cup to his lips, both his hands shaking slightly. He took a delicate sip.

"I'm not sure. He might have stopped on his way up here and spent the night someplace. We moved on this pretty quick. I don't think he would have expected us up here so fast, do you?"

Jasper didn't answer right away, just seemed to be staring at the door leading out to the back yard.

From his seat at the table, Birdie let his eyes roam around the room. "This kitchen doesn't really look like it belongs to a guy who lives alone. You and Pogo searched the place, right? He married?"

Jasper took his gaze off the door and looked at Birdie. "There's some pictures of him with a woman all over the house, some from a long time ago. Same woman, so it must be his wife. Also, she's got clothes in the closets, stuff in the bathroom, perfume and curlers and shit."

"Well, since she isn't sitting here waiting for him, I have to assume they either left together as soon as he got here, or she met him someplace. Is there a car in the garage?"

Jasper shook his head.

"There you go. He must have called and told her to meet him someplace. Maybe he decided to see if the coast was clear before coming back. Maybe he's set up in the woods right now, watching the house."

Jasper shook his head again. "If he was out there tonight, we'd be dead now. Least Pogo and me would be for sure. Probably you, too. I think he's playing it safe, hiding out for a while figuring if we come, we won't stay long. He didn't make it through two tours by being stupid."

"You're probably right. But I'm for waiting it out a while longer. He may show up with or without his old lady. He does, he's dead. He brings the calvary, we can sneak out the back and make our way through the woods and follow the road back to the car."

Jasper nodded in agreement.

"Besides, there's no goddamn way I'm going back out into that fucking cold before I'm good and warm again."

TWENTY-EIGHT

It was slow moving through the trees in the snow at night. Frank was being extra careful not to make any noise. He wasn't worried about being seen; the tall trees and bushes provided ample cover. It was still dark enough, but noise would be a problem. He stopped every so often to view the terrain ahead through the night vision scope. That made it much easier to pick his way past trees and bushes, plus he could follow his own footsteps from earlier in the evening right to where the car was waiting.

He judged that he had covered the full distance to the car in about an hour and a half, though he never checked his watch. When he could see the car, he stopped and surveyed the area through the scope. He didn't expect to find anybody, but better to be sure. When he was fairly confident nobody was around, he moved slowly and carefully to the car and unlocked the hatch with the key. He had disabled the interior lights earlier, so the car remained dark as he opened the hatch. He set his rifle down alongside the shotgun, and then rummaged in a small toolbox that he always kept in his cars until he found the black electrical tape and proceeded to tape over the brake lights. It was getting light out quickly now, but he didn't want to take any chances on his brake lights giving his position away. He made sure to cover the lenses completely, then walked around to the front driver's-side door, opened it, stuck one leg in while looking over his shoulder, and gently tapped the brake. No red light showed. Good. He walked back around to the rear of the car and eased the hatch closed until he heard a soft click. Back to the driver's-side door. He sat in the driver's seat, shifted into neutral, and then loosened the emergency brake. The car began inching downhill. He closed the door as quietly as he could and guided the car as it slowly rolled down the snow-packed road. The only sound he heard was the tires crunching over the hard-packed snow. The car rolled for a good half mile before the road began to level out. When the car would roll no further on its own, he decided to go ahead and start it up. Chances were good that he was far enough away that nobody would hear the engine turn over. Even if the intruders did, they wouldn't be able to isolate the sound since the ridge now lay between he and his property. He started the engine and navigated further along the road, still not turning on his headlights.

A few minutes later he entered the parking lot near the road. There was a car parked in the corner farthest from the road. Frank shifted to park, reached under his seat, and grabbed the loaded .45 he had stashed there earlier. He got out of his car and walked cautiously toward the car, his gun at the ready. He wasn't sure if he was sneaking up on some kids drinking beer or fooling around in the back seat, or maybe another assassin was waiting with the getaway car. He saw no movement inside the car, nor did he hear any sound. He snuck up close and peered in. Empty. He tried the doors. Locked. It was a dirty brown Toyota, older model. A Camry, no, not a Camry. It was a Corolla. Perfect place to hide your car if, say, you were planning to hike down the road, stake out a house, and kill its lone occupant.

He thought about puncturing the tires with his knife, but that would only alert them to his presence. Not a good idea just yet. So, he walked back to his own car, got in, and drove across the car park to the road. He turned right, the opposite direction from the entrance to his road, and drove a short distance before turning on his headlights.

He looked at the clock on the dashboard. It was 5:50 a.m. He drove another half mile or so, then remembered the black tape on the brake lights and pulled over. He got out and walked to rear of the car, pulled the tape off the brake lights and rolled it into a ball.

There was a green road sign directly ahead and to the right of his car. It looked larger now that he was out of his car than it did when he drove past it every day. The sign said Boland City Limit. Frank looked at the sign and then glanced through the glass of his hatchback into the back of the car.

He looked at the road behind him. Empty. Then he peeked around the side of his car and looked at the road ahead. Also, empty.

He opened the hatch, grabbed his shotgun, looked behind and ahead one more time to make sure that no one was around, then took aim at the sign and fired a load of buckshot right through it. Even though he was expecting it, the report from the shotgun startled him. He hadn't thought to put in ear protection before firing, and the morning was so quiet that the sound sent shock waves through his eardrums. The plastic shell casing ejected automatically. He watched it fly through the air and noted where it landed, then put the shotgun back in the car. He found the spent shell casing, picked it up, threw it into the car, and closed the hatch.

He walked around to the driver's-side door and got in. He drove into town down Henry Street, pulled into the parking lot of the town's only bank, and rustled around in his pocket until he found his phone. He turned the power on, waited a minute, then opened his address book and scrolled down until he came to his friend Noah's cell phone number and hit the SEND button.

A voice answered on the first ring.

"Morning, Frank. Everything okay?"

"Morning, Noah. Yeah, everything's fine. Sorry to call you so early. Hope I didn't wake you."

"Wake me? Are you kidding? I've been working the midnight

to eight shift this entire month. I am right now sitting on the side of the road with my radar gun in one hand and a powdered jelly doughnut in the other. As I'm sure you are well aware, eating doughnuts on duty is part of our job description. Now, what's on your mind, Frank? I can't believe you called me at 6 a.m. just to chitchat."

"No, I didn't, Noah. I was heading into town, to the MAC machine, actually, get some cash, and then I'm heading toward Bangor to visit a friend of mine for a few days. He needs some help paneling his basement, and I figured I may as well get of town for a few days."

"I thought you were down in 'New Joisy' visiting with your nephew."

"I was. Just got back yesterday. But, well, you know, I keep moving, and it keeps my mind off things."

"Yeah, geez, Frank, I can't tell you how sorry I am about, well, you know."

"I know, Noah, and I appreciate it. Anyway, the reason I'm calling. I was driving into town, and there was this car passed by as I was pulling out of my road. I got in behind him, was an old Toyota, a brown Corolla I believe, don't know what year. Anyway, there looked to be a couple of old guys in the car. Must have been plastered 'cause the car was weaving all over the road, you know? Anyway, guy on the passenger side suddenly leans out his window swinging a shotgun and starts shooting at road signs just outside of town. Crazy old coots scared the daylights outta me. I slowed right down, let 'em get way ahead, and when I got into town, I called you."

"That was this morning?"

"Yep, just about ten minutes ago."

"I got a call from Kate Henshaw, you know, from the diner, just yesterday. Left me a message about some old hippies in town smoking pot or something. I wasn't too clear on what exactly it was she was talking about. These guys were older, you say?"

"Well, I didn't get a real good look, but that was the impression I got when they drove by. Not real old. About my age, I guess."

"I'll leave that one alone, Frank. If it's the same guys we're talking about, I'd say they've got some kind of bender going. I'll get something out on the radio. Soon as I finish my doughnut, I'll be heading your way, and I'll keep an eye out for these guys."

"Listen, Noah, you be careful, you hear? These guys are whacked out on something, and they're armed. I pulled my car over and took a look at one of the signs they shot, was that city limit sign right outside of town, looks like he's got that shotgun loaded with double aught. This isn't something to fool around with, understand?"

"Yeah, Frank, I got it."

"Sorry, Noah, I don't mean to tell you your job. I'm a little shook up is all."

"Not at all, Frank. I appreciate the warning—and your concern. I've got my vest, and I'll be extra careful should I see these clowns. Also, I'll pass your warning along to the other guys on patrol. It's always the crazies you gotta watch out for. And these jokers sound like they're off their rockers."

"Good, Noah. Thanks. Be careful out there. I'll be back in a couple of days, and I'll see you then. If you'd care to, you're welcome to come over for some homemade casserole. Stop by any time you'd like. I've got chicken, tuna, vegetable. Heck, the whole freezer's full of them."

"Sounds good, Frank. I'll bring some beer."

"Great, Noah. I'll be talking to you." Frank ended the call and then as he was about to power it off, the phone chimed, signaling that he had just received a new email.

TWENTY-NINE

Bill didn't sleep well. He was up most of the night listening to his wife snoring softly at his side. Around five-thirty, he eased out of bed, went into the kitchen, and made a pot of strong coffee. He walked to the front door carrying his steaming cup and checked for the morning paper. It hadn't arrived, so he wandered into the study, turned on the computer, and checked his office email. He answered a few things that needed answering, but he had planned on taking some time off, so he had made sure he had every one of his work projects covered before he left. He checked his personal email and found nothing but junk. Geez, he thought, how popular am I? Not even one stinking email from a live person. He surfed some local news outlets, but soon found himself looking at websites of newspapers up in Maine.

He was worried about his uncle again. He had a bad feeling in the pit of his stomach that wouldn't quit. He wanted to call, make sure that Frank was okay, but it was too early. He checked the time on his computer, not even six yet. Frank was probably still sound asleep. He thought about calling Officer Rudy to find out if there was any word yet on Jasper Sprague's whereabouts, but figured he better wait on that call, too. Rudy had promised to call if he had any news, and it wasn't worth becoming a pain in the ass to the cop who had been so helpful from the start.

He heard soft footsteps in the hallway and turned around

just as Sam appeared in the doorway. She was wearing that old robe of hers, and her hair was a mess, and she had on a pair of funny fuzzy slippers that his kids had given her at Christmas, and he marveled, as he always did, at how beautiful she was.

"Morning, hon," she said, her voice still a little rough from sleep. "Did you make coffee already? Tell me you did. I'd do anything for a fresh cup of coffee."

"Fresh and hot and waiting for you in the kitchen, my dear."

"You are the best!"

"You did say you'd do anything, right?" he said with a smile.

"Well, almost anything," she said. "For absolutely anything, you'd have to make breakfast, too. And then wait for the kids to head off to school."

With that she turned, and he heard her soft footsteps heading toward the kitchen.

He went through his emails again to make sure he didn't miss anything, and then walked into the kitchen to make breakfast for his family. He was thinking with a smile that maybe he'd take Sam up on her kind offer after the kids went off to school.

Sam was sitting at the kitchen table reading the paper.

"I see you got the paper. Sorry, Sweets. I checked when I got up, and it hadn't arrived yet." He headed for the stove. He heard some arguing, which meant that the kids were already up. He grabbed a box of just-add-water pancake mix and a large mixing bowl and began preparing a hot breakfast for everybody.

Sam looked up from her paper. "Pancakes? Hmm, you must have something special in mind for later there, lover boy."

He smiled at her. "Indeed, I do." He turned back to the task at hand.

After the family was fed and the dishes done, and the kids cleaned up and ready for school, Sam said she was heading for the shower and Bill, over the protests of both boys, walked them to the bus stop.

No Officer Rudy patrol car waited there this morning.

Bill saw some other kids waiting at the bus stop, and one of the neighborhood moms was there with her young daughter. Bill waved at her and told the boys to have a good day. Though he wanted to, he didn't kiss them good-bye. Then he headed back to his house.

Sam was lying in their bed with the covers pulled up to her neck, her hair still wet from the shower.

"I don't know what it is that you've got planned there, big boy, but whatever it is, I'm ready, so let's get to it."

Bill smiled ear to ear and shut the bedroom door behind him.

"Don't you move a muscle, Sam. I'm gonna jump in the shower and then brush my teeth."

"Good thinking, Billy. Just because we're going to have crazy monkey sex doesn't mean you have to smell like one."

They lay in bed side by side, slightly sweaty and staring up at the ceiling. With their jobs and their crazy schedules and the kids, it was hard to find the time and the privacy to enjoy each other sexually. Bill was still breathing hard and was feeling a little guilty for going at it with such obvious need and selfish hunger. Like a dog humping someone's leg, he thought. But then Sam snuggled closer and laid her head on his shoulder and stroked his chest. With a pleasant shudder, his guilt dissipated into her caress.

"What time are you planning to leave?" she asked sweetly.

The question threw him, and he looked over at her.

"What?"

"I said, what time are you leaving for Maine? You've been moping around muttering to yourself ever since Uncle Frank left. Why don't you just get it over with and head on up there? If you wait much longer, you'll have to be back at work and you'll miss your chance. I told Mom and Dad that the boys and I would be spending the next few nights with them, and they were ecstatic."

"Sam, I haven't made up my mind whether or not I'm going."

"What are you waiting for? You know, and I know, that if you don't go, you'll be worried sick, and then you'll start calling that poor man so often that he'll be forced to shut off his phone or start avoiding your calls, and then you'll end up heading up there anyway."

"Geez, Sam, you don't have to sugarcoat it. Just tell me what you think." There was an edge to his voice that he hadn't intended.

"I'm sorry, honey. That didn't come out right. What I meant is, you should go. I know you're feeling guilty, and I also know that Uncle Frank didn't want to leave because he was tired of visiting us. It was because he felt that by leaving, he was protecting us. Right?"

Bill made a noncommittal grunting noise.

"So, if you go and visit him, you'll feel better, and maybe he'll feel better, too, having some company. You know, one of us instead of all of us to deal with."

Bill didn't say anything, just lay there staring at the ceiling. Sam stayed quiet, too, her head snuggled into his shoulder. Finally, Bill rolled over and looked at his wife's pretty face.

"I knew there was a reason I fell so much in love with you, Sam. You're one in a million, you know that?"

She smiled back at him and her hand stroked his chest and then tickled his stomach and slowly made its way down between his legs.

"Gee, that's sweet, hon. As for me, it's strictly the crazy monkey sex that keeps me hanging around."

THIRTY

Frank sat in his car looking at his phone. Who would be emailing him at this hour of the morning?

He activated the screen with the touch of a finger and opened his email folder.

There was an email with the subject line "All Star Update".

He touched the file and opened the email.

"Hey Bull, looks like it's game on! I hear you have three batters up already. The good news is they got nobody on deck. Hope you make it through the inning! Keep them hitless for a little while longer, might be you'll get a reliever take some of the heat off. I got some hot rookies ready for the big leagues! Don't be afraid to use the old bean ball. Aim to hit them right between the eyes! Ha, ha!"

He looked at the return email address. Another long-jumbled address that was different from the last email he had received from this guy. He thought about trying a reply, then decided against it.

He wasn't sure how or why this guy was involved or what game he was playing, but he was sure that if he got any intel from him, it couldn't be trusted. The guy definitely seemed in tune with what was happening, and the easiest way to account for that was if he was one of the All Stars himself. Might be trying to set him up, or he might just be hoping to establish communication to gain some type of an edge. Better to ignore it for now. No point in giving anything away to the other side by accident.

He thought how strange it was to find himself in this situation. He was nearing seventy years of age, and three men were trying to kill him for something that happened over forty years ago. Unbelievable. On the other hand, with his Sadie gone, he only had himself to worry about, and he truly wasn't all that worried. If he really thought about it, he wasn't afraid of dying so much as he was afraid of losing to these guys—to that sick bastard Jasper. He wasn't the man he used to be, the professional soldier trained to kill, that was for sure. But the more time he spent thinking about those three men invading his and Sadie's house and bringing trouble to Billy and his family, the more comfortable he was beginning to feel with maybe taking these guys out.

Strange to be thinking these thoughts, but there they were.

He wondered if he should turn off the phone, maybe remove the SIM card so he couldn't be tracked, but he didn't believe that these bozos could possibly be that sophisticated. Besides, he might need to call Noah or nine-one-one if he should find himself in a jam. He found his car charger, attached it to his phone, and then inserted the plug into the slot that had housed cigarette lighters in the good old days. He laid the phone on the passenger seat. Better to charge the phone now so he wouldn't have to worry about it for a day or two once he got up to the cabin.

THIRTY-ONE

Pogo glanced at the digital clock on the mantle over the fireplace in Turd Man's living room. It was eight-thirty already, the sun was up and shining brightly, and still no sign that anyone was coming. No word from Jasper out front, who had relieved him about an hour ago. He was sitting in an easy chair in the living room with the silenced Sig on his lap and the shotgun leaning against the couch next to him. Birdie was stationed in the kitchen with the M16, watching the back in case of a sneak attack. He keyed his walkie-talkie.

"Commo check. Anything happening?"

"Negative." It was Jasper's whispered voice.

A second later he heard Birdie say, "All quiet out back."

Damn, he thought. He wasn't comfortable stuck in the house in daylight. He got up, walked over to the window, and surveyed the property. Patchy snow covered the yard, only one large tree in the front and the rest open space right up the tree line. If someone was out there in the woods—say, up on the ridge—he and Birdie would be trapped. They would never make it to the woods or the road.

He keyed his walkie-talkie again. "I believe our time here is up, boys. I'm for moving on to plan B."

There was silence for a few seconds.

Then Jasper's voice. "I'm gonna move down the road a bit, give me a better angle on that ridge. When you come out, come

out the front. One of you head around to the side of the house
with the M16. Better we got two of us watching that ridge instead
of just one. The other one get's his ass down the driveway and
into the woods. If he doesn't get shot, we're probably in the
clear."

Pogo smiled and spoke out loud to Birdie without keying his
mike. "You hear that Birdman? If you don't get shot, we're
probably in the clear."

"Is that what he meant by one of us? Hell, long as I don't
have to carry that damn machine gun back to the car, I'm cool
with it. Rather get shot than have to lug that thing again."

"Let's give it another half hour," Jasper said, "in case our
boy stopped for breakfast or something. It'll take me that long
to move and get set up at a new spot anyway. Half hour won't
really matter one way or the other. Besides, if they're up on that
ridge, they've probably been up there for hours hoping they can
take us all at once."

"Birdman, you still got that pipe?" Pogo said, again not keying
his mike.

"I do," said Birdie. "Still loaded, too. Forgot all about it
when it was just me and Jasper."

Pogo keyed the mike. "Half hour, no problem, son. Let us
know when you're all set up out there. Me and Birdman, we're
gonna get ourselves mentally ready to evac our position."

Jasper moved slowly, careful to stay behind cover whenever
possible. He tried to stay alert to any movement, directly
around him and especially up on the ridge. If there was going to
be trouble, he felt it would come from there. He was pretty sure
that if even a small force was planning a frontal assault, then he
or Pogo or Birdie would have heard or seen something by now.
That left only two likely possibilities—men coming unawares
down the road in cars, or one or more attackers taking a position
on the ridge. He would put his money on the ridge.

After about twenty minutes of slow moving, he found a spot near the road behind a tree with a trunk that branched out into a V shape just below shoulder height. He laid the barrel of the RPK right in the center where the tree trunks branched off and found he could swing the barrel to cover both the road and the ridge without having to carry the weight of the machine gun. The trunk would give him good cover should anyone return fire.

He carefully and slowly sighted across the span of woods behind the house and then back and forth up the ridge. The only movement he could detect was the occasional sway of branches from the wind. After a few minutes, he keyed his radio.

"I'm in position," he said.

A second later he heard Pogo over the radio: "We flipped for it. Birdman is going to be our runner. I'll cover the back. But since we're the ones taking all the chances here, you get to carry big Bertha back to the car."

Jasper smiled, then keyed his mike again. "And if Birdie has a heart attack from all that exercise running for his life, who carries him?"

Pogo again. "Nobody. We shoot him and leave his ass where he falls."

Jasper stole a quick look at the front door. He watched Pogo come out carrying the M16 and crouch-walk down the front steps and around to the side of the house. A few seconds later, Birdie came out the front door, closed it, and checked to make sure it was locked. He looked over toward where Pogo was set up and then lit out down the driveway as fast as his long legs could carry him, the Mossberg held tight to his chest at port arms.

Jasper turned back to the ridge, moving the RPK from side to side. He was looking for anything that might be a muzzle flash or a reflection from a riflescope. His ears strained for the low thump of a suppressed rifle shot, but he heard nothing.

A few seconds later, he heard clomping footsteps and labored breathing as Birdie reached the end of the driveway and crossed the road, crashing into the brush and the safety of the woods. Birdie ran twenty or so yards into the trees and then stopped and leaned against a tree, doubled over and gasping for breath.

Jasper kept his eyes on the ridge, his right hand grasping the stock of the RPK, his index finger over the trigger. With his left hand he keyed his radio.

"Birdie check in."

There was no response.

A few seconds later, Pogo's voice came over the radio, "Birdman, you better not be having a goddamn heart attack, or I swear I will shoot you dead where you lie."

A few more seconds of silence, then Birdie's breathless, gasping voice, "Fu...fuck...you."

"Fuck me? That's what I get for risking my life and staying behind to cover your sorry ass? Who came out this morning to relieve you when you were pissing and moaning about the cold? Who brought you that Snickers bar yesterday, huh?"

"I got movement on the ridge." It was Jasper's voice, quiet and urgent.

"Where?" It was Pogo, no trace of humor or amusement in his voice any longer.

"About three quarters of the way up, off to the left. There's a big pine tree standing taller than the rest, just past that. Stay out of sight, let me get a bead on 'em." Jasper let go of the radio and grasped the RPK tighter, pulling it with both hands into his shoulder, his finger settling gently on the trigger.

"How many you see up there, Jasper?" Pogo again.

Jasper concentrated on the area where he had seen movement. It wasn't much, someone or something moving in the trees.

"How many, Jasper?"

No answer.

Then Birdie's voice came over the radio, still breathless and labored. "Shut up, Pogo. Let him sort it out. Jasper opens up, you get your ass down that driveway. Stay as far left as you can. Keep the house between you and that ridge as long as possible.

I'll fire from here. Won't hit anything, but it might distract them a bit. Jasper will keep their heads down."

Pogo made his way from the corner of the house back toward the front door. He stayed close to the house. When he found that he was at a straight angle to the driveway, he waited and readied himself to take off. He looked ahead for anything that might trip him up. That would be deadly if he was taking fire. His heart was racing. He breathed in deep.

Man, this is something he thought to himself, all pumped up with adrenaline, a grim smile on his face. This is really something.

He reached down and keyed his mike again. "Boys, if I go down, make sure you give a hundred dollars to each of the dancers at the Mouse Trap Lounge in Rahway for me, you hear? It's the least I could do for those nice girls give me so much viewing pleasure."

There was no sound for a full minute. Then Jasper's quiet voice came over the radio. "Birdie, looks like we're off the hook on paying Pogo's stripper debts unless that deer up there on the ridge decides to come down and stomp that asshole to death."

THIRTY-TWO
RETRIBUTION

It took them over an hour to hike back to the main road. First, they walked deeper into the woods so that they wouldn't be visible from the road or from either of the other two houses along Turd Man's street. It was more difficult hiking in the woods than along the side of the road, but it was also easier going in daylight, and all three men were still jacked up on adrenaline.

It was after 10 a.m. when they reached the car. The car park was still deserted, and they had only noticed one or two cars pass along the main road. They stored the long guns in the trunk, Pogo keeping the Sig in the waistband of his pants and Jasper grabbing his Smith & Wesson .38 out of the trunk where he had left it earlier to reduce the weight he had to carry to the house. Then they all got into the car, Birdie behind the wheel, Jasper in the back seat and Pogo in the front passenger side.

"Man, I can't believe I almost shit my pants over a fucking deer," said Pogo, reaching into the pocket of his coat and bringing out the glass pipe. He loaded it with crystals from a small baggie and then began running the flame from his lighter under it again, holding it up right in front of his face to watch as the crystals began to dissolve into smoke. "We should have greased that motherfucking animal and had us some nice venison steaks for dinner tonight."

He brought the pipe to his lips, inhaled, and then handed the pipe and lighter back behind him to Jasper.

"I gotta tell you boys, when I heard Jasper say he saw movement up on the hill, I started getting jacked up, man. I don't know if it was that shit me and Pogo smoked earlier or making that run that got my heart pumping, but hell, I felt like I was twenty again, you know? I could almost smell the fucking jungle." Birdie took the glass pipe and the lighter and started the crystals smoking again. "I can't remember the last time I felt this good. This shit of yours, Pogo, the secret recipe, it's better than those blue bunnies they used to feed us back in Nam. You should start a business, sell it to the fucking government."

They smoked in silence for a while, Pogo refilling the glass pipe and passing it around until Birdie said, "You hear that buzzing sound?"

"What the fuck are you talking about, Birdman?" Jasper asked.

"That buzzing sound. It's like a million bees floating outside the car."

Pogo smiled and opened the passenger-side door. "Sounds like Birdman is starting on a little trip. I better take the wheel and get us the hell out of here. Let's head back to the truck, regroup and figure out what to do next. I still think we should set up surveillance right here in this lot, stake out the road for a while, see if anyone shows up."

He got out of the car, opened Birdie's door, and then helped him out of the seat. Birdie walked slowly to the other side of the car and slid into the passenger's side. When they were all settled, Pogo started the engine and backed out of the corner near the woods, turned the car around, and headed toward the main road.

"You okay there, Birdman?" asked Pogo.

"Buzzing, man, just like them bees outside. Bzzzz."

They drove in silence for a while, Birdie with the seat tilted back, eyes closed, a sheen of sweat forming on his forehead. Jasper was crapped out in the back, lying across both back seats. He had put on his mirrored sunglasses and had that look on his face, the smile/smirk.

"Jasper?" It was Pogo speaking, calm and matter-of-fact. "We might have us a little problem. I got a cop coming up behind. No lights yet, but he's coming quick. You best stay low."

Pogo reached into his waistband and removed the Sig, which was poking uncomfortably into his leg. He worked it out past his belt and then handed it back to Jasper, keeping his hand low so his movement could not be detected from the car behind them.

"What's he doing?" asked Jasper.

"He's right behind us. There, his lights just came on. I'm gonna pull over up ahead. What do you boys wanna do, take the heat on this shit or take this guy out?"

"Might be he's just looking to give us a ticket," said Birdie, head still back, eyes closed, no discernible expression on his face.

"Could be," said Pogo, "but he takes one whiff of this car, and we're heading for lock up. Then we got to explain crossing state lines with unregistered guns, that silenced Sig, not to mention an M16 and a fucking machine gun in the trunk."

"You mean you never registered that machine gun, Pogo?" Birdie calm and cool, just a hint of a smile on his face now.

"Open all the windows, Pogo. Then pull over and you get out, see what he wants. He starts fucking with us, I'll take him out." Jasper checked the load in his .38 revolver, and then pulled the slide of the Sig slightly back to make sure there was a round chambered. "He hasn't seen me, right? Just make sure he doesn't get too close before I get a shot. You guys good with that?"

"I'm good," said Pogo, "but remember, he's probably wearing a vest, so hit him low, in the legs, or aim for his head. Hell, keep pulling the trigger until you empty the clip. He's got to go down hard and fast, otherwise it's us that's gonna die on this road today, understand?"

"You just sweet talk the man, Pogo. Leave the rest to me."

Birdie opened his eyes and pushed the button on his door, lowering his window. "We should've stowed that damn ma-

chine gun in the back seat with Jasper instead of in the trunk."
Then he stuck his head and arm out the window and let his hair
fly back in the breeze—just like a dog riding in the family car
thought Pogo.

Pogo opened the other windows with the buttons on his
door handle, then put his right blinker on and slowed the car,
guiding it to the shoulder of the road. The police cruiser stayed
close behind, about two car lengths back, the lights flashing but
no siren. When both cars had stopped, Pogo watched in his
rearview mirror to see what the cop would do.

Then an amplified voice boomed behind them from a loud-
speaker.

"Everyone in the car—I need to see your hands out the
windows, gentlemen."

"You ready back there, Jasper?"

"See if you can get him close enough that I can get a shot,
but so he still don't see me." Jasper was moving in the cramped
back seat, readying himself, a gun in each hand.

"How about I ask him to drop his drawers, see if he'll bend
over so you can put one up his butthole?"

Pogo reached both hands out the window and looked back
at the police car, a big smile on his face. "What's the problem,
officer?"

"I need to see everyone's hands. Do it now." Again, the
booming amplified voice from behind.

"Birdie, why don't you wave to the nice policeman?" said
Pogo.

Birdie leaned further out the window, looking back and
waved both hands at the cop.

"I'm going to step out, officer. Got to take a leak." Pogo
slowly opened the door using the outside handle and began to
get out of the car.

"Stay in your vehicle," said the cop. "Keep your hands
where I can see them."

Pogo was out of the car and facing the police cruiser, both

hands up in front of him.

"We've been drinking some beer, officer. I'm about to piss my pants. I'm gonna step over here and take a leak. I'm not armed or anything, I just got to pee."

Birdie opened his door and faced back as well. His hands were up in the air, palms facing the policeman.

"I got to pee, too, officer." He kept his hands up and walked slowly to the back of the car, then around to the side where Pogo was.

The cop opened his car door and emerged with his sidearm drawn. He was around forty years old, tight cop haircut and a gray mounted-police hat on his head. "Both of you, put your hands on the car, feet back. Do it now!"

"I got to take a leak first, officer. Seriously, I'm about to wet my pants. I'll step over there. I can't pee with someone watching me, you know what I mean? I'll pull up my jacket, slow, so you can see I haven't got a gun or anything." He slowly reached his right hand down and opened his jacket, then pulled up his shirt.

"I got to pee, too," said Birdie and he began to lower his hands, "but I can pee right here, officer. I'm not shy."

"I said put your hands on the car! Do it now, both of you!" The cop raised his gun and pointed it at both men.

Pogo raised his hands again and then began slowly walking across the road. "For Christ's sake, you're not gonna shoot us for peeing in the road, are you? Let me just take a leak, then you can go ahead and arrest me, officer. I'm not fooling now. This is an emergency."

Birdie walked to the middle of the road and then slowly lowered his hands and began unzipping his fly.

The policeman advanced toward the two men, both hands on his weapon, which he held out straight in front of him.

"How can you take your pecker out and pee like that right in front of everybody, Birdie?" Pogo kept walking slowly, his hands still raised, to the other side of the road. He heard Birdie's urine begin splattering on the road.

"Jesus fucking Christ," said the cop as he moved closer to Birdie. He was putting his gun back into his holster with his right hand and reaching for his handcuffs with his left when a deafening gunshot sounded, and the back of his head exploded into a fine red mist.

THIRTY-THREE

By 10 a.m., Bill had the car packed and was ready to leave. He had debated calling Uncle Frank and telling him his plans, but then decided against it. He would wait until he was well on his way, maybe until he crossed the Maine state line, before saying anything. If Frank knew now, he would no doubt do his best to talk Bill out of heading up. If Bill waited and said he was already in Maine, he was sure Uncle Frank would just accept it.

He had packed Uncle Frank's old Fox double barrel. He also brought a box of shells, though he wasn't quite sure why he had packed them. All he had were target loads, and those were all but useless for self-defense. He was sure Frank would have something heavier at his house. Given what he had learned about Uncle Frank these last few days, God only knew what the man had lying around, but he figured a shotgun was useless without ammunition, so target loads were better than nothing. His uncle had told him about some of the guns he kept and about the safe he had in his closet, suggesting more than once that Bill get an inexpensive gun safe for his home as well. He always worried about Bill's kids and easy access to firearms, but Bill had a trigger lock that he used on his shotgun and had instructed both his boys, and his wife, too, on basic gun safety. He wanted his kids to be familiar with the gun, so they wouldn't be too curious about it on their own.

Sam walked him out to the car when he was ready to leave.

"Give that big handsome uncle of yours a kiss for me when you see him," she said, hugging him tightly.

"What time are you heading to your folks?" he asked.

"I don't know. I may stop by after lunch and drop some things off, then do some food shopping so we don't eat them out of house and home. When the kids come home, we'll all head on over, I guess."

"Okay, Sam. Do me a favor and stay away from our house at night. Don't stop by to check on things or even if you need something. Wait until daylight. I know I'm being paranoid, but please, just promise me."

"I promise, hon. Now get going. And drive carefully. And call me when you get there, okay?" She kissed him lightly on the lips and watched as he got into the Jeep and started the engine.

She stood in the driveway and watched as he stuck his arm out the driver's-side window and waved. He kept waving as the car headed all the way down the block and away from the house.

THIRTY-FOUR

Frank decided to head over to the town of Oxford to kill some time and stock up on supplies. There was a big Walmart Superstore near there, and he figured he could get everything he'd need and only have to make one stop. He wasn't sure how long he would stay at the hunting cabin, maybe a few days, but he would bring enough supplies to last a week or so. He wanted to pick up a few extra small propane gas tanks for his camping cook stove. Also, two red five-gallon cans so he could bring some gasoline for the generator and a quart of motor oil, too, just in case. And he figured he'd buy a few books to read and a radio and some lanterns and extra flashlights and batteries. Not much to do up there, especially if he chose not to run the generator. Plus, food. Cans mostly, stuff he could heat up.

He had plenty of ammunition, and he couldn't imagine any way Jasper and his crew could find him up there. He had brought the key chain alarms that he had bought the day before. He would rig a few trip wires once he got to the cabin to alert him of any unwanted company. He wondered again if he should also rig up some more deadly traps. He wished he had done so at the house, but then he was expecting trouble. Out at hunting camp, the only thing he could expect to accomplish is to wound or kill some poor animal wandering around the woods. Still, might be worth the risk. He would think about it some more and then decide, even though there was not much chance that anyone would find him up there.

Which reminded him that he would need to shut off his cell phone later. He pulled the phone out of his pocket and checked for messages. There were none. He went to his address book and found Billy's home number, then hit the send button. The phone rang several times, then the message machine came on. He was relieved. It would be better to just leave a message and get it out of the way.

"Hi guys, it's Uncle Frank. Just checking in like I said I would, hoping you're all well." He tried hard to sound bright and cheery. "It's a beautiful morning up here, and I'm up and at 'em, heading into town for a late breakfast, and then I may take a ride into Windham and head over to the Walmart they have there, pick up a few things I need. Billy, I spoke to my friend Noah, the state trooper. As a matter of fact, we may be getting together for dinner later, so there's no need to worry. Also, there's no need to call me back today. I'll probably shut my phone off anyway, since I'll be driving around most of the day. I'll call you guys again tomorrow or the day after. Love you all. Bye."

He ended the call, and then powered off his phone. He'd check for messages a little later, then maybe remove the SIM card. He felt better having left a message for Billy. His nephew was a good man, but a bit of a worrier, and also, he could be bull-headed.

The last thing he needed was Billy taking a ride up here and getting mixed up in all this shit.

THIRTY-FIVE

Jasper watched the cop crumple and go down in a heap. He opened the car door and hopped out, his .38 still in his hand. He had used the .38 because he was used to it, and he knew he would hit what he aimed at. The Sig was quiet, but he had never shot it. With his own revolver, he was pretty sure that all he would need was one shot to put the cop down.

Pogo had turned and run over to the officer as soon as he heard the shot. He had his K-bar in his hand, but there was no need for it. The cop lay still, the back of his head blown clean off, blood and brain matter oozing out the huge hole and forming a muddy puddle in the road.

"Hot damn, Jasper, that was one helluva shot!" Pogo was kneeling over the downed cop. When he looked up, there was a smile on his face, and his eyes were wild and shining.

Birdie finished peeing, then tucked his pecker back into his pants and zippered his fly.

"You see that shot, Birdman? Right out the back window, hit him square in the noodle!" Pogo leaned in closer, looking at the wound. "Knocked his hat clean off."

Birdie walked over to the hat. He picked it up and examined it. "Look at this: no blood or brains on it, good as new." He put the hat on his own head, smiled, and walked back to where Pogo and Jasper were still looking down at the cop's body.

All three men stood and looked down at the dead cop in the

middle of the road until Birdie broke the silence. "So, you guys want to sit around here for a while longer and relive the moment, or you think maybe we ought to move his body off the road before someone comes driving along and wonders what the hell we're looking at?"

Jasper handed his gun to Birdie and then took hold of the cop's feet, one in each hand. He shuffled backwards, dragging the body off the road, into the weeds and to the trees.

When he returned to the car, he saw a trail of blood and gore from where the cop had fallen all the way across the road and into the woods. The dirty snow on the side of the road was stained red. Drag marks led to the tree line.

"Don't worry about that," said Pogo. "Looks like any other road kill. Anyone even notices it, they'll think some possum or raccoon got hit and crawled up into the trees to die. Birdie's right. We got to get out of here before a car comes by." He reached up to Birdie's head, took the hat off, and held it in both his hands.

"Why don't you follow us in the cruiser, Jasper? Birdie's too fucked up to drive, and I don't know of any cops wear their hair in a braid like mine. You put this hat on, and with them sunglasses of yours, you'll fit right in with the rest of them assholes." He placed the hat on Jasper's head, stepped back, and then stepped forward again. He adjusted the hat, giving it a jauntier angle.

"There, that's better. Now you look like a real hard-ass law enforcement douchebag. You just drive around with that normal shit-eating grin you always wear, and we'll be fine."

Birdie had walked over into the woods where the policeman's body now lay. "Jesus, this guy's head is full of worms, white fucking worms," he said. "You should see this! They're all squirming around inside his head."

Pogo looked at Jasper and smiled. "I believe Birdman is tripping."

Jasper looked back at Pogo, but he didn't return his smile.

"Hey." Birdie again. "Should we take his gun?"

"Leave it," said Jasper, still looking at Pogo. "We got enough guns. But grab his radio. And see if he's got a cell phone. He got that on him, they'll find him quick."

Birdie came back to the road carrying a large, black handheld radio and a compact smartphone. He also had handcuffs and a set of keys. Jasper took it all from him, then walked over to the police cruiser and got into the driver's seat.

He started the car, leaned out the window, and said, "Pogo, I'll follow you back to the truck, and then we'll figure out what to do with this car. Birdie get that fucking machine gun out of the trunk. And let me have the M16. I don't want us to get caught with our pants around our ankles again."

Pogo walked to the car, popped the trunk, and then watched Birdie take the weapons out. He put the machine gun into the Corolla's back seat, then went around to the trunk again, grabbed the M16, and walked it back toward the cruiser.

Jasper noticed the big grin on Birdie's face. "What's so funny, Birdman? You don't like my hat? Or maybe I got worms coming out my ears, too?"

"It's not the hat so much, or the worms," said Birdie, handing the rifle through the window to Jasper. "I know I'm a little fucked up from that shit we smoked, but besides that, I was thinking the way things are going, there's a pretty good chance the three of us won't be making it back home from this trip. We're riding a roller coaster now, and we just topped that rise, you know what I mean? We're about to head downhill fast, and there's no getting off, not anymore. And the fuck of it is, I can't remember the last time I had so much damn fun."

Jasper smiled his scary smile back at Birdie.

"Hell, Birdman," he said, patting the M16 on the seat next to him, "the real fun ain't even started yet."

He followed the Corolla, staying about a hundred yards behind. His brain felt like it was on hyper alert, and he wondered if it was the adrenaline rush from shooting that cop, the apprehension he felt driving the stolen cruiser, or just the aftereffects of the crazy concoction he had smoked earlier with the boys.

He had to admit that was some fine shit that Pogo had cooked up. Hell, look what it did to Birdie.

Several cars passed heading in the opposite direction, and Jasper kept his head straight, eyes on the road. With the trooper hat and his mirrored sunglasses, nobody seemed to give him a second look, though each car had slowed down upon seeing the cruiser. But he supposed that was a normal reaction to seeing a cop car. He wondered what it would be like pulling over some fine-looking woman, maybe using the handcuffs on her just for fun, then shook his head to clear it and concentrated on staying in the moment. Not a good time to start daydreaming. He checked the rearview mirror, then looked to the road ahead.

Then a burst of static from the car's police radio caught him by surprise. His body jerked, and he took his eyes off the road and looked at the radio. A woman dispatcher's voice said, "Three-three-four?"

Just like that, three numbers in the form of a question. The voice was friendly and professional. She sounded young. He stared at the radio, then remembered where he was and looked back up at the road.

A minute or so later, he heard static again, then the same voice. "Three-three-four, what's your ten-twenty?"

Ten-twenty. Cop code for location. They were looking for the cop, the guy he had just shot, the guy whose patrol cruiser Jasper was driving now. Jasper pressed a little harder on the accelerator. Sweat formed on the side of his head.

"Three-three-four? Come in, please. What's your ten-twenty?" The voice again, this time with a touch more edge, all business now.

More static, then a man's voice. "This is three-three-seven. What's three-three-four's last twenty?"

"Three-three-four on a ten-thirty-eight about three miles east of Boland. He was traveling north on 117, pulled over a late-model Toyota Corolla, brown, registered to a Warren Hicks, age twenty-five, from Bridgton. Had a report of a man firing a shotgun out the vehicle window."

"I'm on my way. Code three." The man's voice again.

A second later, a different man's voice came on. He heard a police siren in the background coming over the radio. "This is three-three-one heading south on Harrison Road just outside of Norway, running Code three."

Shit thought Jasper, here we go.

THIRTY-SIX

It was close to noon by the time Frank reached the small cabin. The old dirt road onto the property was easier to navigate than he thought it would be. It hadn't snowed the night before, and though there was still a coating of about two inches or so, the road's outline was easy to make out, and traction hadn't been a problem.

Frank pulled up to the cabin and surveyed the area. The windows were covered with wooden shutters secured with small padlocks. This discouraged raccoons and bears when the cabin was not in use. The cabin's front and back doors were solid wood, and each had a sturdy deadbolt lock. A covered porch ran the width of the front.

The cabin sat set in a clearing of a small valley with gentle slopes that led up to the surrounding hills. A good acre or more had been cleared when the cabin was first built to accommodate parking for several trucks or SUVs along with trailers for ATVs. There was even a small, makeshift corral for horses. Sadie's cousin, Nelson Stahl, who was also the owner of the lumberyard where Frank worked, owned the property. Several members of the family, Frank included, had chipped in a few thousand dollars each to buy and help build the small cabin, and the deal was each could use it and the property whenever they liked. The building was a kit log cabin with about six hundred square feet of living space. Inside was a living area with a wood-burning stove and a small kitchen area with sink and portable refrigerator tucked into a corner. There was also a dining table on one side, and a couch and a love seat combination on either side of a scratched and dented coffee table in the middle of the room. Two small adjoining bunkrooms made up the rest of the space, two single beds in one and a set of bunk beds in the other leaving not much more room for anything else. Last, there was a small bathroom about the size of what you might find in a commercial airliner with a toilet, sink and a shower that could only accommodate a child or a small woman comfortably—a small, skinny woman. Luckily, showers were not a priority during the hunting season. When body odors got a little too ripe, some warm water, soap and a washcloth were usually enough to see the men through for a few days. There was also loft space above the bathroom to store supplies and equipment when not in use.

All in all, the space was quite comfortable. Plus, the cabin was wired for electricity, and a generator out back could be plugged right into the electrical panel, providing enough power to run the whole place, even the fridge plus two small electric baseboard heaters, one in each bunkroom. A wood stove in the front outside corner of the living space provided additional heat and, when fully stoked, was usually enough to keep the entire cabin warm and cozy.

Frank drove behind the cabin and parked his SUV near the back door. There was a small wooden shed in the back that they had set up to house the generator and other equipment, and he saw that its door was securely closed and padlocked.

He shut off the engine, put the Colt .45 in his waistband, and then walked through the crunchy layer of snow and used his key to unlock the back door.

The cabin was dark. He walked to a shelf in the small kitchen area and found the flashlight that they always kept there, then did a quick walk through of the cabin. Everything looked neat and in order. The beds were stripped, the kitchen area clean and tidy, with the slightly musty odor of a place that has been shut up for a while. He walked to the front door, opened the deadbolt, went outside to the covered porch, and unlocked and opened the wooden shutters covering the main living area's window. He decided not to unlock the other shutters. With this shutter open, he would be able to see the front area, including the old road leading up the cabin and, if need be, fire out the front window. Better to keep the back closed up for now. He had parked the car parallel with the cabin, the driver's-side door facing the cabin. The car blocked any view from the woods. If he had to run, he could get from the back door and right into the driver's seat in a hurry. Or he had the option of running toward the shed and then into the woods using the car for cover.

He didn't think he'd need to be ready for anything, but he was going to plan for the worst just the same. If he had planned better last night, he might have been rid of this problem already.

He went back to the car and brought in his gear. The first thing he did was lay his weapons out on the lunch table, even the Colt he had tucked into his waistband. He picked up the shotgun off the table. It was a Mossberg Tactical with a modified magazine extension, so it could hold up to eight rounds. With its pistol grip, it would be much easier to aim and fire with only one hand. Also, the synthetic stock and aluminum receiver made the gun relatively light. He reached into one of his packs and opened a box of shells, then took one out and replaced the round that he had shot this morning into the road sign. He double-checked the safety and then put the gun back on the table. He would keep that one always fully loaded and handy. Next, he checked the Glock 9mm. He had it loaded with a fifteen-round clip, and he had two spare clips, also loaded with fifteen rounds each, sitting on the table. He made sure a round was chambered. Next, he picked up his trusty Colt .45. This gun had a seven-round clip, plus he had two spares. He had also unpacked an old holster that he had bought used some years ago in an army surplus store and strapped that around his waist. He slid the gun into it and felt its reassuring weight on his hip. The two spare clips went into his pockets. Last, he picked up the sniper rifle, slid back the bolt back, and ejected the round that he had left chambered. He removed the clip and reinserted the bullet, then replaced the clip on the rifle. He made sure the night vision attachment was turned off, and then he removed it. He would put it back on come nightfall, and then remove it again at first light. He didn't want to worry about having to put it on or remove it should he need the gun quickly.

Next, he brought out the shopping bag with the personal key chain alarms that he had purchased, along with the spool of monofilament fishing line and can of dark green spray paint. He would have preferred to use army issue trip wire, which he knew for a fact was readily available online or in survival and military surplus stores, but there hadn't been time to go shopping for it. Besides, with the snow on the ground, he didn't feel that reflection off the monofilament would be an issue. He would scout out the area around the cabin, particularly any trails leading in from the access road. He would also set trip wire alarms along both sides of the access road, since those all-star fuckups had done that when they'd crept up the road leading to his house last night.

After a momentary bout of frustration trying to get at the key chains in their heat-sealed plastic packaging, he used his combat knife to slice through the tough plastic and then checked all the batteries and tested each alarm. They all worked perfectly and were plenty loud. Out here in the woods, they could probably be heard for miles. It didn't take much pressure to pull the pin that set the alarm off, but enough so he was sure that wind or twigs or even small animals like birds or mice wouldn't trigger any false alarms. The only thing he'd need to worry about were deer or other animals setting them off, but he felt that the chances of that happening were fairly slim, and anyway, he'd rather be safe than sorry.

He gathered up the alarms and the spray paint and went out to the front porch. The alarms were a beige-colored shiny plastic. He sprayed each with a light coating of a matte dark-green paint. He would need to secure the alarms to the bases of trees or bushes, and the dark green would blend in better than the shiny beige. Once the alarms were secured, he would smudge them with dirt and cover them with leaves or small branches to further camouflage them.

Once that was done, he decided to take a quick walk while the paint dried and figure out where to set up his perimeter. He had twelve alarms, but he also had a lot of ground to cover. He wanted to set them out far enough away that he would have ample time to prepare his defense or to run should he detect an intruder.

He looked at the open area around the cabin and then at the trees. The temperature had gone down a few degrees, and the wind had picked up slightly. Dark gray clouds were rolling in, a spring storm, no doubt. Snow for sure, but he didn't know how much. He went back inside and found a small fanny pack that he'd sometimes worn to carry granola bars and fruit and a compass when he went hiking with Sadie. He was usually a little embarrassed to wear it, but his wife had bought it for him, and that was the reason he had used it. He was always afraid that he and Sadie might one day run into someone they knew out on the trail. He smiled at the thought as he belted the pack around his waist. He found a box filled with twenty full-metal-jacket rounds for the deadly rifle, stuffed it into the fanny pack, and closed the zipper. Then he grabbed the M40 off the table.

The shells rested on his left hip, balancing the weight of the Colt on his right. Funny, he thought as he headed out the front door, I sure as hell don't feel so silly wearing the damn thing right now.

THIRTY-SEVEN

Jasper saw the brake lights on the Corolla flash and then watched as the car turned off the road up ahead. They were at the turnoff where the truck was parked. He slowed the cruiser and looked behind and then ahead to make sure there was no other traffic on the road. He didn't want anyone to spot the police car turning off onto the old road.

When he reached the turnoff, he took last looks in both directions and then turned and accelerated over the bumpy road, watching for traffic in the rearview mirror the whole time.

A few minutes later he saw the Corolla stopped by their camper, Birdie and Pogo standing next to the car, Birdie cradling the machine gun with the big, round drum attached to the bottom.

He pulled in behind the Corolla and stepped out of the car.

"Damn, but don't you look all official in your trooper hat and mirrored shades getting out of that big, bad police car." Pogo had a big smile on his face. "Had me breaking into a sweat every time I looked in the rearview mirror. Was just waiting to see them lights start flashing, hear that siren wail, know what I mean?"

Jasper didn't smile back. "We don't get rid of this cruiser soon, we're going to have lights and sirens all over the place. They're looking for our boy right now. It's all over the police radio. Cops coming in from miles around. They got any kind of

GPS trackers on these cars? Can they find it through that fucking radio?"

Pogo's smile faded. "Damn, the guy hasn't been dead but a few minutes. How can they be out looking for him already?"

"Guess he's supposed to call in every time he stops a car. Some lady dispatcher kept coming on the radio asking where he was, then a few of the other troopers volunteered to come looking for him. Next thing you know, the whole fucking police force is heading this way." Jasper looked at Pogo, his eyes hard and mean. "Now, can they find this car through GPS or that goddamn radio, or not?

"Don't know," said Pogo, "but if you still got his cell phone, they can sure as hell track that."

Jasper walked back to the cruiser and found the phone they had taken off the trooper. He carried it back to where Pogo and Birdie stood. Pogo took it from him, and then walked over to the small circle of rocks Jasper had set up when he'd built their campfire. He set the phone down on the flattest rock, then picked up a rounded one and smashed the phone repeatedly until it shattered. He then rummaged through the pieces until he found what was left of the SIM card and ground that between the two rocks until he was satisfied that it was destroyed.

"No one's gonna be able to track us from that no more," he said. Then he ground what was left of the phone under his boot.

"Let's all take a vehicle and follow this road up a ways, see where it leads. Doesn't look like anyone travels on this old road much. Maybe we can stash that cop car in the woods someplace, cover it with brush. We'll have to hide it good. Before too long, they'll have choppers in the air. Better get rid of that little shit box, too," he said, pointing at the Corolla. "He probably called in the plates when he pulled us over. We dump these cars, then we'll take the truck and head back out of here, see what we can see, maybe get the hell out of Dodge. Hopefully them cops will think the kid did the trooper and start chasing a ghost. We got to be long gone by the time they find the cars. Jasper, make sure you wipe your prints off the steering wheel and door handles and seats and such when we're ready to boogie on out of here."

Pogo walked back to where his two companions were standing by the car, smiled broadly, and then clapped each of them once on the shoulder.

"Well, compadres, looks like we're back in the shit. Birdman, you drive the truck. Jasper, you take the cruiser. I'll ride point in the shit box. Let's roll, motherfuckers."

They drove up the rutted road, which seemed to get narrower and more overgrown the farther they advanced. The trees began to get thicker, and after about three quarters of a mile, the road led them over a small rise to a lake that appeared to be frozen over. The road ended at a small boat ramp leading straight down to the ice-covered water.

Pogo pulled the Corolla to the side of the road and waved Jasper forward. Birdie followed in the camper. All three men got out of their vehicles.

"Well I'll be goddamned," said Jasper. He had that combination of a smile and a sneer on his face.

Birdie followed the road down the ramp, put his foot on the ice, and pressed gently. The ice began to crack.

"Ice is about thawed. I wonder how deep it is."

Jasper walked to the water's edge and stood next to Birdie.

"Gotta be a couple of feet at least. Why would anyone build a boat ramp if they were just dropping rowboats or canoes in here? Folks use the ramp to back their trailers right into the water. Probably bass boats with them big outboards."

Pogo walked into the woods and began dragging branches toward the cruiser.

"Hey, why don't you two lovebirds stop holding hands over there and help me gather some brush? We'll tie what we can to the top of this cop car, then we can run it right into the fucking lake. Hopefully the goddamn thing will sink right under. Even if it doesn't sink all the way, we get enough brush on it, it won't be visible from the air, will buy us some time."

So, they all went to work dragging branches and brush and twigs. Jasper used the butt end of the shotgun to smash the emergency light bar that ran across the top of the car, and he knocked off both side-view mirrors. He then went to town on the police radio under the dash and smashed the front and rear windshields. Once that was done, they took rope that they had found in the camper and tied on as many branches and downed tree limbs as they could pile on. They stuffed brush in where the windshields used to be and jammed twigs and small bushes into the car's back bumper.

"Looks like a goddamn brush pile," said Pogo with some satisfaction.

"Wish we could torch the damn thing," said Birdie.

"Too much smoke," said Jasper. "Better we sink it and get gone. Who wants to drive it in?"

"Well, you done the dirty work taking care of that cop and driving that cruiser all the way up here," said Pogo, "I guess I'll finish it off. Let's wipe down the inside real good, then open all the side windows so that the water can get in. Once that's done, you boys get out of the way. I'm going to back up and then get her rolling a bit. Once I get close to the ramp, I'll jump out. Hopefully, she goes all the way under. Look at that sky, clouds rolling in, the air getting colder. Can ya feel it? With any luck that water will freeze up again tonight, maybe we get a little snow and we'll be good for a few days. Maybe even a few weeks if the weather stays cold. Next, we wipe down that little shit box, cover it up with brush, and park it under those trees. Probably won't get found until some asshole hauls his boat up here come summertime."

Jasper said, "Birdman, let's find some rocks and break up that ice, make it easier for the car to get through."

Jasper and Birdie walked back down to the water's edge and began heaving rocks into the lake, making huge cracks and leaving gaping holes in the ice. Pogo got into the driver's seat and backed the cruiser up thirty yards or so. He had the door open, one butt cheek on the car's seat and the other hanging in air, one foot near the gas pedal, the other braced near the edge of the door. When his friends had cleared out of the way, he put the car in drive, hit the gas, and accelerated toward the ramp. He let out his Indian war whoop and at the very last second dove out the door and rolled away from the car.

The car didn't seem to be moving fast, but it hit the water with a loud splash and crashed through the ice, sending sprays of water high into the air. Jasper and Birdie watched as the car's momentum carried it through the ice and into the lake. It surged a few feet into the lake, slowed abruptly, then began sinking. It rolled further and settled into the mud of the lake bottom. Pogo brushed himself off and walked over to where his friends stood watching. After what seemed like little more than a minute, the engine sputtered. Only a portion of the back bumper could be seen where some of the brush and branches had come off.

"Hell, boys, that's better than we could have hoped for. Even if the lake don't freeze over tonight, it's still going to be hard to tell what's under that water from the air. With all that brush, looks like it could be a downed tree that fell off the bank. Tying those branches on was a good idea. If it ices up a bit more, they won't find this car till summer."

Birdie looked at Pogo. "That was something, jumping out of that car like that. You're damn lucky you didn't run yourself over."

"Luck had nothing to with it, my friend. I honed that skill years ago dodging bullets from hostile VC commie bastards and irate husbands. But, truth be told, I don't relish the thought of further practice with live rounds from our friends in law enforcement. So I suggest we get to work on hiding that other car and then haul ass out of here in that camper, pronto like."

The three men turned away from the sunken police cruiser and began gathering more brush and branches to cover the Corolla.

THIRTY-EIGHT

It took about two hours for Frank to finish setting his trip wires. Though he was familiar with the land around the hunting cabin, he hadn't walked it with an eye toward stalking someone inside. He walked about two hundred and fifty yards down the old access road he had driven in on, then turned around and looked for the stealthiest approach. There were several paths, and he figured they would probably split up and each follow one. He laid four of his trip wires about a hundred and fifty yards out on either side of the road. That would put them within easy range to pick off, even with his old eyes, plus it would give him enough time to bug out if he decided to run. Next, he hiked the perimeter of the cleared area just inside the tree line. He set the rest of his alarms and trip wires at places he might choose if he planned to scope out the cabin. Then he scouted out what he thought might be the best routes out of the cabin and into the woods should he need to flee. He looked for places where he could take cover and fight if he had to. He knew these woods from his old hunting days and from time he had spent at the cabin with Sadie, both of them enjoying the solitude and the exercise of hiking the surrounding hills. He felt confident that if he got ahead of them without getting shot, he would be able to pick them off if they tried to follow. The trick would be getting past the open ground and into the trees. They were well-armed. He thought back to when he'd watched through the riflescope

THE DEAD DON'T SLEEP

as they approached. One had an M16, the other maybe an AK47, the last guy a shotgun. Probably carrying sidearms as well, though he wasn't too worried about that. He would have to make his decision to get out of the cabin quickly, and then get to the trees as fast as possible. If they had time to set up before he made his run, he was a dead man. He was sure that both the M16 and the AK47 had automatic fire capabilities. Even a lousy shot could spray a fairly open area and have a good chance of hitting something, even a moving target. If both fired at once, he would have no chance.

He walked out of the woods toward the cabin's front porch. He leaned the M40 against the porch, sat on the top step, then surveyed the area in front and to the sides. He believed he had placed his trip wires well. He pulled out his cell phone and turned it on. Reception at the cabin had improved markedly over the last few years, with new cell towers going up across the state. Two bars showed on his phone. He checked his email and his messages. Nothing.

He hoped to hear some news from his friend, Noah, the state trooper, that he or one of the other officers had pulled Jasper and his friends over, maybe arrested them for carrying those assault rifles. He wasn't sure having assault rifles was a crime. He knew several people who owned them. But shooting at road signs out of a moving vehicle had to be illegal. He hoped the police would be careful approaching these guys. He couldn't imagine Jasper and his two buddies doing anything crazy since they hadn't committed any crimes yet, but crazy was crazy.

He dialed Noah's number, but the call went to voice mail, and Frank decided not to leave a message. Noah would see his number and call back if he had the time, or if he had any news to report.

He thought about calling Bill, his nephew, but decided against it. Billy was a good man, but he worried too much. Frank thought it might be best to give Bill some room, give him time to get back into his own routine, let him worry about his family and his job instead of worrying about Frank.

He was about to power down his phone when it emitted a tone signaling the arrival of a new email.

Subject: *Incoming!*

Hey Bull, I hear you're back in the bush, outnumbered and outgunned, just like the old days! Wish I was right there with you! Well, no, not really. But don't you worry son, just keep your head down and your butt cheeks clenched, and you'll be fine. Say, maybe medevac will to come to the rescue—or just show up in time to pick up the pieces! Isn't this fun! Anyway, best of luck-

Frank read the email again, hit "reply" and typed "Who are you?" then hit the "send" button.

He stared at his phone. After a few minutes, the new-email tone sounded again. He opened the file, but his message had simply been returned: invalid email address.

He decided to power down the phone. Best to conserve the battery. He would check it again later tonight or maybe tomorrow.

THIRTY-NINE

They drove the camper away from the lake back down the old road they had come in on. When they got to where they had camped earlier, they got out and checked the area for any garbage they might have left.

The air had begun to chill, the sky to darken, and a few solitary snowflakes began making their way slowly and silently to the ground. Birdie and Jasper were already in the cab of the truck and Pogo took one more walk around the area looking for anything they might have missed. He found an empty plastic Poland Spring water bottle, picked it up, and carried it back to the truck. He opened the driver's-side door, tossed the bottle onto the back seat, and then got in.

"I think we're going to be okay here, boys." He started the truck and began making his way back towards the main road.

Jasper was sitting in the passenger seat, Birdie in back. Their weapons, except for the silenced Sig, which was under Jasper's seat, were in the storage bin under one of the bunks in the back of the camper.

Jasper turned so that he could see Pogo and Birdie at the same time. "Well, boys, I guess we better decide what the hell we want to do next," he said. "Way I see it, we can leave right now, head on back home, and come back in a few weeks, start over again. Or we can sort of mosey around a bit, see what kind of heat we're dealing with."

Nobody said anything for a few seconds. Then Pogo looked over at Jasper, turned his head and looked at Birdie, then turned back and looked straight ahead at the road and said, "I think we're okay, I really do. Jasper, you were listening to that radio. Did they say anything about a trooper being shot? Did they call any type of emergency, officer down, anything like that?"

"No. Just asked the guy to call in, and then everybody and his brother started volunteering to come look for him. They were running hot, though. I could hear their sirens coming in over the radio."

"So, far as they know, the guy's just not answering his radio, right?"

"I don't know that for sure, but that's what it sounded like."

"So, for all they know the guy might have radio trouble or maybe hit himself a moose with his car, or maybe he stopped off at one of these farmhouses to get himself a nice blow job from the farmer's daughter, right?"

"So you're saying we should stick with it, that's what you're saying, Pogo?" Birdie was sitting on the edge of the seat, his forearms across the backs of both front seats, his head now right between Pogo and Jasper.

"What I'm saying is, we're not at DEFCON One yet. Until those cops find the body or the car or something that says this guy is dead, then they're chasing their tails. We're more like DEFCON Four right now. I realize that they're going to find something sooner or later, probably be the guy's body. They gotta know about where he stopped us, so at some point they'll start searching the side of the road, maybe get dogs in. But I can't see that happening yet. Right now, they'll keep after him on the radio, get troops in to search the back roads in case he skidded off in this snow, maybe hit his head. And they'll keep looking for somebody driving that little shit box we were in. That's gotta be the last thing he radioed in. I say we got maybe a few hours until we go DEFCON Three. That's when we should start thinking about hitting the bricks. Until then, I say we still got unfinished business."

"I don't know, boys," said Birdie. "I'm thinking it might be good to get going while the going's good, you know? What do you think, Jasper?"

Jasper looked out the passenger-side window. Pogo was driving slowly down the old rutted road. He could just make out the main road about a quarter of mile away. The snow had picked up a bit, now coming down steadily, the larger flakes having given way to smaller, grittier ones that ticked off the windscreen as they drove.

"I think you're both right. We've got to boogie soon, that's for sure. I want to be gone before they start setting up roadblocks and get a chopper in the air. I think we sunk that cruiser pretty good, and it was a great idea Pogo had piling on that brush, but I don't know what it will look like from above. Maybe they'll be able to see the hood through the ice, but like Pogo said, I think we still got some time before that happens. This snow is gonna help us too." He looked at his friends, that weird, scary grin on his face again. "Let's go back to the car park, set up like we planned, and watch his road. He may have stopped overnight on his way here like we said earlier, or maybe he took his wife to the airport or to visit the grandkids. We can watch and wait and see what happens. If we see too much activity, cop cars, or if we hear a police helicopter or if we hear something on the local radio, then we nice and easy start making our way out of here and back home. I can't see them stopping three nice old guys like us on vacation driving in a stupid fucking camper, can you?"

"Hiding in plain sight, just like the VC, eh, Jasper?" said Pogo with a smile.

"Just like the VC," agreed Jasper.

"Remember how we dealt with those VC?" asked Birdie, not really addressing either man. "We fucking killed them all."

Nobody said anything until Pogo turned around and looked Birdie in the eye. "You really know how to put a damper on a good time, you know that, Birdman?"

FORTY

It didn't start snowing until Bill hit the Maine border around 2:30 p.m. He listened to his MP3 player on and off most of the way up, but he tuned his radio into the local news station once he crossed the border from New Hampshire into Maine. They were predicting a spring storm with maybe six-inches of snow. He remembered Uncle Frank mentioning that a storm was on its way. He thought back to the beautiful sixty-degree weather he had enjoyed yesterday back home and remembered Uncle Frank telling him at the trap range how he had left sixteen-degree weather on his trip down to Jersey.

Jesus Christ, he thought. Middle of April, and it's sixteen degrees and snowing. Well, not sixteen degrees outside now, but wait until tonight, he thought.

He pulled out his phone and took a quick glance down to see if he had any messages. None. He thought about calling Uncle Frank now that he was close, let him know that he'd have company soon. He was sure that Frank wouldn't be all that happy to see him, especially not a surprise visit like this. Frank didn't seem like someone who enjoyed surprises, but then Bill had to admit that he wouldn't have taken too kindly to this either if the roles had been reversed. He started thinking that maybe this wasn't such a great idea, but then shrugged and thought I'm here already, and it's too late to start thinking like that. If Uncle Frank gets pissed, so be it. He'll get over it just like Bill got over him not saying anything about knowing Jasper.

Bill looked at his gas gauge and saw that it was getting low and decided to pull over at the next station and fill the tank. He wanted to double-check his map again as well. He knew how to get to Uncle Frank's and Aunt Sadie's, had in fact stayed at their home several times over the past few years, but he didn't make the trip often enough to be totally comfortable with his directions. He had brought an old road map with him, along with the phone numbers of some of Aunt Sadie's relatives that he had written down on a piece of paper, just in case. He had his GPS, but Uncle Frank had told him that his street address didn't show up on most GPS units. No matter. Bill was sure he would recognize the turn-off when he saw it.

He saw a sign for gas at the next exit and followed the arrows to a Shell station. He filled his tank, then pulled off to the side near the service station restrooms and called his wife's cell phone.

Sam answered on the second ring. "Hi, hon. Where are you?"

"Hey, babe. Just crossed into Maine. I'm sitting in the parking lot of a gas station, thought I should fill up the tank before I get to Frank's. It's snowing like crazy here. How are you doing?"

"I'm good. Heading over to pick up the boys from school, then going to Mom and Dad's. I locked up the house and called Officer Rudy. He said he'd keep an eye on the house for us, but he said he didn't expect any more trouble. I don't either, but I still feel better going to my folks. The boys are thrilled to be staying overnight. Dad says he's got a surprise for them. I swear, Dad is like a kid himself. I think he's as thrilled as the boys are. Like they're all going to sleepaway camp or something. Did you talk to Frank yet?"

"No, not yet. I'm going to call him as soon as I get off with you. I've been sort of putting it off. You know Frank. I'm expecting him to give me a hard time about coming up, and though I can certainly understand, I'm just not in the mood to listen to it, you know?"

"Oh, don't worry about him. He'll huff and puff, but by

dinner tonight, he'll be happy as a clam to have someone to hang out with. Maybe you can take him to that diner they have there in town, or maybe be a sport and drive to a real town and splurge on a steak or a burger at Applebee's or one of those other chain restaurants, throw a few beers down him. I think he needs someone to talk to, you know, about Sadie. I really do. I think your driving up there is going to end up being a good thing for him, good for both of you. I'm glad you decided to go."

"Geez, hon, I'm glad I called. I was starting to second-guess this trip. Was thinking maybe this wasn't such a good idea, you know, surprising him and all."

"Well, it's too late now, don't you think? Better to head on in and get it over with. Call and see what he says. I'm sure it's going to be fine."

"Yeah, I'll call him at home. I should be there in an hour or so."

"Be careful driving, Billy. And call me later, okay?"

"I will. I love you, Sam."

"Love you too, hon. And don't forget to give Frank a big kiss for me."

"I will if I don't get punched in the mouth first."

FORTY-ONE

They reached the main road and turned left, heading back toward Turd Man's house. The road was now coated with a thin film of white snow. Pogo drove slowly with his headlights on, the windshield wipers scraping over the icy glass intermittently, making a chattering sound. They saw no other cars on the road until they drove around a bend and over a small rise and saw two state trooper cars parked on the opposite side of the road. They were side by side facing in opposite directions, so the drivers could talk through their driver's-side windows, their light bars were flashing, the blue and red lights visible from a distance through the falling snow.

"This a roadblock?" asked Jasper. He reached under the seat, took out the Sig and checked to make sure there was a round chambered, then slid it back under the seat.

"I don't think so, brother." Pogo slowed up a bit as they approached the cars. The cops seemed to take no notice of them as they drove past.

Birdie turned his head and looked out the side window as they drove on.

"They're just sitting there shooting the shit," he said, keeping his eyes on the cops until they rounded a curve and the police cars were no longer visible.

"It's like I said before," said Pogo. "We're at DEFCON Four. They still got their heads up their asses and don't know what's going on yet. This snow is going to slow things down for them considerably. Make flying a chopper a whole lot harder, and it will cut visibility if they can even get one up in the air. Also, it's going to wash away any blood that got spilled on the road where we shot that guy and cover up any drag marks on the side of the road. We're golden, man, at least for a while longer. I bet they're thinking car accident right now. That will last for another hour or two. There are just so many roads near here that they can check. When they don't find that car, then they're going to start thinking funny business."

They drove for another few miles and then saw the lights and heard the siren of another state police car approaching from the front. Pogo veered to the right side of the road and slowed nearly to a stop, giving the cop plenty of room. The car sped past them in a blur of flashing lights.

"That's three cars we've seen already," said Jasper. "Looks like they got themselves the beginning of a convention."

"When we get to that car park, I'm going to light us up a fatty," said Pogo. "We'll get out and smoke it so as not to stink up the truck, you know, in case we get pulled over later."

"Now that sounds like plan. I must be getting old, but all these cops are making me nervous. Maybe you got some of those magic crystals left in your kit there, Pogo, give us that edge back."

"Give us that edge, Birdman? Shit, you were tripping back there for a while," Jasper shook his head, smiling now. "You smoke any more of that shit, you'll be flying right off that edge."

"It's like I told you before: we're on that rollercoaster ride now, Jasper. We're short timers. Who gives a shit?"

"Don't worry, I got plenty more crystals boys, my own homemade Blue Bunnies. Let's get to the car park and get set up, smoke that fatty and get us straightened out some, see what happens. Birdie, we'll save that other shit for later. Hopefully, we'll get a chance to put it to good use. We get lucky and find that motherfucker, take care of this business, we still got us a bottle of Beam to drink."

"Amen to that, brother," said Jasper.

Birdie leaned his head back and rested it on the top of the back seat. He put both hands on his knees, then reached his left hand over and pushed the button, and the side window rolled down about six inches. Cold air swirled in and filled the truck's cabin. He breathed deeply and felt the cold air fill his lungs.

"That's it, Birdman. Let that fresh air on in." It was Pogo yelling from the front seat. "Breathe it in boys, that there is freedom. We're living the life, the warrior's code. It's nature's way my friends, fuck the man, stick it right up his ass!"

Jasper started laughing, and kept at it, hunching over in his seat and holding his stomach like he was going to be sick.

Pogo let loose his Indian war whoop again and then slapped Jasper on the back.

Birdie leaned further back into his seat and closed his eyes.

He knew they were all crazy, he and Jasper and Pogo. And he knew that probably none of them were going to make it home from this party.

But he really didn't give a shit.

FORTY-TWO

Bill was thinking that there must be some sort of emergency. He had seen three or four state police cars with their lights flashing in the last few minutes. It was probably some sort of accident. The roads were getting a bit slick, though not anywhere near treacherous yet.

He saw a sign that said the town of Boland was coming up in five miles. He knew Uncle Frank's road was nondescript turnoff two or three miles from the center of town. It was easy to miss, so he slowed down a little and began looking for familiar landmarks. After a few minutes, he came upon a small parking area that hikers and snowmobilers used that he remembered from the last time he was up visiting, and he slowed down even more until he saw Frank's road.

He put on his blinker, made the turn, and drove slowly up the road past the houses of Frank's two neighbors. Bill had only been up to Frank and Aunt Sadie's home in the summer. Then, with the trees green and full and the sun shining, it had been beautiful, bucolic, even. Now, with snow coming down and low cloud cover and ice forming on his windshield, *bucolic* was not a word that came to mind.

Desolate was more like it.

He thought about Uncle Frank living up here with his wife all these years. It must have been lonely with just the two of them.

How was he going to live up here all by himself?

He could see the barrier up ahead indicating the end of the road. He drove on and saw Uncle Frank's house up on the left and pulled into the driveway and followed it up to the house.

There were no lights on.

He got out of his Jeep and walked up to the front door and rang the doorbell.

No one answered. He knew Frank wasn't home, but he knocked on the door anyway. The air was cold, and he looked at the front yard and the driveway and saw that the tire tracks he had just made driving up were quickly disappearing.

He walked back down the front steps and followed the walkway back to the driveway and then walked over to the garage. He opened the garage's side door and peeked inside. No cars.

He walked back to his Jeep, got in, turned on the ignition, and fired up the heater. He had called Frank's house number before and left a message. He hoped that maybe with the snow, Frank would've been home by now.

He dialed Uncle Frank's cell and waited. Once again, he reached a voice mail.

He sat in his truck not really knowing what to do next. He thought back to his conversations with Frank. He remembered his uncle saying that he might go visit friends, or maybe stay at the cabin they use as a hunting camp.

He didn't know how to look up any friends that Uncle Frank might go visit, but he could probably find the cabin. Maybe stop at the lumberyard where Frank worked and talk to the owner if he was around. He was Aunt Sadie's cousin, owned the land where the cabin was situated. What the hell was the guy's name? Neville or Nelson—something like that. He could ask one of the other employees discreetly what the guy's name was when he got there. He should probably ask permission to stop by that cabin and see if Frank was there. Probably be good to ask directions while he was at. It had been quite a few years since he had been up there, before the cabin was even built and that had been over ten years ago. No way he could find it on his own.

He looked up the address of the lumberyard on his phone and then punched it into his GPS. He also looked up the number and address of a few motels in the area in case he couldn't find Frank and needed a place to spend the night. He didn't want to be driving too far in this weather, especially at night.

That done, he turned the jeep around, so he wouldn't have to back down the long driveway, and then headed back toward the main road.

He glanced occasionally at his GPS as he drove. It seemed like it was taking unusually long for the system to acquire satellites, but by the time he reached the intersection, it had calculated time, distance and directions, and he did as the mechanical female voice instructed and turned right toward Boland. The lumberyard address was calculated to be about fifteen minutes or so away, on one of the main roads on the other side of town. He was driving slowly because of the weather, but there didn't seem to be many other cars on the road. Up ahead he could make out red taillights of some sort of car, but with the low light and the snow coming down, he couldn't see what kind of car it was. He checked his rearview mirror and saw what appeared to be a pickup with a cap of some kind, maybe a toolbox across the top of the bed, or it might even be a camper in back. It was hard to see because it was a ways back and the guy had his headlights on. There was no traffic coming out of town for the first few minutes until he saw a police cruiser heading in his direction. The cop car had its emergency lights on but was driving slowly and the officer wasn't using his siren.

He wondered again if maybe there was some kind of accident. It was strange to see so many cop cars, especially out here in the middle of nowhere. When he got into the town of Boland, he drove down the main drag. He stopped at a traffic light, and at the corner directly to his right he saw the diner that Sam had mentioned. It made him smile. Boland's finest dining establishment. He noticed an ambulance parked in the lot and thought again about all the cop cars he had seen since he arrived in the vicinity of Boland. He stared at the ambulance without really thinking about anything, and then he noticed a bunch of antennas and even a small satellite dish on the roof. He looked at the license plate. It wasn't a Maine plate. He squinted a bit to try to see better. It was a white plate with blue lettering. He thought it might have said Virginia across the top, but then someone behind him honked the horn, and he saw that the light had turned green, and he continued on his way.

He drove through town, staying on basically the same road, and, after a few blocks of small storefronts and a municipal building and one convenience store he was once again driving with nothing but woods and fields and the occasional small house on either side. The lumberyard was about four of five miles past Boland. It was two large warehouse-type buildings, one was more like a huge shed with lumber and feed supplies and bags of what Bill assumed were fertilizers and seed and other farm supplies on shelves or in large bins, and the other seemed more a retail store. There were also several tractors parked next to each building. Some of the tractors looked brand new, and he assumed that the place probably sold and rented to local farmers. Bill knew from Uncle Frank that the guy who owned this place was one of the wealthiest guys in the area. He could certainly understand why, as it was quite an operation.

He drove to the retail building, parked in one of the spaces in front, and then walked into the store. He introduced himself to an older woman working the register, explained that he was Frank's nephew, and asked if the owner was around. She was round and friendly and just pleased as punch to meet Frank's nephew, and Bill was afraid she might try to pinch his cheek. He found out that the guy's name was Nelson Stahl, and he was indeed in his office, which was up the stairs behind the register. Bill looked up and saw office space through some windows high above the store. The woman picked up a phone, punched in a few numbers, and then told Mr. Stahl that Frank's nephew was here to see him. She smiled and hung up the phone and told him to head on up.

Nelson Stahl got up from his desk and walked around to shake Bill's hand. Bill had met Nelson once before when Bill was just a kid. Nelson had stopped by the hunting camp once when he and his father and Uncle Frank had been up there camping.

"Mr. Stahl, I'm Bill Thompson, Frank's nephew."

"Bill, how nice to see you. Come in, sit down, and please, call me Nelson, Mr. Stahl makes me sound like an old man."

Bill shook Nelson's hand and smiled warmly. "I believe we met once when I was a kid. My dad and I went camping up on your property with Uncle Frank, geez, I don't even remember how many years ago that was. Anyway, it's nice to see you again."

"It's nice to see you too, Bill. What brings you up here? I thought Frank was down visiting for a few days."

"He was. Something came up on my end and, his trip got cut short. I got things straightened out and had some time on my hands, and so I decided to come up here for a visit, maybe spend some time together. What with Aunt Sadie passing, well, I just wanted to spend some time, you know."

"That's nice, Bill. I am so sorry about Sadie. She was a wonderful gal, my cousin was. Frank is taking it hard. He doesn't say much, but they were very close. I think it's good he has some company. Everyone around here has been trying to visit, or get him to visit, but he's dealing with it in his own way, I guess. So, you looking for him? He hasn't been back to work. He said he was taking a week or so off. You been by his place?"

"Just left. I spoke to him yesterday, and he said something about maybe going up to the hunting cabin. I don't know if he's there, or maybe he's out visiting a friend, but I stopped by to ask your permission to head over there and see if maybe he decided to get out of town for a few days."

"I don't know why he'd head up there in this weather. But you're welcome to head on up and take a look if you'd like. I got a key if you want. You're welcome to stay there, too, if you'd care to. Better yet, if you don't find Frank, why don't you come stay with my wife and me? I fear the weather will get worse before it gets better, and we've got plenty of room. My wife would love to have someone besides me to talk to."

"That's very kind of you, Nelson, but I've got the numbers of a few motels."

"Nonsense." He walked over to his desk, sat down, opened a drawer, pulled out a pad and pen, and began writing. He opened another drawer and rummaged around until he found some keys. He walked back around the desk and handed the paper and keys to Bill.

"That's my address and phone numbers, both house and cell. You got a GPS?"

Bill nodded.

"Just punch it in, and it'll come up. Also, I wrote down directions how to get to the cabin. It'll take you about twenty minutes to get there, probably more with this snow. The turnoff is a bit tricky. It's an old dirt road. There's a pole gate across the road, painted yellow so it's easier to see. That small key with the black dot on it is to the padlock on the gate. The larger key opens the cabin door. The other opens the locks on the shutters should you decide you want to spend the night. Place is wired for electricity, and there's a generator in the shed in back, but if you're planning to stay, you better bring fresh gas."

"Thank you, Nelson, but I'm going to see if Frank is there. If he's not, I'll bring these keys back or drop them off at your house. I appreciate the offer to stay over, and I may take you up on it, but I'd just as soon play it by ear. If I don't find Frank, I may try to get a jump on heading back home."

"Okay, Bill, but you're more than welcome."

They shook hands again.

"I appreciate your help, Nelson. My uncle speaks highly of you, and I can certainly see why."

"Well, Frank's a good man. I admire him very much, and I'm privileged to have him working here with me. Anything I can do, Bill, just let me know. If I don't see you later, well, I'll assume that you found Frank, and you can have him bring those keys back when he comes in to work."

"I'll call you regardless, Nelson, and thanks again." Bill left the office, headed back down the stairs, waved to the woman at the register, and walked to his Jeep.

They were parked on the opposite side of the road facing back towards Boland, about a hundred and fifty yards past the lumberyard. They had followed the Jeep from Turd Man's road and then driven past the lumberyard after the Jeep had pulled in. They drove about a quarter mile, then U-turned and slowly drove past the entrance again and then pulled over. Jasper had walked back along the road a ways skirting the edge of the woods with high-powered binoculars so he could watch the parking lot. Pogo was kneeling and fiddling with one of the tires in case someone drove by and noticed the truck on the side of the road.

They had watched Bill's Jeep turn into Turd Man's road shortly after they had smoked a joint and set up in the car park. Jasper was pretty sure it was the nephew's Jeep as soon as he saw it, even though they didn't see the driver or the car's license plates through the falling snow. They debated following him in, but then reasoned that they could always go in later if the kid didn't come out. They were pretty sure that Turd Man hadn't returned home and, if that was the case, they planned to follow the kid, hoping he would lead them right to their man. If he didn't come out, they would wait a while longer and then go in and grab him, use the kid as bait, call Turd Man from his own home phone, and set up a place to meet, and then kill them both.

But the kid did come out, and here they were.

Jasper had his eyes on the front door of the retail building and as soon as he saw Bill walk out, he whistled a loud, short burst through his teeth and began sprinting back toward the truck. Pogo was already in the driver's seat with the engine running when Jasper jumped into the passenger seat.

"He's leaving! Get ready to roll! Soon as his car gets to the gate, start moving. If he comes this way, I want us to be far enough ahead, so we can turn off and get behind. If he goes the other way farther out of town, as I expect, we've got to be able to turn around quick without him seeing us."

"Take it easy there, son, I got this," said Pogo, speaking calm and easy. "It's not like we're going to lose him in traffic. Why don't you give them glasses to Birdie? He'll be able to see better from the back seat. Once we get behind him again, you take over and then keep that Jeep in sight."

Jasper handed the glasses back to Birdie, who had already opened the back window and was positioning himself at a better angle to watch the road.

"He's coming to the gate," said Birdie, "Start moving, Pogo. Looks like he's headed the other way."

The truck began moving off the shoulder and onto the road. Pogo and Jasper were looking out the side-view mirrors when they heard a siren in the distance. They looked at the road ahead, Jasper reaching almost unconsciously for the gun under the seat.

"What do we got?" asked Birdman, reaching the glasses over the front seat. Jasper took the binoculars and put them to his eyes.

"I see lights, maybe a cop...no, wait, looks like an ambulance. Yeah, it's an ambulance. Wait till he passes and then let's turn quick. Kid will probably pull over to let him go. We can gain on him then."

A few seconds later, the ambulance went screaming by with lights flashing and siren blaring. Pogo waited a few seconds more, and then pulled a U-turn right in the middle of the road. By the time he was fully turned and heading down the road, the ambulance was a speck of flashing lights in the distance.

"Maybe they found our trooper," said Birdie.

"I don't think so," said Pogo. "Guy had half his head blown

216

off. It wouldn't be an ambulance. They'd have called an ME, probably one of them crime scene investigation units, too, like they have on TV. Besides, if they did happen have our boy in there, then they'd have had a whole convoy of police leading the way, don't you think?"

Nobody said anything, and they drove in silence.

They didn't see any traffic ahead or behind and Pogo began increasing his speed. Jasper was peering through the binoculars, but the road curved every so often, and with the snow coming down, visibility was limited.

"Okay, I got him," said Jasper, excitement back in his voice. "Let's get a little closer, and then back off. Damn, I was afraid maybe he turned off on some little shit road like we did the other night and we drove right past him. Hold on, he's turning left. He just put his blinker on. Pogo, slow down. We don't want to run too close up his ass."

They continued following the Jeep, making the occasional right or left turn onto rural back roads, getting further off the main roads. There was nothing but woods or fields on either side, not even farmhouses.

Birdie said, "Let me have that map, Jasper. I want to see if I can figure out where the hell he's headed. Maybe our boy is squirreled away in some little hot sheet motel or campground. That would be perfect."

Jasper opened the glove box, found the map, and handed it back to Birdman. Then he brought the glasses back up and looked at the red taillights of the car ahead in the distance.

"I wonder where this motherfucker is going. We're gonna need a fucking snowmobile soon. Birdie, you figure out where we are yet?" asked Pogo.

"This map has no detail. It only shows the main roads. Shit, we've been turning onto these little fucking farm roads, I can't even tell what direction we're headed. I followed that main road out of Boland, but this map doesn't show anything out this way for miles. No towns. We may be in a state park, or at least bordering state land."

"It doesn't matter," said Jasper. "The farther out we go, the better off we are. Ain't nobody going to find any bodies out here. And I don't mind getting away from those cops back there either. One way or the other, this thing is going to get settled. We'll teach them the meaning of fear this night."

"What'd you just say?" asked Birdie.

"I said the farther out we go, the better."

"No, that other thing. We'll teach them to fear the night. That's what it was. Where'd you get that from, Jasper? I remember that."

"The fuck you talking about, Birdie?" asked Pogo, glancing over his shoulder.

"Must still be tripping," said Jasper, the binoculars still glued to his eyes.

Birdie leaned back and put his hands behind his head, relaxing into his seat.

"It was that spook that said it, guy looked like an accountant. You remember that guy? What was his name? Had glasses, was this little wormy guy. 'Just call me Robert,' that's it. Remember him?"

"You mean Bobby Vegas?" Pogo sounded delighted. "He wasn't a spook. He was the guy from Psyops. I remember that little fucker. 'Just call me Robert.' Guy would come up with these suicide ops and send you off with a smile. Anyone called him out on the operation, he'd say, 'Yeah, it's a gamble.' That's why we called him Bobby Vegas. He was nuts, used to take NVA prisoners up in a chopper, come down ten minutes later, and it was just him that'd hop out."

Jasper dropped the glasses from his eyes for a second and looked over at Pogo with that eerie grin of his. "Enhanced interrogation technique."

Then the glasses went back up again, and he watched the Jeep ahead.

"Yeah, I guess." Pogo grinned sheepishly and shook his head.

"I remember I was on patrol one night," Birdie said, looking up at the roof of the truck, hands behind his head, "and we captured these two dinks riding bikes along a trail outside a VC village. 'Call me Robert,' he told us the way to kill them, put two holes in their neck, puncture the artery with this thing he gave us, like an ice pick or something, and hang them upside down. Said to drain all the blood out of them, then cut 'em down and leave them on the trail. You believe that shit? Said he wanted the villagers to think there were monsters roaming the trail. You know, vampires. Try and scare them so they'd be afraid to move weapons and supplies at night. 'We'll teach them to fear the night,' that's what he said. I think that's what you just said, too, Jasper."

"He was one crazy motherfucker," said Pogo.

"He was right, though, Pogo. There were monsters roaming that trail at night."

"Hell, yeah, Birdman," answered Pogo good-naturedly. "We were the goddamn monsters."

"Still are," said Jasper, his eyes never leaving the red taillights ahead.

"Damn right," said Birdman, closing his eyes, remembering the sight of those two men hanging by their feet, hands bound behind them, blood pulsing out the holes in their necks and dripping down their heads, pooling on the ground. "We still are."

FORTY-THREE

Bill saw a flash of yellow on his left and jammed on the brakes. Even though he was going fairly slowly, the Jeep skidded and careened almost sliding off the road. Cursing under his breath, Bill pumped the brakes lightly to control the skid, and when he finally stopped, he backed the car up until it was even with the gate that Nelson had told him about. He could see a chain with a lock, but the chain was only wrapped around one post. That meant that even though the gate was closed, it wasn't locked. There were faint tire ruts in the snow. Someone had driven through that gate recently, maybe as recently as earlier today. The new snow had started to cover the tire marks, but the outline of the ruts was still clearly visible. The road was only discernible by the ruts and the cleared path that led through the trees. If he hadn't been looking for that yellow gate, he would have driven right past.

He got out of the Jeep and checked the road both ahead and behind. It was clear in both directions. He had seen an occasional vehicle behind him in the distance, some idiot driving with no headlights, but there seemed to be no one else on the road now. The snow had begun to slow down a little, coming down more as frozen rain or sleet than snow. He hoped that the worst of it was over but knew from the weather stories he had heard from Uncle Frank over the years that you couldn't count on anything up here. He walked over to the gate, swung it open and then got back in the Jeep. He drove through the gate and onto the road, then got out again and closed the gate. He wasn't sure why he closed it, but felt somehow that he should, like closing someone's front door.

The then got back into the car and began driving toward the cabin in four-wheel drive. He drove slowly, trying to stay in the ruts of the previous vehicle. It was a little unnerving driving when he couldn't see the road. He put on his bright lights, but the falling rain and snow made it harder to see ahead with the brights than with the low beams, and so he switched back.

He didn't know how far in the cabin would be. He couldn't remember how long it had been since he'd last been up here. They had camped here when he was a kid, but Bill had also come up to visit with his parents when they were both still alive, maybe fifteen or sixteen years ago. He had driven them up to visit Frank and Sadie for a long weekend, and one day they had all decided to take a ride to this campground and have a picnic, just for something to do to get out of the house.

After ten or fifteen minutes of slow going, he saw what might be a clearing in the woods ahead, though visibility was still very poor. He continued on until the woods cleared out some into what might turn into a beautiful meadow come summer and up ahead near the edge to the cleared land he saw the log cabin. Uncle Frank was standing outside on the porch, a scoped rifle in his left hand.

Bill pulled up to the front of the cabin facing the front door, and Uncle Frank began circling his hand in the air, apparently directing him to do something.

Bill rolled down his window, not sure what to expect.

"Pull the car around this way Billy, the front facing that way," said Frank, pointing off to his left. Bill noticed that Frank was not looking at him, but rather his eyes were looking down the road in the direction he had just come from.

Bill did as directed, then opened the door and smiled at his uncle.

"You're a hard man to find, Frank."

"Not hard enough, I guess. You got a bag, bring it on in." He turned and headed into the cabin. Bill went around back, opened the tailgate, grabbed his overnight bag and the old Fox, then carried them both inside.

Uncle Frank was standing at the window, looking at the road through black binoculars.

"What's going on, Frank? You expecting more visitors?" Bill carried his bag into the living area, dropped it on the floor, and laid the old Fox on the dining table.

"What are you doing here, Billy? How'd you find this place?"

"Well, I kind of felt bad about how our visit ended, and I already had the time off and, well, I didn't like the thought of you up here all alone. I stopped by your place, then remembered you saying that you might take a ride up here for a few days, so I stopped by and saw Nelson at the lumberyard, and here I am. By the way, here are Nelson's keys before I forget." He dropped the keys on the table.

Frank hadn't looked at him at all, just kept looking out the window.

"Did anyone follow you? Did you see any cars behind you, even at a distance? Maybe a brown Toyota, one of them older little ones, Camry or Corolla?"

"What? No, I didn't see anyone."

"Think, Bill. It's important. Did you see anyone behind you? Anyone at all?"

"Well, there weren't many people on the road once I left the lumberyard. I saw a bunch of cops in and around Boland though. Might have been some sort of accident. And let's see, an ambulance passed me just as I left Nelson's, and I saw an old truck with a camper behind me for a while, but I lost them on one of the turnoffs coming here. That's about it."

"What did the truck look like? Did you see the plates at all? Did you see what state they were from?"

"No, too far off. What's going on, Frank? Why the rifle? Why the shotgun over there and those two handguns on the table?"

"You shouldn't have come up here, Bill. Shit, you didn't call me or leave a message. I told you I was fine. Why'd you have to come up here? What the hell is wrong with you?"

Bill didn't know what to say, so he said nothing.

Finally, Frank put down the binoculars and walked over to Bill, putting both hands on his shoulders, and brought him close for a hug.

"I'm sorry, Billy Boy, I know you mean well. But my problems have escalated some. Sit down. Go ahead, please. Sit down."

Bill sat at one of the chairs by the table. Uncle Frank absently picked up the old Fox, flipped the lever and broke the gun open, then reached up onto a shelf and into an opened a box of double-aught buckshot shells, removed two and loaded the shotgun, then snapped it shut.

"I'm afraid, Bill, that we might be having some company soon. Now I'm not totally sure, but pretty sure."

"You mean Jasper and his friends?"

Frank nodded. "They came to visit me the other night. They meant to kill me. Had some heavy firepower, snuck up the road, even entered the house through a window."

"How did you escape? What happened?"

"Well, as a precaution, I spent the night up on the ridge behind my house with this." He picked up the M40. "Watched them come in and set up right inside the house. They were waiting for me, I guess. One guy was hiding in the woods near the road, the other two inside. Hunter/killer team, just like I taught them."

"Did you call the cops? Is that why all those police cars are driving around Boland?"

"I don't know. I didn't call them last night. I was afraid someone might get killed. Those boys, they're well-armed. I saw an M16 and an AK47, plus a shotgun. And that's just what I saw. If I'm right, those assault guns will fire on automatic. Any police try to take those boys out while they were set up at my house and they had no escape, someone was going to get killed. I don't care about these assholes, but I do worry about the police up here."

"So why all the police?"

"Like I said, I'm not sure. These guys were driving a brown Corolla. That's why I asked you about it before. I called my buddy Noah, the state trooper, the next morning and told him I saw some older guys firing a shotgun out the window of their car. I asked him to call it in, let his people know that these guys had loaded weapons and were dangerous. I can't see even these nitwits getting into a firefight in broad daylight with state cops over a traffic stop. Least I certainly hope that's the case. Did you hear anything on the radio while you were driving?"

"No, but then I wasn't playing the radio much," said Bill, reaching for his phone. "How's the reception up here?"

Frank walked back over to the window carrying the M40, laid it against the windowsill, and grabbed the binoculars again.

"Should be okay. I tried to call Noah an hour or so ago, had two bars on my phone, got through to his voice mail."

Bill fiddled with his phone, browsing the internet for any stories having to do with Boland, Maine. He didn't find anything that seemed like breaking news.

"I'm not seeing anything, Frank, but I don't really know where to look."

Frank put the binoculars down and walked back to the table where Bill was sitting. He grabbed the Glock and brought the slide back to check the load again.

"You know how to use this?" he asked, handing the gun to Bill butt end first.

Bill took the gun carefully and pointed it away from Frank.

"It's a Glock, right? They make these things out of plastic or something. That's why they're so light."

"Ever fire one?"

"Yes, I have. A friend brought me to a range with him once. Had all sorts of handguns. But I'm no expert or anything. I wasn't very good with the 9mm. He had an old Colt 38 Police Special that I could shoot a lot better with."

"Well, Billy, I'm afraid I didn't bring one of those." He reached up on the shelf again and grabbed the two extra clips. "Fifteen rounds in each clip. You know how to reload the clip?"

Bill nodded.

"Good. Keep the Glock with you while we're here at the cabin. Put those extra magazines in your pocket. Do it now." Frank walked over to where he had laid the shotgun and brought that over to where Bill sat.

He pulled up a chair and handed the shotgun to Bill.

"Tactical shotgun, semiauto. Be careful, it's loaded. Don't let the short barrel fool you. Some people think with the short barrel you get a much wider pattern and just have to point in the general direction of a target to hit it. Not true. You still have to aim if you intend to hit anything, but it'll fire as fast as you can pull the trigger. Loaded with double aught, like the Fox. Let's keep that handy and loaded, too. Here's some more shells, just in case." He put another box of shotgun shells on the table.

"What are you expecting, Uncle Frank, a war?"

"Billy, I don't want to scare you, but if those boys come any-where near us, they mean to kill us. I wish you hadn't come up, I really do, but now you're here, and that means you're in danger, too. There'll be no talking to them, no reasoning or bargaining." Frank put a hand on Bill's shoulder and looked into his eyes. "Do you understand that? You really need to understand that."

"Why don't we just get out of here, Frank? If you know they're up here, let's go to the police, right now."

Frank got up and walked back to the window. He picked up the binoculars and began searching the edge of the woods around the clearing.

"We can't right now, Bill, because if they did follow you from town, they could be making their way here right now through those trees. You drove down that road into here. Goat path is really more like it. With that snow, we can't move fast.

If we get stuck or if they ambush us while we're in the truck, we're dead. If they come, they'll block the road just out of our view, probably with their own vehicle. Two assault rifles on auto and a shotgun, they'll make mincemeat out of us. Ever see *Bonnie and Clyde*, that old movie? Warren Beatty and Faye Dunaway get ambushed in that old car and get cut to pieces? Think about it."

"Jesus, Frank, I thought you said you didn't want to scare me."

"Well, Bill," said Frank, turning away from the window for a second and looking at his nephew, "I'm afraid that right now, we might both have good reason to be scared."

If it hadn't been snowing, they would have missed it. As it was, they drove right past the gate. They had decided to hang back a bit further so as not to be seen and Pogo was following the tire tracks in the snow. He was moving relatively slowly, as he didn't want to turn on his headlights and visibility was poor, but there was nobody else on the road, and they only had one set of fresh tracks to follow.

Just past the gate, the tracks swerved and ran over each other as if the car had skidded off to the side. The tracks moving forward ended abruptly and Pogo drove past and then slowed to a careful stop. He turned to look at Jasper and then backed up until he saw the gate.

"I think we just hit pay dirt, boys." He backed the camper up further so that should anyone driving down that trail on the other side of the gate happen to look back, they wouldn't see the old camper sitting there.

"Jasper, why don't you take that M16 for a little stroll down there a ways and see what you can see? Let's make sure there's nobody on lookout or waiting for us. We need to get this truck in there and off the road, then we can all head in on foot."

Jasper opened the door and headed around behind the truck.

They heard the camper door open, then felt the truck drop slightly as Jasper climbed into the camper and retrieved the M16. A few seconds later, the back door closed quietly, and they saw a shadow skirt the fence and begin making its way through the trees parallel to the trail.

Pogo turned around in his seat and looked at Birdie. "It's show time, Birdman. Our boy's definitely here. I swear I can sense it, you know?"

"Me, too, Pogo. Feels like we're about to hit a VC vil, doesn't it, just like in the day."

"Yeah, I'm juiced up. Soon as we get the truck in there, let's break out that pipe and get our heads right, then we go in, S&D, and we waste that motherfucker."

"Waste 'em all," said Birdie.

"Take no prisoners," said Pogo.

There was sudden knock on the window and both men were startled for a second, then Pogo turned and saw Jasper's face looking at him, his mirrored sunglasses on and an old jungle bush hat on his head. He had that crazy grin on his face, something between a smile and a snarl.

Pogo powered the window down halfway.

"We're good," said Jasper, and then he turned and trotted over to the gate, lifted the latch and pulled it all the way open.

Pogo drove the truck through and followed the trail for about thirty yards, then cut the engine.

He and Birdie got out, closed the doors as quietly as they could, and walked around to the back and opened the camper door.

Once inside, they checked their weapons, each staying with the one he had carried to Turd Man's house before. Pogo showed Birdie again how to load the machine gun and made sure that everything was in working order. He then checked the shotgun, making sure the magazine was full. Birdie handed him three extra boxes of the Hexolites shells and Pogo opened them and stuffed the loose shells into his jacket pocket. He didn't want to be fumbling around trying to open a box if he needed those in a hurry.

"Jasper come on in here," said Pogo quietly when they were locked and loaded.

When Jasper was in, he handed each man one of the radios.

"I put in fresh batteries." Each man turned on the radio and put the ear buds in, testing to make sure they could all hear each other.

Jasper looked at his two friends. "I guess we go in like before. Birdman is hunter, we're killer team. We'll stay off the trail and head up both sides, just inside the tree line. Gotta be an old cabin or trailer of some sort up this road. He can't be staying in a fucking tent in weather like this. Good thing is, we don't have to worry about our guns making noise out here. We're miles from anywhere."

He handed Pogo the Sig that he had grabbed from under the front seat. "You take this. I'm going with mine."

"Damn, Jasper, that's awful nice of you. I thought you were going to carry a gun in each hand and shoot that M16 with your dick."

Jasper looked at Pogo, then at Birdie. "Whoever we find up there, we waste them all, agreed?"

Both men nodded.

Jasper reached into his jacket pocket and came out with several old baseball cards. "I didn't forget to bring these," he said holding the cards up. "When this is done, I'll leave a half for each person we take out. If the cops find 'em later, it'll let those that matter know who did this and why."

Each of the other two dug into a pocket and brought out cards. One of Pogo's was torn in half. He held it up and smiled at the other two.

"That kid," he said.

Birdie had a torn card as well. "The cop. I slipped it into his pocket back there. Just seemed right, this being a mission and all."

"National League fucking All Stars, man, we're tearing the ass out the world all over again," said Jasper, with a big smile on his face. Then, "Pogo, you want the Savage? Got a scope in case we have to snipe that fucker."

Pogo thought for a second, and then shook his head. "We ain't sniping anyone this trip, Jasper. This is going to be up close and personal. Besides, this crappy weather, I think I'm better off with this." He tapped the shotgun. "We'll leave the Savage on the front seat, loaded. If for some reason things turn to shit, we make our way back here to the truck and use it to keep their heads down, cover our assholes on the way out."

"That makes sense. We get this done, we carry the bodies out and dump them someplace else. I don't think we have to worry about roadblocks or cops this far out, but it would be best if we don't keep them bodies with us for too long. We'll drive out of here, then dump them in the woods up the road like we planned."

Pogo sat down on the bunk and began loading the glass pipe with crystals. "Think I'm going to start calling this special concoction of mine Rabbit Turds since Blue Bunnies is already taken. What do you boys think of that? Keep you sharp as a bunny's butthole."

"That's a good selling slogan," said Jasper, reaching into his pants pocket and removing an old Zippo lighter. "You always gotta think advertising."

"You think he's got any other hard chargers with him up there?" asked Birdie.

"I think he's hiding," said Jasper. "I can't believe that he's got more backup than just that kid in the jeep, and maybe his wife."

"Besides," said Pogo, "whoever he's got up there with him, we've got 'em outgunned and outclassed."

"Yeah," said Jasper, striking the flint on his lighter, "sharp as a bunny's butthole, that's us."

"Well," said Birdie, gently patting the RPK light machine gun, "at least we've got 'em outgunned."

FORTY-FOUR

"Billy, why don't you come over here and take over for a few minutes?" Frank stepped away from the window and handed the field glasses to Bill. "Look down the road and then slowly scan from side to side. Keep an eye out for movement anywhere in the woods. If you see something, or even think you see something, let me know."

Frank walked to the shelf where he had left the night vision attachment and began remounting it to the scope.

"What the hell do you have there?" asked Bill from the window.

"Night vision for the scope."

"Night vision? I thought you said you weren't into this Rambo stuff. Geez, who the hell has night vision? You get that from some buddy in special ops or something?"

"Nope. Borrowed it from Matt."

"Matt, your neighbor? He was in special forces, too?"

From the sound of his voice, Frank could tell that Bill was getting nervous. He could see the tension on his face, the jaw muscles drawn tight, his eyes bright, skin going pale and a light sheen of perspiration beginning to form. He remembered seeing men with that look before.

"Well, Billy, I don't believe that Matt ever served in the armed forces. Told me that he ordered this off the internet. It's used for varmint hunting at night. I told him some animals were getting into the trash at my house, and he offered to let me borrow it for a few days. Sun going down, I thought it might help us keep a better watch."

"How long do we have to stay, I mean before we can be pretty sure they're not out there?"

"Let's give it a while longer. Soon as it gets a little darker, I'll take a walk outside and look around a bit. With this scope, I'll be able to see anyone out there before they see me."

"You really think that's a good idea? What if those guys have buddies that go varmint hunting at night too?"

"I guess that's a possibility, but I've been in these woods already earlier, I know my way around. They haven't. That will make a big difference. But unless something happens soon, then I think we're probably in the clear. I think it's best if we drive my car out of here, leave yours. I'm driving Sadie's; they won't know that one. We'll call my friend Noah with the State Police, maybe meet him somewhere and tell him what's going on, tell him the whole damn story. I already called him and told him to be on the lookout for these characters. After that, we'll ride on over to Portland, get a room at the Holiday Inn for a day or two. I'll buy you a nice steak dinner tonight. Tomorrow, we'll ride around town some, maybe go see a movie at night. Then we'll come back here the day after and get your car and you can head on home. I'll work with the police until these characters are rounded up, get this whole goddamn circus over with already."

Bill looked at his uncle but didn't say what was on his mind, didn't ask him why he hadn't already met with Noah or any other law enforcement people. Frank looked up at him and met his eyes briefly, and then turned back to attaching the night vision scope.

"I wish you hadn't made this trip, Billy Boy, I truly do."

Bill didn't know what to say. At this moment he felt the same way and wished he'd just stayed home. He was scared. He was starting to understand the situation he was in. He wasn't an ex-recon marine like Uncle Frank. He wasn't a decorated war hero who'd served two tours in Vietnam no matter how long ago that was. Bill had never experienced anything remotely like combat, had never been in a situation where he feared for his life. Almost unconsciously, he moved his body closer to the side of the window to present less of a target. He had a wife and two kids, he had to be back at work in a few—

His thoughts were interrupted by a sudden, loud blaring in the distance. Uncle Frank was up and at his side almost immediately. Frank put a hand on his shoulder and moved him away from the window, then undid the latch and opened the window about six inches. He grabbed the scoped rifle and, kneeling, about a foot from the window, rested the barrel on the sill and began sighting along the road and into the trees.

"What's that noise?" Bill's voice cracked slightly, his throat suddenly very dry.

"Something triggered a trip wire," said Frank, his voice calm, lacking almost any emotion or inflection. "Grab that shotgun, Bill. Make sure you've got extra shells handy. Keep that Glock nearby. You have those extra clips in your pocket?"

"What do you mean a trip wire?"

"I set a few perimeter warning alarms. Someone or something set one off."

The alarm was still sounding, and Frank was trying to get a bead on where the sound was coming from. He looked through the scope, but nothing moved. They must have hit the dirt and made themselves small as soon as the alarm went off.

"Might be a deer," said Bill, but even he knew he didn't sound convincing. He was breathing fast, but he couldn't seem to get any air into his lungs.

Uncle Frank didn't say anything, and about a minute later, the alarm stopped abruptly

"It's no deer, Billy. Someone silenced that alarm." Frank moved away from the window, staying low, and made his way to where Bill stood. He pulled Bill down and duck-walked him to a spot near the bedroom doors where they could see the front door, the open window and the back door. He took the shotgun from Bill, double-checked again to make sure it was loaded, and then handed it back to Bill.

"It's ready to fire. Remember, you have to aim. Then, just pull the trigger. Keep those extra shells nearby." He then grabbed the Glock and checked it and put it on the floor next to Bill. "Use the shotgun first. Reload if you can, but keep that handgun ready, just in case."

"Jesus, Frank, this is crazy."

Frank pulled the Colt .45 from its holster and checked it again, made sure the clip was full and it was ready to fire, patted his pockets to make sure he had his extra clips.

"You have your phone, Bill? Call nine-one-one. Tell them we got people shooting at us. Then give me the phone. I'll let them know where we are." Frank grabbed his coat off a hook on the wall and put it on. He felt in his coat pocket and found an extra loaded clip for the M40. He had a handful of loose shells in the other pocket. He made his way back to the partially open window, staying low, and sighted the scope down the road again.

He thought he saw movement off to the left and then focused on a shadow where the movement seemed to have stopped. He thought about turning on the night vision, but there was still enough light out to see. He tried to hold the spot in his vision, and he pushed the barrel a bit further forward and began adjusting the focus dial on the scope until things became slightly clearer and he could just make out the form of a man who seemed to be crouching and resting the end of something long on a log or rock. Frank pulled the rifle away from the window and dove on the ground just as all the glass in the window shattered and rained down on him and the concussive force of an eight- or ten-round burst of machine gun fire exploded into the wall behind him, blowing coffee mugs and glasses and dishes off a shelf. The cabin seemed to shake and rattle with the force.

Frank looked back at Bill and saw that he had dropped the phone and the shotgun and was curled up in a ball on the floor, his arms covering his head and face.

He worked his way over to where his nephew lay, staying low and away from the window.

He put a hand on Bills shoulder and shook him gently. "Billy? Billy, you okay?"

Bill moved his arms from his head and looked at his uncle.

"What the hell was that?"

"Light machine gun. Are you okay?"

"A machine gun? They're fucking shooting a machine gun at us?" Bill's voice was loud and high, and his eyes looked wild.

Frank squeezed Bill's shoulder hard, saw Bill wince with pain, and said urgently, "Bill, are you okay? Are you hurt?"

Bill quieted and shook his head.

Frank nodded once and then looked around on the floor until he found Bill's phone. He handed it to Bill.

"Here. Call nine-one-one. When you get them on the phone, make sure you keep them on. Tell them someone is trying to kill us. Tell them they're shooting at us. Understand?"

Bill took the phone and looked at his uncle blankly.

"Call nine-one-one. Understand?" Frank squeezed his shoulder again, not quite as hard as before.

Bill nodded once, looked down at the screen on his phone, and then began hitting numbers.

Frank made his way back near the window, careful to stay down and away from any direct line of fire from outside. He checked the wall below and around the window with his eyes and then with his fingers to make sure no rounds had gone through the walls. The cabin was made of logs, and the walls were thick and solid. There were cracks in the plasterboard, but nothing got through. He crawled past the window, staying low and then raised himself up slowly and stood flat against the wall on the window's left side, his back facing the inside of the room. He peered out quickly and noted the area where he had seen the figure with machine gun. He took the Colt out of its holster with his right hand and let it hang at his side, took three deep, slow breaths, then quickly slid right so his right arm could extend straight while he kept most of his body behind the wall and fired three quick shots at where he thought the shooter was and then slid back behind the wall.

Almost immediately he heard a short, a three-round burst of gunfire from somewhere ahead and to the right, and bullets flew past his head buzzing like bees and then slammed into the wall behind him. The M16, he thought. Hunter is set up right in front with that machine gun. Killer team is working its way around behind. He reached through the window again and returned fire, moving his aim farther to the right. He knew he wasn't going to hit anything, but he wanted to slow them down a bit.

He ducked, and as he worked his way back to Bill, a loud report came from somewhere outside and something like a sledgehammer hit the front door.

"What the fuck was that?" Bill's voice was loud and a little shrill.

"Never mind, Billy. You get through?"

Bill shook his head. "I don't get it. I'm getting bars, I was online just a few minutes ago, remember? But all I'm getting now is static. I can't call out, can't get online. Something's wrong."

Frank reached into the inside pocket of his jacket and brought out his own smartphone. "Here, try mine. Keep trying, you hear? Maybe we're getting jammed somehow. Keep trying."

He went back near the window and retrieved his rifle, which was lying on the floor amidst the shattered glass from the window, and then crawled back to where Bill was punching numbers into the phone. The shelf where he had placed several extra boxes of ammo had fallen, and loose bullets and shotgun shells were all around him. He popped the clip from his Colt, gathered a few .45 caliber shells and began jamming rounds into it, reloading. Once it was full, he slammed it back into the gun and checked to make sure a round was jacked. He then began gathering additional bullets off the floor and put them into his jacket pocket.

"Billy, I have to go out there. They're making their way around behind. If I don't go real soon, I won't be able to leave. I'm going to go out the back door. You lock that door behind me, you understand? It's a deadbolt. These doors are solid; they can't get in. You've got to watch the windows. These side windows are shuttered, but the locks are flimsy. You hear someone fiddling near one of these shuttered windows, use the Glock and pop one or two rounds right through the window, wait a few seconds, and then watch that front window. They'll want you looking out back. Understand? Two rounds through the back window, grab that shotgun, and watch the front. You see someone, you shoot. Remember what I said: these men are here to kill us. You can't talk to them, you can't reason with them, they are not going to let us go. We have to kill them. Or they'll kill us."

Bill looked at his uncle.

"Uncle Frank," he said, almost like a child. "I'm scared. I'm really fucking scared."

"Me too, son. Me too. Now I'm going to go over to that front window and fire one shot. You stay down. I think that machine gun is going to open up on us again, so be ready. Soon as the bullets stop, I'm going to open this back door and head up into the trees. You lock the door behind me, come right back here to this spot. You can see both doors and all the windows from right here. They won't get too close for a while yet. You keep trying the phones, keep your eye on that front window."

Frank duck-walked over to the love seat in the living room and pushed it over to where Bill was crouching.

"Stay behind this. Watch that busted-up window. Keep calling nine-one-one. If you get through, don't hang up. Tell them to call Nelson, Nelson Stahl, and he'll be able to tell them exactly where the cabin is. I'm going to see if I can't even up the odds some. At least silence that machine gun. I know where that motherfucker is hiding."

Bill looked at his uncle, amazed at how calm he was. He didn't seem afraid at all. He didn't even seem nervous. He looked younger somehow, his face flushed, his eyes bright and sparkling. Frank was smiling when he finished that last sentence, and for some reason it sent a chill down Bill's spine.

"All right, Bill, I'm going over to the window. I'll shoot once, then hustle over to the back door. Don't forget, they're going to put some rounds in here, so get yourself ready. Soon as I'm gone, you lock that back door, you hear? Don't forget to lock the door! Then stay down behind this chair. Wait a few minutes, then shoot one or two rounds out the front window. Use the Glock, not the shotgun. You shoot from right here. Do not go near the window. You understand?"

Bill nodded.

Frank patted him gently on the shoulder, like he was petting a dog.

"Good. Now tell me, slowly, what are we going to do?"

Bill cleared his throat. "You're going to shoot, then run out the back door. I'll lock it, wait a few minutes, and shoot out the window from here. With the handgun, not the shotgun. And call nine-one-one, I've got to call nine-one-one."

Frank looked at his nephew, got in close so he was looking at him right in his eyes. "That's good, son. We're going to be okay. You remember when I told you that when I was in the army, I was just an ordinary grunt? That I wasn't some kind of hardcore Rambo type?"

Bill nodded his head slowly, mesmerized by the look in his uncle's eyes, his hot breath in his face, the dust floating in the air and the broken glass on the floor, the numbness in his shoulder where Frank had squeezed him earlier and the ringing in his ears.

"Well, Billy Boy, I lied."

Then Frank smiled and his whole face lit up and he turned away and made his way back to the window. When he got there, he turned again, faced Bill, and said loudly enough so that Bill could hear him clearly. "You ready to rock and roll, son?"

FORTY-FIVE

Jasper didn't see the trip wire, never even felt it, just heard the alarm go off directly to his right, and he dove left instinctively, his body tensing, waiting for the steel balls of a bouncing betty to shred him to pieces like he'd seen happen to other guys in the jungle so many years ago.

But nothing happened.

He stayed down with his face buried in the snow. The alarm was blaring to his right. He didn't move for about twenty long seconds, and then slowly and carefully started crawling further away from the sound toward a thick tree.

Once he got behind the tree, he looked up, his heart racing, wet snow clinging to his face and blurring his vision. The alarm went silent and he turned and saw that Pogo had smashed at something with the butt of his shotgun and then had quickly moved back and away, disappearing like a ghost into the trees and snowflakes.

He heard Pogo's voice come softly through his earpiece. "He's got perimeter alarms set. Looks like a trip wire. He's probably got more of them set up out here. Let's make sure we stay alert, watch where you step. He may have set something more lethal closer in. Jasper, you okay?"

Jasper took one deep breath trying to calm himself.

"Yeah," he whispered. It was all he could get out without letting the panic he felt from tripping that wire come through.

"Birdie, you okay?" Pogo's voice again, soft and soothing.

"Right as rain."

"He knows we're here, boys. Let's move slowly. Remember, silent and deadly, watch for wires. Jasper, I'm gonna go past you on the right. I'm betting the other side is wired, too. We should be clear here for a bit. Birdie, you follow behind me, not too close, stay in my tracks. Soon as we see where he's at, you find a good spot and set up with the RPK. You see any movement, give them a blast from that pig you've been toting around, show him what the fuck he's dealing with. Me and Jasper will circle around behind, get him in a crossfire. I'm of a mind to collect us an ear after all, and send it down to Beezer, just like he asked for."

Jasper's heart rate began to slow, and his breathing returned closer to where it was before the alarm. He took another deep breath and spoke softly into the radio: "Listen for a car engine. They might panic, try and make a run for it right down this road. If they do, we'll rip them a new asshole."

Birdie's voice came over the radio. "He won't panic. Let's stay sharp and get this done. Pogo, I'm right behind you."

Jasper didn't see Pogo go past, but a minute later he saw Birdie slowly making his way forward to his right carrying the RPK at the ready. They made eye contact, and then Jasper began moving slowly and carefully forward, eyes scanning the ground in front looking for wires.

A minute or two later he heard Pogo's voice again. "It's a cabin; the kid's Jeep is parked in front. I don't see another car, probably around back. Cabin's got a window in front, might be open. Watch out for sniper fire. Birdie let us know when you're set up."

Jasper continued moving slowly forward and further left until he saw the clearing and could make out the cabin. He saw the Jeep and the window that was slightly open through the snow.

"I'm in position." Birdman was ready.

Jasper was looking intently at the window and he saw

movement, maybe a rifle barrel or some type of spotting scope.

"I got some kind of movement in the window," he said softly into the radio.

Suddenly, Birdie opened up with a burst from the RPK and glass shattered as rounds burst through the window and chips of wood and mortar flicked into the air as other rounds hit the log walls on either side of the window. Jasper moved a bit further left and stood behind a tree, aiming his M16 at the cabin. He had it set to fire three-round bursts, and he waited to see what would happen next. Nothing happened right away, but Jasper sighted on the window, then moved to the door.

Suddenly he saw movement, and three quick pops sounded from the cabin. Jasper moved his sights from the door back to the window and let go a three-round burst.

Then all was silent again.

"Birdie?" It was Pogo's voice over the radio.

"I'm good."

More movement and another three pops in quick succession from the cabin. Jasper heard the bullets impact the ground or trees about fifteen yards to his right.

Then he heard a loud blast from his far right that had to be Pogo with the shotgun, and something thudded hard against the front door.

"He's firing blind," whispered Jasper into his radio. His blood was pumping again, and the adrenaline was flowing, and he was feeling fired up.

"Should I take out the Jeep?" Birdie again.

"No," said Jasper, "let them think they can run. If they make a break for the Jeep, hold your fire and let them get in the car and start it up. Soon as they start moving, then rip it to pieces, Birdie. We'll sort them out later."

It was quiet for a few seconds, and then Birdie's voice came back over the radio.

"Goddamn, boys, this is the best hunting trip ever."

Frank popped up and fired one shot out the window, then ducked down again and moved right. Another hail of bullets concussed against the plasterboard, and the wall behind him exploded, sending dust and debris into the air. Frank made his way to where Bill knelt, grabbed him by one arm, and led him to the back door. The firing stopped, but the noise still rang in their ears. "Lock the door behind me," Frank said. "Wait a few minutes, and then fire out the window from behind the couch. Got it?"

Bill nodded, and then Frank turned the deadbolt, took a quick look out the door, and was gone.

Bill closed and locked the door behind him, then felt terribly and utterly alone. He slid down the door, clutching the shotgun to his chest like a lover. He felt a sob coming on and mustered all his will to stifle it. Then he crawled back behind the couch and tried to think again about what he was supposed to do. The Glock was sitting on the floor where he had left it, and he remembered that he was supposed to shoot out the window right from this spot. But he had to wait a few minutes. How long? His stomach knotted, and again he wished he had just stayed home. He silently cursed his uncle for not going to the police right away and for not staying with friends and for coming to this secluded goddamn cabin.

He tried to get hold of himself and saw his phone on the floor. He picked it up and tried nine-one-one again. Nothing happened. He looked at the phone stupidly. Now there were no bars. He had stuffed Uncle Frank's phone in his shirt pocket and took that out and tried making the call again. No bars on his phone, either. Shit.

He looked up at the shattered window and had an inexplicable urge to crawl across the floor and peek outside, see what was happening. But one glance at the back wall changed his mind quickly.

He put Uncle Frank's phone down and grabbed his own off

the floor. He tried to access the internet. Nothing. He stifled another sob, and then grabbed the handgun.

How much time had gone by since Uncle Frank left the cabin?

Frank made his way down the steps and crouched behind the Subaru. He decided to move right toward the storage shed and then into the trees. He shuffled his way to the right front tire, took a quick look over the hood, and then in a crouching jog headed toward the shed. Snow was still falling, and the light was fading quickly. He hoped that would work to his advantage. He made it to the shed, stopped for a minute, and listened hard. He heard nothing. He hoped Bill had locked that door behind him. Stress could make or break a man, and he wasn't sure how Bill would react. He hoped Billy would be able to keep it together. He wished again that the kid had just stayed home.

The tree line was about twenty yards away. Frank made his way behind the shed and then, as quietly and quickly as possible, along a route he had scouted earlier. He made it into the trees, stopped again, and listened intently. The falling snow seemed to muffle all sound. He stayed low now, moving carefully from tree to tree. He hadn't marked where he had set his wires, but he knew where he hadn't, and he headed toward an area that he had found earlier that would give him a view of the terrain in front of the cabin. There was a spot with a downed tree that would give him a good shooting perch and would also provide cover once he had taken his shot and had to move. He had to hurry. He didn't know how long he had before Bill took his shot, or even if he would take a shot.

He made it to the downed tree and crouched behind it. He had a pretty good idea where the hunter was set up and scanned the area with the scope. Light was fading quickly and visibility was poor. He flipped the switch, turned on the night vision, and things took on an eerie green glow. It was still hard to see, but he found the spot where he thought the shooter was and kept the scope trained on it. He listened intently for any sounds around him, tried to breathe deep and even, and then he waited.

Pogo was taking his time, moving slow and cautiously. His shoulder ached a bit from the recoil of those tactical shells that Birdie had given him for the Mossberg. He hadn't expected the wallop, and it threw off his aim. He had been trying to put one through the window but had hit the door instead. He was surprised that door hadn't blown open from the impact, and he smiled. He'd be ready for it next time.

He was moving right, making his way toward the back corner of the cabin while Jasper moved left. His head was buzzing, all of his senses razor sharp. That dusted meth they had smoked was coursing through his body and dialing in his brainwaves, and he wanted to take another hit, but he knew that would be a bad idea. He wasn't wearing gloves or a heavy parka, just a light field jacket with big pockets, but he didn't feel the cold. Not at all.

He stepped carefully and then looked down saw some light indents in the snow. He stopped and bent down low, then reached over his shoulder and drew the combat knife from its sheath on his back. He crawled along slowly, moving the knife with the sharpened blade first until it snagged. He stopped and, using his finger, felt the tension. He stopped and whispered into the radio.

"Found another trip wire. Lay low for a minute and let me see what we got here." He followed the wire with his finger to a tree and carefully moved snow and leaves until he saw the green plastic key chain alarm. He looked closely to make sure that it was nothing lethal.

"Just a perimeter alarm." He cut the line carefully with his knife and then began advancing again.

He heard two muted shots from inside the cabin, and then Birdie opened up with a short burst from the RPK. A half second later he heard another shot, but this one seemed to have come from up ahead and to his left. He froze and made himself small.

The shot had come from somewhere in the trees. He keyed his mike and whispered, "Birdman?"

Nothing came back.

He keyed his mike again. "Birdie, say something, brother."

Then a three-round burst far off to the left that had to be Jasper. Then nothing. Then another three-round burst.

"Shot came from the trees, your side, Pogo." It was Jasper's voice. "Birdie, you okay?"

Pogo shook his head. "I think Birdman is down."

Frank crouched behind the downed tree looking through the scope at the same spot with both eyes open. He tried to quell the voice in his head that kept repeating, "Shoot, Billy, shoot."

He heard nothing except the occasional sound of loose snow falling off branches behind him. He didn't flinch. He just kept looking though the scope and tried to concentrate on his breathing. It had been many years since he sat motionless like this, looking through a riflescope, but he seemed to settle back into it easily and naturally.

Two muffled pops sounded from inside the cabin. Nothing for a second, and then a burst of light through the scope and the thunderous sound of machine gun fire erupted startling him for a second. It was a relatively short burst, but enough for Frank to breathe deeply once, hold, exhale, and adjust his aim. He saw the barrel clearly now and from this angle had a better view of the man's head and shoulders. He squeezed the trigger lightly as the fire from the machine gun barrel stopped and the sound of the bullets exploding began to fade. The recoil and the loud report from his own rifle shot almost surprised him. The figure in his scope flew back and went down, and the barrel of his gun fell off the log, and Frank knew he had hit his target.

He didn't move for the first few seconds, and then he heard a three-round burst from off to his right, and still he didn't move. Then another burst, and he heard bullets fly overhead and hit trees directly above him, and still he didn't move. A full minute passed. Then he slowly lowered his head and gingerly removed the rifle from its perch on the downed tree. He slid on his belly using the log for cover and carefully made his way toward where he had heard the incoming gunfire.

"Birdman just key the mike if you can't move," Pogo said softly.

No response.

Damn, he thought, I wish I had that Savage now.

"Pogo, that fucker is out here. What do you want to do?" There was an edge to Jasper's voice.

Pogo thought for a few seconds. He didn't like their chances against Bull out here in the woods. The man was deadly, no doubt about it.

He keyed his mike and said with a smile, "Well, Jasper, we're really back in the shit now, ain't we. He's gonna start hunting us. We got two choices: hightail it back to the truck and make tracks, hope he doesn't pick us off before we get there, or try and get inside that cabin and see if we can trade whatever we find, his old lady or that kid or both of them. Very least, we can use them for cover and take one of his vehicles and drive on out, disable the other."

"Think we can smoke him out?"

"Maybe, but unless we get real, real lucky, it's gonna cost us. One or both—probably both to some degree. Look, I'm sure Birdie's dead. Turd Man doesn't know where I'm at, at least I don't think he does. But he's probably headed your way now. Keep your head down and start swinging back around to the front, see if you can recover that RPK, give us some firepower. I think we have to assault that cabin and get inside. I don't see much choice. There's a shed off to the side in back. I'll make my way down there. Once you get set up, I'll sneak down and stay on this side of the cabin, try and get inside. You provide cover."

It was quiet for a few seconds as Jasper thought things over.

"Come on, son, nobody lives forever," said Pogo cheerily, "not even the National League fucking All Stars. We go down, let's go down fighting."

"Okay, Pogo, we started this thing, let's finish it."

"That's the spirit, you ugly fucker! Now, let's have some fun."

FORTY-SIX

Frank moved slowly and carefully. The falling snow and the failing light were both a blessing and a curse. He was pretty sure he would be a hard target to spot. On the other hand, he couldn't see much either. He couldn't use the scope until he found a place to set up, but his hunter's instincts were coming back, and he sensed that his quarry was moving away. So, he kept moving, stopping every so often to listen.

He heard no gunfire, and no sounds came from the cabin. He hoped Bill was still okay and holding things together. He was proud of Bill for giving him the time to set up and then firing those shots like they'd planned. Some men would have panicked, maybe fired too quickly or not at all. Now the odds were a little better. Now he was sure he could kill these other two. In fact, he looked forward to it.

That's when he hit the trip wire and the fucking alarm started blaring.

Jasper heard the alarm and sprinted to where he had seen Bird-man set up earlier. Birdman was on his back, his head surrounded by a dark halo in the otherwise white snow. A large part of his skull had been blown clean off, one eye socket gone, the halo was blood that had leaked from the gaping wound. The RPK lay next to the log in the snow. Jasper grabbed it, then crouched down to take cover behind the log.

He aimed where he thought the sound was coming from and let loose a short burst with the RPK, then another.

He saw nothing but falling snow and shadows. He blinked away tears from the cold and snow and scanned the area again. He thought he saw movement, fired a burst, and then waited. Nothing happened for a few seconds, and then the alarm went quiet. Jasper's ears were still ringing. He took careful aim and fired a slightly longer burst, peppering the area again, moving the gun in a circular motion to cover more ground. He pulled his head away from the machine gun. Spent shell casings littered the area. Tendrils of steam rose where the hot metal had hit and sunk into the cold wet snow.

He wiped his brow with his sleeve, and then sighted up the hill once again. He was going to wait until he saw movement, and then empty the rest of the fucking drum into that mother.

Pogo worked his way to the edge of the woods. He heard Jasper firing the RPK and judged roughly where the rounds were hitting from where snow kicked up and branches fell.

He got to the tree line and stopped at a spot he judged to be nearest the shed. He could make out footprints in the snow leading all the way from the back door of the cabin right to where he stood, and then up into the trees.

He shook his head and smiled. That Turd Man was a true warrior. He looked at the cabin and then down at the footprints and thought about following the footprints instead of going to the cabin, but without the Savage and the scope, he'd have to get pretty close to have any chance of finishing him with the shotgun. He'd probably catch one in the head before he got near enough to fire a shot.

No, it was best to get into that cabin instead.

He readied himself to make the run to the shed. He'd have to cross about twenty or twenty-five yards of open ground. Once there, he'd have another short run to the cabin, but an old Subaru SUV parked in back would give him cover.

He keyed his mike and said quietly, "Jasper, you there?"

He waited about fifteen seconds before he got a reply.

"Yeah, I'm here. Birdman's dead. Took one in the skull. Our boy is up on that ridge. I saw movement. Not sure if I hit him."

"I'm going to try for the shed in back. Count to twenty, then give me a short burst. If he's up there, I need you to keep his head down."

"No problem."

Pogo made sure the Sig was secure in his waistband, then reached into his pocket and took out one of the extra tactical shotgun shells and replaced the round he had fired into the door earlier. Then he got ready to make his run.

He heard Jasper open up with the RPK, and he sprinted for the shed. The snow slowed him down some, but not much. The adrenaline was pumping, and he could feel his heart beating, and he crossed that twenty or so yards in a flash and then braced his back against the side of the shed, giving Turd Man no shot whatsoever. He was breathing hard, and he concentrated on calming himself. He peeked around the side of the shed. The Subaru SUV was close, and he knew he could cover the distance in a few strides. He wasn't sure where Turd Man was, but if he was anywhere near where Jasper was firing, it would be a difficult shot for any trained marksman, let alone an aging man shooting through a snowstorm.

Still, he didn't want to underestimate the old Recon marine.

He was going to take another quick peek, but then surprised himself by just taking off around the corner and running in a low stoop until he made it to the safety of the car.

He sat on his haunches, his back to the driver's-side door, and looked at the cabin. It was a small prefab log cabin. The back had what looked like a solid door, and off near the right-hand corner was a shuttered window. He remembered looking at the cabin from the front and the side as he had made his way to the back woods. There was no window around the left side; there was a front window, now just an open hole after Birdie had blown most of it out with the machine gun. He suspected one more window along the other side of the cabin, probably because there were two small bedrooms on that side. That window would be shuttered as well. Doors locked, windows shuttered. That left just one avenue of assault: the blown-out front window.

He keyed his mike and whispered, "Jasper, I'm around back of the cabin. Got a back door, one shuttered window. I believe there's another window around the side, your left. I'm thinking the only way in is that front window."

Nothing for a few seconds, and then, "You got a plan?"

"I can cause a bit of a diversion, maybe rattle this back window some, get whoever's inside looking this way, then quick as shit make my way around to the front and get through that window, fast. Same time, you fire a burst up that hill and finish off whatever we got left in the drum, then ditch the RPK and charge the cabin. We time it right, we should get there about the same time. It'll be tough for him to get his head out of his ass, get re-set, and then get a bead on you while you're moving, especially in this weather. If I don't get shot going in through the window, we should be fine. What do you think, son?"

Once again there was no reply for a few seconds, and then Jasper's quiet voice came through his ear buds, "Sure could use another hit or two of those Rabbit Turds you mixed up, get my head straight for this."

"Me too, brother, but it will have to wait till later. Time to tighten your jock strap 'cause we're all in now. I'm by the back window. Give me a short burst whenever you're ready. I'll get their attention inside, then you let loose on that hill with all you got, and get it in gear. I'll meet you in front. We got to go in quick. We stay on that porch, we die, simple as that."

Pogo removed the Sig from his waistband. He would throw the shotgun through the window ahead of him. He didn't want it getting caught on anything while he was going through. Speed was the key here. He held the shotgun in his left hand and the silenced pistol in his right.

He crouched under the window and looked up at the tiny lock that held the shutters closed.

Now all he had to do was wait for the next round of bullets to start flying.

Bill crouched behind the love seat, keeping a cautious eye on the blown-out front window. He had his phone in his hand, repeatedly trying to get a call through to nine-one-one. The Glock was on the floor next to him, as was Uncle Frank's tactical shotgun. He had also crawled slowly and carefully over the broken glass and ceramic shards from shattered dishes and coffee cups and retrieved the old Fox from the floor, where it had fallen from the table when the shooting started. That gun was leaning up against the back of the love seat right next to him.

Bill was scared, more frightened than he had ever been in his life.

He had done as Uncle Frank had instructed and fired two shots with the Glock, aiming from this very spot out the window. He felt the recoil of the gun and watched the two spent cartridges fly through the air and heard the distinctive clink they made as they hit the floor. Then he hunkered down as a blast of machine gun fire ripped through what little glass remained in the window frame and smacked the back wall, shaking the whole cabin again.

The machine gun went quiet, but almost immediately after that, he heard the rat-tat-tat of a three-round burst in the distance. Not the same sound the machine gun made, different, more muffled. Nothing came through the window or hit the cabin. Then silence for a few seconds, then another three-round burst.

Shit, they must be shooting at Uncle Frank. They must have seen him.

It was dead quiet for a few more seconds and Bill shivered, even as sweat poured down the sides of his head, one drop of moisture making its way annoyingly into his left ear canal.

Then he heard the faint sound of another of those alarm things, the trip wires Frank had set up. It went on for about ten seconds, faint but clear, and Bill wondered who or what had set this one off and where it was coming from. He heard another short burst, different from the last two. It was louder, and he knew it was the machine gun again, only not firing at the cabin. The firing stopped briefly, then another burst.

The gun and the alarm went silent. Suddenly the firing started again with a burst longer than any of the others.

Bill was shivering again and had a sudden urge to urinate. He wondered if Uncle Frank was dead, and a thought popped into his head so unexpectedly that it caught him by surprise—if he's dead, then they're coming for me next. He put the phone down, crawled to the end of the love seat, and vomited onto the floor. He had tears in his eyes though he wasn't crying. He spit on the floor, then wiped his eyes and mouth with the back of one hand. Then he crawled, moving backwards, to where he had left the phone and picked it up and tried nine-one-one again.

His hands were shaking, and he found it hard to hit the right buttons on the small screen, but he knew it didn't matter because the phone wasn't working anyway.

He heard another burst from the machine gun, and something clicked in his head, and he realized that if they were still shooting and nothing was hitting the cabin, then they were shooting at something or someone else.

Uncle Frank.

For some reason a wave of shame and guilt overwhelmed him. Uncle Frank was out there fighting for his life, for both their lives, and he was all by himself.

Bill picked up the Glock and looked at it. Who could have imagined that he, a boring family man from Hackensack, would end up fighting for his life in a secluded cabin in the wilds of Maine?

Then the window rattled in the back bedroom.

* * *

At the very instant the alarm sounded, Frank dove to his right and flattened himself in the snow. Nothing happened for a second or two, and he began crawling toward the alarm that he could barely make out at the base of a large tree. He could almost reach the screeching alarm and, as he started his grab, he heard a burst from the machine gun, and bullets tore into the ground ten feet to his left. He hunkered down and waited, wondering if he had only wounded the gunner with his shot earlier.

Another slightly longer burst. Bullets began working their way toward him, and he pushed himself down into the snow, grinding his body into it. He waited to see if a bullet would find him.

Then the shooting stopped. He reached out slowly and grabbed the vibrating alarm, found the kill switch and the noise suddenly stopped.

He knew what was coming next. He was crawling quickly around a tree trunk when the machine gun opened up again. This time bullets ripped into the area where he had lain just a second or two ago, and peppered the tree above him, sending wet snow and leaves and tree branches down on his head. The bullets landed all around him, and he didn't move, not even after the bullets had stopped flying.

Silence.

He waited a bit longer, then slowly lifted his head.

The snow was still coming down, but was starting to mix with sleet, a fine rain making the snow around him wet and heavy. He couldn't see the cabin or much of anything from where he lay, and he inched up onto his knees, careful to keep the tree trunk always between him and the position where the machine gun fire had come from. He peeked around the tree trunk and had a view of the open ground, one entire side and most of the front of the cabin. He could also make out part of the front grill of the Subaru parked around back, but nothing beyond that.

He brought the rifle up slowly and looked through the scope, first scanning the front of the cabin and seeing most of the window shot out, then slowly swinging back to where he had last seen the machine gun. He could make out some movement. Someone was still there, staying low behind a log, and he wondered if that meant there were two more men out in the woods, or if one had run out to retrieve the weapon from the man he had shot earlier.

Two muffled shots rang out from the cabin, and the guy with the machine gun suddenly popped up. Before Frank could get a bead on him and fire, the tree where he knelt started shaking, and bullets kicked up snow and dirt and ice, and then more snow and leaves and twigs were raining down on him, and he brought the rifle around and leaned against the tree. He watched and waited, and the bullets kept coming. The burst seemed to go on forever, and then it stopped. Frank waited two beats and then brought the rifle and scope around again and tried to find the spot where the fire had come from. He saw movement and followed with the scope. Someone sprinted towards the cabin carrying an M16. Frank tried to line up a shot and pulled the trigger too quickly. He shot way wide, leading the target too much. He pulled the bolt back to chamber another round and lost the man in the scope for a second and then reacquired him, still running. Frank took a breath, held it, and steadied himself for another shot. As he was squeezing the trigger, the man flew forward, his rifle flying through the air as the man tumbled face first into the snow.

Frank kept the scope on him, but he didn't move.

Everything seemed to happen at once. The window in the back bedroom rattled as if someone were trying to break the lock. Bill held the Glock and looked down at it, then raised it out in front of him and fired two shots at the window. The glass shattered and rained down back inside onto the floor. Bill stared at the window, his ears ringing. He wondered if he should shoot again. His eyes moved across to the other bedroom door, and he waited to see if they might try to get in through that window, too.

Suddenly the machine gun started again, a long burst, longer than any of the others. Bill put the Glock down on the floor and closed his eyes and covered his ears, just wanting the noise to stop and wishing he was someplace else, any place other than this stuffy cabin with the dust stinging his eyes and the broken glass all over the floor and the sharp odor of spent powder burning his nose.

He was breathing rapidly, and he was trying to think of what he should do next and trying to remember what Uncle Frank had said about the back window. He opened his eyes and saw the old Fox there right in front of his nose leaning against the back of the love seat. He removed his hands from his ears, grabbed the shotgun, and put the stock to his shoulder. He rested the barrel along the cushions on the backrest of the love seat and aimed at the shattered front window just as an arm appeared. The arm lowered a shotgun onto the floor, then shot back out the window and returned with a long-barreled gun that coughed rather quietly twice. Something hit the love seat hard, and a man appeared, trying to get in through the window, one foot on the broken window frame, his body trying to squeeze itself in. Bill saw the man's long gray hair, which seemed to be tied back. Something about his face looked familiar. He was smiling, and he looked right at Bill, right into his eyes, and then Bill let go with both barrels, and the man flew back out the window as if he had been hit by a train.

FORTY-SEVEN

Frank heard the boom from inside the cabin and moved the scope quickly in that direction. A man flew backwards off the front porch and landed on his back in the snow. A pool of blood formed around him, and even from a distance Frank knew that he had taken a massive hit, his chest and part of his shoulder ripped open. The man lay still for a second, then tried to sit. He almost made it, then slipped back down again into the wet snow.

All was quiet for about a full minute.

Then a voice sounded from the woods in front of the cabin, someone yelling.

"Recon, we have your position marked. The area is secure. Come down off that ridge, both hands on your rifle, hold it high above your head. I want to see that bolt back."

Frank moved the scope back towards the woods, trying to get fix on where the voice was coming from. Nothing moved, and he could make out no shapes that looked like they could be people.

A minute later the same voice. "Frank Thompson, come down off that ridge. The area is secure. I repeat, the area is secure. We have your position marked."

Frank played the scope slowly across the woods in front of the cabin.

Then the voice again. "Wingo, why don't you assure that old recon marine up there that we have him marked?"

Almost immediately bullets began peppering the ground about three feet in front of Frank, but he heard no gunfire, saw no muzzle flash from the woods.

"William Thompson, we need you to exit the cabin from the front door. Put your hands on your head and step forward away from structure. You will not be harmed. The area is secure."

Frank heard Billy's shrill, shaky, voice from the cabin. "Who are you?"

The voice from the woods: "This is the authorities. Come out, put your hands on your head. You will not be harmed. Do it now."

"Okay, I'm coming out. Don't shoot."

The front door opened, and Bill walked slowly out onto the porch, his hands on his head. He stopped and looked around, then walked slowly down the front steps and out into the open. He stopped again when he got near the man on the ground in the bloody snow, then turned away, bent over, and appeared to vomit, his hands never leaving the top of his head.

"Recon, we were sent here to help. But hell, it looks like you didn't need much help at all. Come on down. Let's get this cleaned up and move on."

Frank lowered his rifle. They had Billy, and they had him. Whatever would happen next was going to happen anyway.

"I'm coming down," he yelled, and then he opened the bolt on his rifle, ejecting the live round and he stepped from behind the tree. He held the rifle over his head with both hands and began making his way through the trees and down the ridge toward the cabin.

A figure appeared like a ghost out of the trees. He wore a white military camo suit. The white was broken up with soft gray splotches, making him hard to see as he emerged from the trees. He held a short assault rifle, a model Frank had never seen before, with a white suppressor attached to the barrel. He wore no helmet, but instead wore a tight white military balaclava, which hid most of his face. He had on a headset with a thin wire microphone that floated off his cheek near his mouth.

Two similarly dressed men emerged from the woods about thirty yards on either side of the first.

The lead man said, "Wingo, check the cabin. Biz, ID these two and upload."

The other two men went silently about their business. The one called Wingo trotted toward the cabin. The other walked over to Jasper, who lay face down in the snow, a stain of blood surrounding a small, dark hole in his back. The man turned Jasper over, then removed a glove from his hand and felt Jasper's neck for a pulse.

"Dead," he said. He pulled something like a smartphone from his pocket, stood over Jasper's body, and took a picture of his face. Then he pulled out another small electronic device, grabbed one of Jasper's hands, and scanned each finger for prints.

The one called Wingo emerged from the cabin and said, "Clear."

He was carrying the silenced Sig, which apparently had fallen from Pogo's hand when he was shot in the chest going through the window.

He walked over to Pogo, who lay face up, the wounds in his chest and shoulder still leaking blood into the snow.

"This one is still alive." Pogo coughed softly, his mouth opening and closing like a landed fish, blood gurgling from his mouth and down the side of his face. The man photographed Pogo's face and then began scanning his fingertips.

The first man had his weapon trained on Frank.

"I read your file, Recon. Impressive. I can't believe this group of morons even tried to take you down. I'd say they had balls, but I try never to confuse balls with stupidity, and these clowns take stupid to a whole new level. We were tempted to let this comedy play out a little longer. Wingo there was betting that Mr. Sprague wouldn't make it within ten feet of the porch before you got him, but you missed that first shot and, well, shit, the truth is we were sent here to help, so I popped him."

"We got confirmation on both these guys," Biz said looking at his phone, "I'll see what I can get on the other one." He trotted over to where Birdie lay and repeated the procedure used on the other two.

"What about this guy?" asked Wingo, looking at the man who had addressed Frank and who was apparently the leader of this assault group.

"Do him," said the man calmly, his eyes never leaving Frank, who stood a few feet in front of him, still holding the rifle over his head.

Wingo used the silenced Sig and put two bullets into Pogo's chest while standing directly over him.

The leader touched something on his belt and spoke softly into his mike. "Bring the vehicles forward."

"Can I put this rifle down?" asked Frank.

"Drop it behind you, put your left hand on your head, use the right to take that .45 off your hip. I want to see the underside of your wrist the whole time. Use just your fingertips." He shifted the barrel of his assault rifle and aimed it at Bill. "Do it slow, Recon."

Frank complied, and then dropped his Colt into the snow a few feet to his right. Then he put his hand on his head and stood facing the leader.

"You're professionals," said Frank, speaking calmly to the leader. "What are you doing here? You're too young to have had anything to do with these old psychopaths. You're not part of the All Stars."

"Not All Stars yet," said the leader with a smile. He moved his rifle back until it was aimed at Frank's chest.

In the distance Frank saw two vehicles driving up the snow-covered access road. An old pickup truck with a camper in the bed was in the lead; an ambulance followed, both vehicles moving slowly. A man wearing the same white camo gear was driving each vehicle.

Bill walked slowly over and stood next to his uncle, his

hands, too, on top of his head, fingers laced together.

"Uncle Frank, what's going on? I think I saw that ambulance in town today. Who are these guys?" He was whispering, even though the man with the assault rifle was standing just a few feet away.

"I'm not sure Billy," said Frank quietly.

Bill asked the leader, "Who are you? You said you were with the authorities. You're not the police; your friend just shot that guy. Who are you?"

"You ever hear that old joke, the one that goes I could tell you, but then I'd have to kill you? Well, Mr. Thompson, in this case, it's no joke."

Frank said, "Hush, Billy."

"You'd do well to listen to your uncle, Mr. Thompson." The man with the rifle pointed it at Bill.

The vehicles pulled up close to the cabin and the drivers got out.

"Wingo, get some shots of the cabin, inside and out, then upload." The leader then called over his shoulder to the two drivers, "Scooter, C-Man, get those bodies and put them into the camper. Biz, round up the weapons and any brass you can find, put them on the porch. We got a clean-up crew inbound."

"How'd you find us?" asked Frank.

"Phones. Yours and his." He nodded at Bill. "Was us jamming you once we got zeroed in."

"What are you going to do with the bodies?" Uncle Frank was unfazed. He spoke like he was asking what time it was.

The leader didn't answer right away. Frank just looked at him. Finally, the leader said, "These three are total fuck-ups. You should smell the inside of that camper, smells like a goddamn meth lab. Good thing they had that Russian machine gun, otherwise I don't think they could have hit the side of a barn. As far as disposal, these roads up here are mighty dangerous. Three old guys mixing booze and illegal substances, reliving the sixties, man, that's a recipe for disaster. End up driving off a cliff in a snowstorm. Truck goes up in flames. No questions. Simple."

They stood like that, Frank and Bill with hands on their heads watching the two men drag the bodies and load them into the truck while the other man, the one called Biz, gathered the weapons and scooped up brass, the leader with his assault rifle still pointing at them, not saying anything.

When they were done, Wingo walked over to the leader and said, "Ready."

"Is everything prepped for transport? I don't want anything to go wrong."

"We're set here. We've got a rendezvous point for the exchange."

"What's that you have there? Is that a Sig?"

Wingo handed him the silenced gun. "P226 9mm with a suppressor. Found it in the cabin, on the floor."

"Why, young Mr. Thompson, is this your weapon? You're just full of surprises. Chip off the old block, eh? I didn't figure you for the silent-killer type."

Bill shook his head. "I never saw that gun before."

"Well, then, I guess old Willy Nelson over there must have dropped it when he was trying to climb in that window and ventilate your head for you. Okay, I need you two to turn around and face the cabin. Keep your hands on your head. Wingo is going to put some plastic restraints on your hands, one at a time. Mr. Thompson, I'm going to need you to move away from your uncle a few steps. Do it now, gentlemen. We need to roll."

Frank and Bill looked at each other. Bill looked scared.

"Uncle Frank?" His voice cracked.

Frank said, "It's okay, Billy. Do what he says."

Bill moved away from Frank. Both men turned and faced the cabin, their backs to the two men in white camo. Wingo grabbed one of Bill's wrists and brought it down behind his back and then the other. Then he locked them together using plastic restraints.

He nudged Bill to the side and began walking him toward the vehicles.

The leader held the gun on Frank and talked quietly to his back.

"I'm sorry about this, Bull, really, but I got orders."

With that the leader extended the Sig with his right arm, aimed at Frank, and pulled the trigger.

FORTY-EIGHT

Bill hated hospitals. He hated the smell of them, the odor of disinfectant mixed with something medicinal. That, plus old-people body odor, seemed to hang in the air, turning his stomach.

He looked around the room, the heart monitor with its redlight pulsing, the oxygen tubes and IV drip bottle and the old-style TV up on the wall with a game show playing, the volume turned way down so that it was indecipherable background noise.

He remembered being in a hospital like this a few years ago, his father smiling bravely up at him as he wasted away from an aggressive form of cancer, knowing he was dying, telling Bill over and over not to worry, that he was ready to go. And now, here he sat looking at his uncle in his white patient smock, his hair greasy and disheveled, skin pasty white, oxygen tube across his face with two nubs sticking into his nostrils, his breath shallow, his eyelids fluttering, as if he couldn't decide between being asleep and awake.

For the first time ever, Uncle Frank looked old and helpless.

Bill never heard the shot that hit his uncle, not even a little cough from the silenced gun.

He had watched the two drivers, Scooter and C-Man, race the ambulance, a first-aid kit already on the stretcher as if the scene had been orchestrated, like they were expecting to care for a wounded man. When he turned to look, the man called Wingo shoved him hard, hustled him into the back of the ambulance, and made him sit on a fold-down jump seat up near the cab.

A minute or two later, they brought Uncle Frank in on the stretcher. There was a blood-soaked bandage wrapped around his shoulder. Bill was shocked, shocked and outraged, and he remembered that he had begun yelling Frank's name and had tried to get up out of the jump seat, that Wingo had stepped into the ambulance and pushed him back down and hit him open-handed hard across the face. He'd told Bill to shut up, that his uncle would be okay, and Uncle Frank had looked over at him, and they'd made eye contact for a second, and Uncle Frank had said, "Easy, Billy." So Bill had sat quietly, letting the men strap Uncle Frank in and ten to his wound.

C-Man rode in the back with Frank and Bill as the ambulance started down the bumpy road. They drove for twenty minutes, and Bill knew they had made it past the gate and back out onto the old country road.

He heard C-Man talking softly to Uncle Frank, heard him say, "It's through-and-through, Recon. You'll be okay. Get you fixed up good as new," and then he heard nothing more.

The ambulance stopped, and C-Man put a black hood over Bill's head so that everything was darkness. Bill heard the ambulance door open, and they rolled the stretcher out, and he heard men speaking quietly. Another door slammed shut and then the sound of a siren, loud at first, then diminishing quickly and fading into the distance and Bill sat in his jump seat, scared and alone in the darkness.

A few minutes later he was gently removed from the ambulance and his wrist ties were cut, but the hood remained on. He was led to a waiting car, put in the passenger seat and told to leave the hood on. He heard vehicles coming and going and men shouting and talking, and then a car door opened, and someone got in next to him and lit a cigarette. He smelled the tobacco smoke right through the hood.

A voice said, "Your uncle is going to be okay. I want you to listen to what I say, and you need to listen very carefully. I am going to tell you a story. You are going to tell that story to anyone who asks you what happened today. Only that story. Nothing else. Do you understand?"

Bill nodded.

"You found your uncle at the cabin. He was shot. He told you that he was about to start cleaning his gun; it was on the table in the cabin. He got up and turned to get his cleaning kit and bumped the table, the gun fell on the floor and went off, and he got hit in the back. That's all you know. Do you understand?"

Bill nodded again.

"You called nine-one-one and then helped Frank into your car and began driving him to the hospital, and you were met by an emergency services ambulance. Have you got that?"

Bill nodded again.

"Tell me," said the man. "Tell me what happened."

Bill repeated the story.

"Good. Now, Mr. Thompson, you will not deviate from that story. Not to the doctors, not to your wife, not to anyone. I assure you that your uncle will tell the same story. You will never speak about what happened up here again. The police and other authorities will not bother you. If anyone should ask, you repeat that story. Keep repeating it until you are absolutely sure that it is the truth. Until you believe it is the truth."

Neither man said anything for a full minute.

"Mr. Thompson, you have a nice family—a lovely wife, two beautiful kids. You have a good job and a comfortable life. But everything can change in an instant. Do you understand what I'm saying here? Everything can change, just like that, and you'll never know what hit you."

He was removed from the car. Keys were put in his hand, and he was told to count to sixty slowly, and then to remove the hood and get into his Jeep, which was parked nearby, and drive to the hospital. The address was already programmed into his GPS.

The door to the hospital room opened and a nurse walked

in, startling him.

"Mr. Thompson, you have a call. It's the police. I can transfer the call in here if you'd like." Bill nodded, and the nurse disappeared.

The phone on the small stand next to Frank's bed rang a few seconds later, and Bill picked it up.

"Mr. Thompson?"

"Yes." Bill's throat was dry, and the word came out more like a cough. He cleared his throat and then said it again.

"Mr. Thompson, this is Noah Porter. I'm with the State Police. I'm a friend of Frank's."

"Noah, yes. My uncle told me about you. He said that you and he were supposed to get together. For dinner."

"Yes. I'm calling to see how he's doing. I'd have stopped by, but we've got an emergency situation. One of our guys is missing. I tried to get some information on what happened to Frank, but things have clamped shut. Nobody is talking. I couldn't get anyone to tell me anything. I guess everyone is busy with this other thing right now. How is he? How's Frank doing?"

Bill was quiet for a second. "He's okay, I guess. Doctors don't say much other than that he's no longer critical. He's sleeping now."

"What happened?"

Bill was quiet again, then repeated the story he'd been told.

"Really? That's what Frank told you? That doesn't sound like Frank. He knows guns, and he's careful. He's always careful. He's got a Glock 17, right? Or was it that .45 of his? What was it he got hit with?"

"I think it was the Glock," said Bill.

"I never heard of that happening with a Glock. Not ever. Did he have a round chambered? Why would he clean it without first making sure there was no round chambered? Weird. Did he do any modifications to that gun?"

Bill didn't know what to say. "Noah, I don't have much information. I'm sorry, but I've got to go. The doc just walked in."

266

Noah began to say something, but Bill hung up.

It was strange. When Bill got to the hospital, there were no police. Nobody questioned him. At the front desk, he was directed to the third floor. When he got there, he saw a man in a suit talking to the doctors. The man reached into his breast pocket and removed an ID, which he showed to a nurse. Then he pointed at Bill. The nurse nodded, walked over, took Bill by the arm to a waiting area, and sat him down. She told him Frank was in surgery and then brought Bill a cup of coffee. He sat for a few hours, afraid to call his wife, not sure what to tell her, and then a doctor showed up and told him that Frank was out of surgery and doing fine. The doctor told Bill to go down to the cafeteria and have something to eat.

Now he sat, his body tired and his brain numb.

A cell phone began ringing, and Bill automatically reached to his belt, where he normally kept his phone. He felt for the clip, but there was none and no phone. Then he remembered seeing his phone on the car seat next to him in the Jeep. One of those men, the commandos, must have put it there after the shooting.

Bill slid open a drawer in the rolling stand that held the hospital phone. He saw Uncle Frank's phone, along with his keys, a wallet and some loose change.

The phone stopped ringing. Bill looked at it, and then he heard that distinctive chime he knew meant an email had just arrived. He touched the icon and opened the email program.

There was one unread message. Bill looked uneasily at the closed door to the hallway. He then looked at Uncle Frank, still sleeping, his eyeballs moving behind closed lids. He opened the email and began reading.

"*Hey Bull, told you I was sending in some relievers. Made it a live fire training op. Babes in the woods. I heard the bambinos done good. As you might have guessed, I'm with the spooks now. Always been trying to keep an eye on them All Stars. Crazy motherfuckers. Sorry about the shoulder. Well, not really. Kid was just following orders. My orders. I owed you one. I figure now we're even. Ha, ha."*

There was no sign-off at the end, but there was an attachment. Bill opened it.

He closed out of the email program, shut down the phone, laid it back down next to the wallet, and shut the drawer.

He thought about what he had just seen, about what it meant.

He looked at his uncle and gently brushed a sweaty lock of hair that had fallen near his eye.

The attachment he had looked at was a low-resolution jpg, obviously downloaded off the internet.

It was a small, adorable cartoon bunny with big, warm eyes and floppy ears, a small pink nose and two large padded feet.

Bill had seen that bunny countless times on his TV screen. He remembered sitting on the couch, an arm around each of his children, wondering how the kids could stand to watch the same thing over and over. They loved watching that Disney DVD of Bambi, and he never tired of listening to them squeal with delight whenever Bambi's sidekick came on the screen.

The adorable little rabbit that, coincidentally, shared its name with a M79 40mm grenade launcher.

It was insane. All of it was insane.

He closed his eyes tight, and a tear rolled down each. He wiped his eyes with the back of one hand, then laid the hand on his uncle's head.

He was tired, more tired than he had ever been before. He kissed his uncle on the forehead.

Frank's eyelids fluttered, and then opened. Bill looked at his uncle and saw his eyes, at first clouded and confused, begin to focus.

"Water," he croaked.

Bill grabbed a plastic cup from a shelf next to the phone and put a straw to Frank's lips.

Frank took a sip and looked at Bill.

"Are you okay, Billy?"

Bill nodded.

"What happened?"

Bill didn't answer right away. Then he leaned in and said softly, "You were at the cabin. You were about to clean your gun. You got up to get your cleaning kit and knocked the Glock off the table. It went off, and you got hit in the back."

Frank didn't say anything, just looked at Bill.

"That's what happened. Do you understand what I'm saying?"

Frank kept looking at Bill and finally he said, "Spooks?"

Bill nodded.

"It was a ghost that got me, then," said Frank softly, almost to himself.

Bill nodded again.

"I guess it's as it should be," said Frank, turning away.

He said to the wall, "I got pulled back into the shit, Bill, and I pulled you in with me. It lays a stink on your soul, and I'm sorry for that, I truly am. That fucking goddamn war."

Bill said, "The war is over, Frank."

Frank looked at his nephew again. "It'll never be over, Billy, you'll see. The dead don't sleep."

Then he smiled. "You did good, Bill. I'm proud of you. But you look terrible. What will Sam say? Go back to my house. Lay down for a while. We'll talk about this again later."

Now it was Bill's turn to look away.

"No, Uncle Frank," he said, "we won't. You dropped your gun, it went off, and you got shot in the back. There's nothing more to talk about."

Uncle Frank said nothing, just looked at the side of Bill's face.

Bill looked down. His hands were trembling. "Those men, they were sent there to the cabin. They were tracking us. They knew, someone knew what was happening, what was going to happen, all along. This whole thing, it was like a game to them."

He clasped his hands together, trying to stop them from shaking. "Why'd they let it go so far? I don't understand. They could have stopped them, could have arrested them."

He looked at his uncle, looked in his eyes. "They warned me,

Uncle Frank, those men back there. They put a hood over my head and they threatened me—me and my family. I don't know who they are, but I do know what they're capable of. We are not going to talk about this later. We're not going to talk about this ever again."

EPILOGUE

Six months later
Twelve miles outside Indiantown, Florida

Beezer sat at the scarred kitchen table in the dingy shack that he called home on the edge of Everglades National Park. He stared at the road map once again. It was an old map he had probably gotten at a gas station back when you could still find maps at gas stations. He followed with his finger the route he had traced with a highlighter he'd bought a week before at the Dollar Tree.

Make his way up to Kanner Highway, head east to I-95, then north until somewhere's around St. George, South Carolina, and start looking for Interstate 26. Take I-26 to Route 64, and that should take him pretty goddamn close to the Hendersonville, North Carolina, Econo Lodge.

He rubbed his hands together like a small child. Hot damn!

The van was all packed. He had clothes, a sleeping bag he'd found at a secondhand store, his crutches should he need them, and his spare leg. He wasn't anticipating needing the spare, as he was to be the wheelman, but what the fuck. He also had a Smith & Wesson snub-nosed .38 revolver, a box of ammunition and two little surprises he had managed to salvage from his past.

He opened the old cigar box he had brought out of its hiding place in his bedroom closet and peered inside. He reached in almost reverently and fingered his old dog tags, then brought out the string with what looked like dried figs, ears he had taken from men he had killed during the war. He laid the string on the kitchen table. It made him smile. Then he picked up one of the two lemon grenades he had smuggled home when he was discharged. They were over forty years old now, and he wondered if they would still explode. Then he remembered hearing stories of ordnance that had been buried since WWII and even from the first World War occasionally blowing up. He thought, hell, compared to that shit, these grenades were still practically new.

He put the grenade on the table, and then reached into the box and removed the other. Then he took out his dog tags. They were still on the chain he had used in the service. He put the chain around his neck, picked up the string of ears, and put that around his neck as well.

He wasn't entirely sure that he would return home from his trip up north, but he didn't really care. He was stopping in North Carolina to meet up with some of the boys, Spider, Tools, and maybe Smash. Some of them knew how to work computers and would be bringing key information. Seems there was a suspicious car accident, and then a fire. Seems someone got himself all shot up. They were going to share intel, make a plan, and then head up to Maine.

Up to where their old friends Pogo and Jasper and Birdie had met their end.

They were planning on meeting up with another old friend.

That's when the real fun would start.

ACKNOWLEDGMENTS

Susan, thank you for being such an important part of my life. You inspire me in more ways than you'll ever know.

I want to thank my friend John who introduced me to trap shooting and other outdoor pursuits. For some reason he, along with his family, friends and acquaintances, seem to influence and inhabit many of my stories. I would also be remiss if I did not mention the wonderful author Andrew Grant, who showed much kindness and enthusiasm early on and even offered an editorial jewel that helped kick-start this story.

Lastly, to my friends and family who read early drafts of this book, I thank you all.

STEVEN MAX RUSSO has spent most of his professional career as an advertising copywriter and agency owner. He got interested in writing fiction after one of his short stories was accepted by an online literary journal in 2013. After that, he caught the bug and began writing seriously. His first novel, *Thieves*, has garnered praise from renowned crime and thriller authors from around the globe. Steve is proud to call New Jersey his home.

StevenMaxRussoBooks.com

On the following pages are a few
more great titles from the
Down & Out Books publishing family.

For a complete list of books and to
sign up for our newsletter,
go to DownAndOutBooks.com.

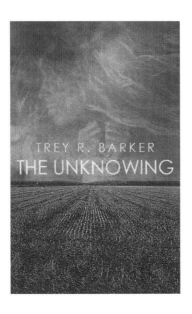

The Unknowing
Trey R. Barker

Down & Out Books
September 2019
978-1-64396-033-3

Runaway. Victim of domestic battery. An older, married boyfriend. Pregnant. And ultimately, dead and forgotten in a cornfield. For Sheriff's Deputy Wes Spahn, this case has too many similarities to his first case as a detective, similarities that will leave him questioning everything.

He tries to work both cases simultaneously and soon understands someone is gunning for him.

Which case is drawing this attention? Who wants him dead?

Regret The Dark Hour
Richard Hood

Down & Out Books
August 2019
978-1-64396-028-9

When Nole Darlen kills his father, the single resounding gun-shot sets up a dark patchwork of memory and expectation. A tangled tale involving the dead man's wife, his neighbor , a des-perado, and a grizzled muskrat-trapper. There is never any doubt about who killed Carl Darlen, but the story turns and weaves through the day of the murder and ends with a startling, dark, surprise.

A story of family violence set against the clashing tensions of old-and-new, fiddle-tunes and factories, among the hills and coves of prohibition-era East Tennessee.

Guillotine
Paul Heatley

All Due Respects, an imprint of
Down & Out Books
February 2019
978-1-64396-009-8

After suffering a lifetime of tyranny under her father's rule, when Lou-Lou sees a chance to make a break with the man she loves, she takes it. Problem is, daddy's also known as Big Bobby Joe, a dangerous and powerful man in the local area—powerful enough to put out a sixty grand bounty on the head of the man she's run off with, who also happens to be one of his ex-employees.

But Big Bobby Joe hasn't counted on his daughter's resolve to distance herself from him. No matter what he throws at her, no matter what he does, she's going to get away—or die trying.

The Furious Way
Aaron Philip Clark

Shotgun Honey, an imprint of
Down & Out Books
May 2019
978-1-64396-003-6

Lucy Ramos is out for blood—she needs to kill a man, but she has no clue how. Lucy calls on the help of aged hit-man, Tito Garza, now in his golden years, living a mundane life in San Pedro.

With a backpack full of cash, Lucy persuades Garza to help her murder her mother's killer, ADA Victor Soto. Together, the forgotten hit-man hungry for a comeback and the girl whose life was shattered as a child, set out to kill the man responsible. But killing Victor Soto may prove to be an impossible task…

Printed in Great Britain
by Amazon

35349973R00166